Richard Hough is a naval historian and biographer of Admirals Lord Fisher and Mountbatten. He has for long had a special interest in the Royal Navy of Victorian and Edwardian times, and his books such as *Admirals in Collision* and *The Big Battleship* have been widely acclaimed. He is well equipped to write this trilogy of naval novels, of which the first two were *Buller's Guns* and *Buller's Dreadnought*, set in the period 1875 to the end of the First World War.

Mr Hough is Vice-President of the Navy Records Society. His account of the mutiny of the *Bounty* won the annual Book of the Sea Award, and was made into a major film, starring Anthony Hopkins.

Mr Hough is married to the publisher, Judy Taylor, and they live in an old farmhouse in the Cotswolds.

GW00385179

Also by Richard Hough

BULLER'S GUNS
BULLER'S DREADNOUGHT
THE BOUNTY

and published by Corgi Books

BULLER'S VICTORY

RICHARD HOUGH

CORGI BOOKS

For advice and information I would like to thank Warren Tute and Captain John Coote RN

BULLER'S VICTORY

A CORGI BOOK 0 552 12413 3

Originally published in Great Britain by
Weidenfeld and Nicolson Ltd.

PRINTING HISTORY

Weidenfeld and Nicolson edition published 1984
Corgi edition published 1985

This book is set in 10/11pt Plantin

Corgi Books are published by Transworld Publishers Ltd.,
Century House, 61–63 Uxbridge Road, Ealing, London W5 5SA,
in Australia by Transworld Publishers (Aust.) Pty. Ltd.,
26 Harley Crescent, Condell Park, NSW 2000, and in New
Zealand by Transworld Publishers (N.Z.) Ltd., Cnr. Moselle
and Waipareira Avenues, Henderson, Auckland.

Printed and bound in Great Britain by
Cox & Wyman Ltd., Reading, Berks.

Contents

I

The Quest for von Spee

Richard Buller could overhear what the two young midshipmen were saying, and it did not make good listening.

'What sort of chance have we got with this rum collection of old tin cans?' one was asking, and the other answered at once, as if there were no argument, 'None whatever, old boy. At least *we* might get away if there's a fight, but as for those two' – and he pointed towards the ancient armoured cruiser and the armed liner – 'they won't last long – "ten-minute ships" I call them.'

Richard was torn between curiosity at what they might say next and his sense of duty which told him he should stop this defeatist talk. The two midshipmen were walking towards him but were still hidden by the forecastle 6-inch gun and its shield.

There came the shrill sound of a bosun's whistle, a distant shouted order from somewhere astern and the inevitable echoing 'Ay ay, sir'. Then, only a few yards away now, the first midshipman said, 'The flagship'll help – if she ever joins us.'

His companion could not agree. 'The *Good Hope* might last another ten minutes, no longer. What we need is a battleship. And the chances of that are 100 to one against. Want a bet Johnny?'

Before the midshipman, the Hon John Letchworth, aged eighteen, could reply the two young men almost bumped into Richard.

'Sorry, sir,' they said together.

'You'll be sorrier if the captain hears your views on the future of the squadron,' Richard said crisply. 'And it wouldn't help if the men knew what you thought. Your duty as future officers is to keep up the spirit of the lower deck – didn't you ever learn that at Osborne or Dartmouth?'

Letchworth, the taller of the two, and his good-looking fellow middy, Arthur Richardson, stood at attention looking embarrassed and chastened. 'Yes, sir.'

'Well, remember it now, when it matters. The Royal Navy does not lose engagements at sea. Read some history tonight before you sling your hammock. Carry on, gentlemen.'

As the two young men paced away across the forecastle, silent now, Richard experienced a double sense of guilt, first at his pomposity and second because what they had been saying was true enough. Somewhere in the vast expanse of the Pacific Ocean lay Admiral Maximilian von Spee's East Asiatic Squadron of two powerful armoured cruisers and goodness knows how many light cruisers in support. Since the beginning of the war back in August 1914 they had eluded all efforts by British, Australian, New Zealand, French and Japanese ships – dozens of them – to track them down. Allied trade had almost come to a halt. Merchantmen on the west coast of South America had been prohibited by their owners from leaving port. Troop convoys with vital reinforcements for the armies in France and Flanders had not sailed from Australia and New Zealand for fear of interception by the enemy.

And now what was the Admiralty in London doing about this continuing threat? They were sending a pair of armoured cruisers which should have been in the scrapyard years ago against this crack German squadron. There was the *Monmouth* ahead of them, steaming at eight knots through the calm waters of the Magellan Straits, her four tall funnels, 'like a packet of Woodbine fags when you've 'ad one' as an old tar called them, belching black smoke, armed with nothing bigger than 6-inch guns and most of them disposed in casemates so low in the hull that they were swamped in any sort of a seaway.

And astern steamed the squadron joke, the converted liner *Otranto*, nicknamed 'the sardine-tin'. A few months ago there would have been deck chairs instead of a scattering of old 4.7 guns on her upper deck, a ripe target for the most incompetent German gun-crew. And it was well known by now that there was no such thing as an incompetent German gun-crew. In fact Admiral von Spee's big ships held the top gunnery prize in the German Navy.

Admiral Christopher Cradock, their commander-in-chief, was due to join them soon in his flagship *Good Hope*. But even this cruiser did not live up to her name as she was almost as long in the tooth and ill-armed as the *Monmouth*. Meanwhile here they were, approaching the Pacific Ocean, where they might meet von Spee at any time of day or night as he headed for the Atlantic to cause more destruction and paralysis of trade.

While Richard had to admit that the omens were not good, and that the midshipmen had been probably right in suggesting that they might survive in their little light cruiser *Glasgow* only because of their good turn of speed, the sights and sounds about them for the present were beautiful and awe-inspiring. It was spring down here in the uttermost south. The shoreline of Patagonia two miles distant to the north was a varicoloured splash of wild flowers spread over gently rising hills. Farther away to the south, off the port side of the *Glasgow* and under a bright blue sky, the mountainous islands of Tierra del Fuego, bright green rising to the craggy snowline, stretched far into the distance among the maze of channels. Beyond them lay Cape Horn, the end of the American continent. The *Glasgow* had been down there recently, among the glaciers, searching for one of von Spee's cruisers, and

Richard had drawn the Cape roughly, for the cruiser was pitching and tossing violently and spume splashed the paper. The island was like a giant crouched bear, he had thought, a bear about to reach out for another victim.

But here, in this strait through which Ferdinand Magellan had sailed in 1520 to discover the *Mar del Pacifico*, it was as peaceful as a village pond on a windless day, contradicting the evil reputation of this part of the world.

Ahead of them the *Monmouth* put over her helm for a four-point alteration of course to conform with the strait's change of direction to the north-west, the dark headland of Cape Froward marking this turn. Distantly to the south, the highest mountain of the region, Mount Sarmiento, thrust its white conical peak high into the sub-Antarctic sky, trailing a long vapour cloud from its summit like a signpost to the South Pole.

It was the end of the forenoon watch and, as the bells sounded out, Richard made his way below deck and aft to the wardroom, walking swiftly and with his characteristic loose-limbed gait. His elder brother, Harry, used to say teasingly, 'Mother forgot to tighten the bolts when she gave birth to you, Rich.' But Richard could beat him over a hundred yards, or any distance for that matter. And at Dartmouth he could shin up the simulated rigging on the parade ground as fast as anyone.

For a 4,800-ton light cruiser, the *Glasgow* had a spacious and comfortable wardroom, although it had been stripped now in preparation for action, the piano, wood panelling on the bulkheads and much of the furniture removed and left behind at Port Stanley. Officers' Steward Thompson from Cardiff was on duty and Richard ordered a pink gin from him.

'A beautiful day, sir. Not what I expected of this part of the world.'

Richard agreed. 'It must have been a day like this that

tempted the early Spaniards to set up a colony here nearly four hundred years ago.'

'What happened to them, sir?'

'They all starved to death – all but a handful,' said Richard cheerfully.

'That's what's going to happen to us, if we don't take on some more stores soon.'

Richard was well aware of the problem. The officers were eating no better than the lower deck – bully beef or salt pork and biscuits day after day, with no fresh fruit or vegetables for weeks now. Half 'Bare Navy', the rations were. 'Issues on repayment' of peas and haricot beans, flour, tea, jam and sugar had long since ceased.

'There was more than thirty outside the sick-bay at 8.30 this morning, sir. Boils and ulcers mostly. The men are getting low and weak.'

'Any more cheerful news, Thompson?' Richard said with a laugh. He sipped the sweet gin, feeling its warming effect on his empty stomach. That's one thing the Navy was never short on, hard spirit – gin and rum. That's what had fired them for battle in the sailing Navy, that and the lure of the prize money. He put down his glass and told the small, dark Welshman, who was always a true source of information on the mood of the lower deck, 'You tell the men we'll be putting into a Chilean port as soon as we can for stores. Everyone's in the same boat – as you know – literally.'

The German light cruiser *Dresden* was the culprit. They had been chasing her for weeks now, all the way from the Caribbean where she had slipped through the net Admiral Cradock had laid for her, right down to Orange Bay behind Cape Horn where a scratched message on a rock told them that their quarry had recently been there. And now there seemed every likelihood that she had escaped up the west coast of Chile, searching for British merchantmen before joining up with Admiral von Spee.

Other officers came drifting into the wardroom for a gin before luncheon, the staff paymaster, the engineer officer, the first lieutenant, or 'number one', Lieutenant-Commander Jerry MacTavish, and Lieutenant Jerry Phipps, the gunnery officer, Richard's boss. Phipps was a rather heavy, serious officer, with a square-cut face and prematurely grey hair. He was only about twenty-eight but looked older. His eyes were deep blue and unusually sharp, too, as Richard had long since learnt while observing him supervising practice firing. And he was a friendly enough officer with whom Richard got on well, respecting his policy of giving praise rarely and only when it was earned, and indicating disapproval to range-takers, gunlayers and range-finder crews alike by a heavy silence which no one could fail to note and attempt to avoid in the future.

Phipps greeted Richard unsmilingly. 'The captain's ordered firing practice as soon as we get past Cape Pilar and out into open water.'

'4-inch and 6-inch?' asked Richard.

The *Glasgow* was armed with two 6-inch guns, one fore and one aft, and ten guns of the smaller calibre disposed along either beam behind shields and with a range of around 10,000 yards, or six land miles. In accordance with family tradition, Richard had specialized in gunnery from his days as a midshipman, and had passed out from his course at HMS *Excellent* with a first-class certificate. These had earned him, as a sub, a plum appointment as assistant gunnery officer in this crack modern light cruiser at the age of twenty.

Like his father before him, Richard had a lifetime love affair with guns, from his first 20-gauge Greener (with which at nine years he had first gone partridge-shooting over dogs), the 12-bore Churchill his father had given him at the age of fourteen, to the 12-inch Armstrong Mark VIII 35-calibre naval gun he had first handled at Portsmouth only three years ago. His dream had been to fire one of these monsters at extreme range and hit the target with one of its great shells. Maxims, .303 rifles, polished brass signal-guns, the new Vickers machine-guns, ancient muskets – he loved them all. As a musicologist relishes the sight of a finely led and conducted orchestra, so Richard's first pleasure was to witness a well-drilled gun crew in action, packing home the silk bags of charge powder behind the projectile, slamming shut the breech and firing.

All the officers of the *Glasgow* except the officer-of-the-watch, the navigating officer and the captain had assembled in the wardroom awaiting luncheon. They knew one another well now, all fourteen of them, their foibles and mannerisms, accents and tastes, in many cases their family histories. In the course of peacetime leave in South America, friendships had been formed ashore while riding and shooting on the Argentine pampas or on the nine-hole golf course outside Port Stanley, and during the long weeks at sea, from the heat of the tropics at Abrolhos Rocks to the stinging cold off Staten Island. Richard had had his fair share of rough teasing as the 'baby' of the wardroom, but that was over now. He was treated as an equal who had shared the same pleasures on leave, the same evening wardroom larks, and the same dangers and discomforts of patrol and search since war had broken out more than two months ago.

Richard's closest friend was Lieutenant William 'Sparks' Latchmore, the *Glasgow*'s signal officer, who introduced Richard to the secrets of his new Marconi wireless set. Neither fully understood the workings of the other's skills, but Richard was often invited into William's wireless office to listen to the shorts and longs of Morse code cipher signals transmitted from hundreds of miles away and received in the earphones together with a medley of static and interference like the sound of breaking waves on rocks. To Richard it all seemed a wonderful sort of magic, mysterious by contrast with the scientific practicality of naval gunnery. William was a cheerful, fair-haired extrovert, an out-of-doors man, you would judge on meeting him, not the sort whose first joy in life was to play with wires, knobs and crystals like some wizard in the confined space of a small man-o'-war's Wireless/Telegraphy Office.

'What's the news from the outside world?' Richard asked him.

'None from now on – not for a while,' William answered.

'Why's that?'

'Something called the Andes. Signals don't like mountain ranges. We'll have to go ashore and collect cables from our consuls at Coronel or Valparaiso.'

Not much more than ten years earlier, before the first W/T sets had been fitted to British warships, all signals from the Admiralty in London were sent by undersea cable and had to be collected from cable offices in the chief cities of the world. But now, as a result of the genius of Marconi, it was not normally necessary to send a ship ashore to collect information and instructions. Cabled signals from London to Admiral Cradock were transmitted in cipher from Montevideo in Uruguay to the Falkland Islands, and thence re-transmitted to his ships at sea.

But the Chileans were not so obliging, and refused to allow either German or British signals to be transmitted from Chilean soil in cipher. And now, as the squadron approached the Pacific through the deep gorge of the western end of the Magellan Straits, William was no longer able to pick up a signal from the Falkland Islands.

'What was the last message?' Richard asked.

Several of the *Glasgow*'s officers stopped talking to listen to William's answer. 'One of our consuls in Chile says the buzz there is that von Spee is heading for Valparaiso for coal and stores. The German colony in the town is preparing a reception, apparently.'

'Did he know how many ships?' someone asked.

''No,' said William, and turned to Lieutenant-Commander MacTavish. 'But he would be concentrating his squadron, not splitting it up, wouldn't he, sir?'

MacTavish nodded. 'If he wants to get into the Atlantic, wreck our shipping and then head for home, which is what I'd want to do if I was him, von Spee could go north or south. North to the Panama Canal, which was opened a few weeks ago, or south to Cape Horn where we are now. One way he escapes, the other way he meets us. And we don't want another *Goeben*.'

There was not an officer in the wardroom who did not know what the Commander meant by 'another *Goeben*'. The *Goeben* was like a mark of shame on the whole Royal Navy. Richard could remember his father saying of the flag-officer responsible, 'They ought to shoot him – like Admiral Byng.' At the outbreak of war there had been a powerful German battle-cruiser, the *Goeben*, in the Mediterranean. Like von Spee's in the Pacific, this ship with its accompanying light cruiser posed a threat to Allied trade and the French troop convoys from North Africa to French ports. Admiral Sir Archibald 'Arky-Barky' Milne was the C-in-C of the Mediterranean Fleet which, unlike Admiral Cradock's squadron, was far more powerful than the enemy's. There was a frantic hunt for the *Goeben*, then a pursuit when she was sighted. Four armoured cruisers under the command of Admiral Sir Thomas Troubridge could have intercepted the German ship at dawn. Instead, they turned away and lost any chance of damaging or destroying the enemy because the admiral calculated that he was not powerful enough and in an action might lose all or some of his ships.

There had been a court martial. Admiral Troubridge had not been shot for cowardice, like Admiral Byng in 1756. But he had been disgraced, along with his flag-captain who had advised him against the attack, and Admiral Milne. After that awful example it was certain that no British naval officer would risk similar disgrace by failing to attack the enemy, whatever the odds.

'We are in the Pacific Ocean,' announced Captain John

Luce,' crossed by Francis Drake in 1578 and charted by Captain Cook two hundred years later.' The *Glasgow*'s lower deck had been cleared and the entire ship's company, with the exception of those engaged on essential duties, was assembled on the cruiser's upper deck for their captain to address them. The captain, Richard had noted before, liked to bring a bit of history into his speeches. Luce was a fine commanding officer, a Wiltshire man, forty-four years old, tall and well-built, with a heavy jaw, strong mouth and close-set piercing eyes which recognized danger quickly and never flinched from it. The men feared and loved him.

'But for us,' the captain continued, 'this ocean is not likely to be pacific. We are searching for a powerful enemy and it's very unlikely that we'll return to port without meeting him. And I have news for the ship's company,' he continued puckishly. 'When we meet Admiral von Spee, we're going to lick him – you mark my words. Admiral Cradock will be joining us shortly with his flagship. And he will have with him . . .' He paused to add emphasis. 'He will have with him a battleship.'

A spontaneous cheer arose from the men. There were more than three hundred of them standing packed on the deck, some of them on the capstans and the roof of the 6-inch gun-shield. They were a motley crew at first sight, many of them dressed in makeshift coats run up from bits of tarpaulin or old blankets. A peacetime commission on the South American Station did not normally include steaming about the islands of Tierra del Fuego and doubling Cape Horn, and the men had found themselves as short of warm clothes as of adequate rations. Now their spirits were raised by the prospect of reinforcements on a powerful scale. A battleship was the one class of ship they needed. A battleship, even an old one, meant 12-inch guns, against von Spee's 8.2-inch batteries. It had been rumoured that the armoured cruiser *Defence* with 9.2s and 7.5s might be joining them. But a battleship, a battleship for certain –

now that was worth a cheer. And the next piece of news the captain had for them was worth a cheer too.

'Before we rendezvous with our C-in-C and his flagship and battleship, we're going to put into Valparaiso for provisions and "slops".'

Fresh meat, bacon, eggs, fruit! Warm clothes, new underwear, socks and boots! After weeks of cold and an unvarying diet, the prospect of Valparaiso, a big warm city – oranges, steaks, pretty young Chilean girls – now that was more like it!

This information was as much news to Richard and the rest of the officers as it was to the lower deck. He was already doing rough navigational calculations in his head. They were now about one thousand sea miles south of Valparaiso. At a steady nine knots, allowing for adverse weather and twenty-four hours for coaling *en route* – that would mean they would be there in about six days. Today was 9 October. They could be anchoring in Valparaiso roads on the 15th.

Captain Luce stepped back and responded to the first lieutenant's salute. 'Carry on Number One,' he said, and made off to his cuddy aft. It was a lonely job being commanding officer of a man-o'-war on a distant station. Meals on his own, and too much time for brooding in his cabin. What was the saying in the Navy about rising in rank to command? 'Years of hard labour, followed by years of solitary confinement.' Still, for Richard Buller, four thick rings on his sleeve instead of one thin one seemed like a gap that was impossible to span. That was his father's rank – Captain Archibald Buller DSO, RN.

As the men dispersed, the group of officers began to chat about this welcome news, and the *Glasgow* steamed north into the long shallow swell of the Pacific. Richard cast his mind back briefly to the last time he had seen his father. It had been at Rosyth in Scotland, on the River Forth, the great naval port upon which the Battle-Cruiser Squadron was based, Admiral Sir David Beatty's 'ocean

17

greyhounds', as the First Sea Lord 'Jackie' Fisher called them when he first conceived them.

Richard had eaten luncheon in his father's cabin on the *Incontestable*, the steward treating him as if he was an admiral of the fleet instead of a sub-lieutenant. The battle-cruisers had been battle-tested already, racing into a brisk action between German and British light forces off Heligoland, risking minefields and U-boats to sink three German cruisers with their heavy guns in very short order. 'It wasn't fair really,' Captain Buller had told his son. 'Like shooting pheasants out of season.'

Richard had shot all manner of game with his father, from pheasant and grouse and geese to deer with a 7 mm Mannlicher. But never German ships. What that would be like he could only imagine, for, unlike partridge or pheasant or hares, they could fire back! And kill.

Richard possessed the traditional Buller quality of courage in full, there was no doubt about that. He had once talked to his father about fear. He recalled that his father had been discomfited by the conversation as if it was 'bad form', but he had told Richard about climbing up to the truck in the old training-ship *Britannia* when he was a cadet. It was a feat few cadets attempted and it was frowned upon by the authorities, who normally applauded initiative. 'The only fear I felt', Richard's father had said, 'was of being afraid. But I enjoyed the challenge. Now,' he went on gruffly, 'a good many years after that I *did* feel afraid.' And he had told Richard about an incident in the Battle of Colenso during the South African War when he was a commander in the Naval Division and was trapped out on the veldt, pinned down by Mauser fire – the occasion when he earned his DSO. 'Now that was fear all right, and it wasn't good at all. Bullers weren't born to fight on land.'

And that was that. They never spoke of it again, nor did Richard wish to do so. He did not want it to be known that he thought so much about things. But he did, and he knew it. Once his mother, who was as straight-talking as his father and certainly did not believe in introspection, had called him 'Dreamy Dick'. Life was not about thinking – that was for poets and clever johnnies who taught at varsity. Ordinary people got on with things, like getting a good left-right with your Churchill when you put up a covey of partridge, and sending off the dog to bring in the brace.

For a young man who enjoyed his shooting – all shooting – so much, and was so good at it, it was curious that Richard did not enjoy the consequences of it: the warm, soft dampness of a dead snipe in his hand, and least of all the great stretched out body of a Highland stag which, seconds before, had been leaping so gracefully and skilfully from rock to rock in an attempt to avoid this fate, the blood already drying round the fatal wound in his chest.

Shortly after the visit to his father's ship, Richard had rejoined the *Glasgow* in the Caribbean – the *Glasgow* now at war. With the daily increasing likelihood of live action against the enemy, Richard's imagination played more and more on what it would be like when the time came. At gunnery practice at noon on that day, with the *Otranto* towing a canvas target at 5,000 yards range and the *Glasgow*'s 4-inch batteries firing in ripple salvoes, Richard tried to envisage the muzzle flash of the enemy's guns firing at him, at the *Glasgow*, hear the whooshing sound of the 'overs', the crack of the explosion of near misses sending up tall fountains of water, feel the shudder of the ship when she was hit, the dead and wounded lying about the smashed gun.

But all he could see were the neat patterns of falling practice-shell about the towed target, and – through his glasses – the torn canvas hanging in tatters where the *Glasgow*'s gunners had scored hits. All harmless sport. Twenty rounds a gun, the teams working in fine co-ordinated rhythm at the hot breeches of the port batteries. Then, at a signal from Lieutenant Phipps, Richard put the megaphone to his lips and shouted into the wind, 'Cease fire!'

'The gunnery officer says that was capital shooting,' Richard said later to the gunner's mate. 'Let the men know.'

'Always give encouragement where it's due,' Richard's father once told him when he was still a cadet. 'If they're good, let them know. They'll be better still next time.'

Coming from a long line of naval officers was a great help. It had never crossed Richard's mind, as far back as he could remember, that he would do anything else with his life than become a naval officer. When his father talked 'navy', Richard's ears were always open, his memory receptive, so that he rarely forgot anything, from direct advice to reminiscences of people and places, storms and actions against the enemy.

The name Buller had been synonymous with the Royal Navy since the days of Henry VIII, when the Navy was young indeed. Then, in October 1743, the fortunes of the family were suddenly altered in the course of a brisk action between the frigate *Frobisher*, captained by Alastair Buller, and a Spanish treasure-ship. When the enemy's colours were struck and Captain Buller boarded his capture, he increased his wealth many times over with the prize money. This Captain Buller bought a thousand acres of best Cotswold pasture and built a magnificent residence, Weir Park, which was now the family's ancestral home. This was the seat of Richard's uncle, Captain Sir Guy Buller Bt, although he was unlikely to see much of his residence until the war was over for he commanded one of the Grand Fleet battleships.

Then there was Captain Henry Buller, Uncle Guy's twin brother and in the same Battle Squadron. They were identical twins, which had led to much confusion in the Navy (and in their families) over the years. Both were tall men, prematurely grey-haired, able and vigorous, who commanded their dreadnoughts with a light touch and were much loved by the ships' companies. With Richard and Uncle Henry and Uncle Guy's four sons in the Navy, that made eight Bullers on active service, as many as in the Napoleonic wars when the name Buller had been so feared by the French and Spaniards, and three of the family had served at Trafalgar.

But Richard was the only Buller serving in foreign waters in October 1914, and not even his own father knew where he was except that the *Glasgow* was somewhere off South America – not that he was 50° 41′S, 76° 22′W, eighteen miles due west of Cabo Santiago on the coast of southern Chile, skies grey and overcast but visibility unlimited and the dark coastline clearly in sight on the starboard quarter, saw-toothed and threatening.

Admiral Cradock, impatiently awaiting the arrival of his battleship at the Falkland Islands, knew little more than Captain Buller at Rosyth of the whereabouts of his own squadron; and no one, not the British Admiralty nor even the German Admiralty, knew the whereabouts of Admiral von Spee.

II

Sounds from the Enemy

Some of the *Glasgow*'s officers became edgy under the
strain of the long hunt for the German squadron. Others
remained excited by it, among them Richard Buller whose
country upbringing had prepared him for the demands of a
long pursuit. He had ridden to hounds in Gloucestershire
from the age of eight, had enjoyed beagling and hare-
coursing. The tense excitements of fishing and shooting
had instilled in him a love for the uncertainties of the sport
with its sudden crises punctuated by the rattle of guns as
the quarry was sighted. Hunting for German warships in
the South Pacific and the gunfire that would mark their
discovery was not altogether unlike the field sports of the
West Country in England.

There was one marked difference between a run over the
Wolds with the mid-Gloucestershire Hunt and this search
for their human quarry over the wide oceans, which
surprised and shocked Richard. In all the fox-hunting in
which Richard had participated there was no hatred of the
prey, indeed there was a respect for it if it eluded pursuit
cleverly and bravely. In the wardroom of the *Glasgow*,
however, there was only hatred and contempt for the
Germans they were hunting, and, now that the British
were to be reinforced by a battleship, no uncertainty about
the outcome of any engagement. 'The bloody Boche' and
'the damn Hun' were the terms used to describe their
adversary. There had been stories circulating in the early
days of the war when the Germans advancing into Belgium

22

were reported to have committed atrocities against civilians. German soldiers were called 'murdering swine' and were depicted in cartoons with babies spiked on their bayonets.

Richard was as keen as anyone to hunt down and destroy the enemy. But this bitterness and hatred of German sailors, who were fighting for their country just as they were, mystified him. When the talk in the wardroom took a bloodthirsty turn and one of the officers attracted the laughter of the others by describing how he would use swimming German sailors for target-practice after their ship was sunk, Richard was the only one who did not join in. William Latchmore noted this. 'It's only high spirits – they don't really mean it,' he would reassure Richard quietly when they were alone.

'I suppose so,' Richard agreed. 'Do you think the German officers talk like that?'

'Of course they do. You're still wet behind the ears, Richard. When we sink the bastards we'll risk our necks diving in to rescue them – you'll see. Even that fire-eating Jerry Phipps.'

Richard laughed disbelievingly. He could not imagine Lieutenant Phipps, who had vowed to use 6-inch shells on any German lifeboats or rafts of von Spee's squadron, diving in to pick up the wounded.

'It's all part of the war-dance to build up their courage,' William continued. 'Like animals "displaying" or roaring before a fight. It'll be all right. Don't worry, Richard. We're all feeling a bit on edge.'

Suddenly realizing what his friend was thinking, Richard felt himself flush. 'You think I'm scared, don't you?' He controlled his voice with an effort. 'I don't blame you. But I'm not really. I'm more interested in what it's going to be like, and putting on a decent show. I just don't feel bloodthirsty. Perhaps I ought if I'm going to be any use. But I'll admit, I'm not much looking forward to the bloody part.' He paused, and then added quietly, 'The dead and wounded. Ours and theirs, poor blighters. I honestly don't

23

mind much about myself.'

William said philosophically, 'Well, that's what they say, "War is hell." And we're not in this rotten part of the world for the good of our health.'

Richard laughed, shrugging off his morbid thoughts.

The cheerfulness and fitness for battle greatly improved and matched the crew's bloodthirstiness after the visit to Valparaiso. Warm, rested and with good fresh food inside them, the *Glasgow*'s ship's company steamed towards the rendezvous with the commander-in-chief at a secret and lonely anchorage on the Chilean coast, Vallenar Roads. Here the *Otranto*, the *Monmouth* and the *Glasgow* awaited the arrival of the *Good Hope* and the promised battleship, coaling from colliers sent ahead from Port Stanley. For two backbreaking days the entire crew of the *Glasgow*, officers and men alike – except the captain, the surgeon and sick-berth attendants, the chaplain and cooks – handled the baskets of coal winched in from the collier alongside, lowering them down chutes into the bunkers under the mess-deck. Here it was trimmed by the stokers, 450 tons of it, until the bunkers were full. During all this working time, a black cloud of coal dust hung over the ship, obscuring the light and lingering chokingly in everyone's throats.

At four p.m. on the second day, the work was complete. The rocky cliffs became visible again, thick with booby and gannets' nests, and distantly they could see the high white undulating Andes. The captain ordered the main-brace to be spliced. Richard looked around him, the weariness like a clamp on his body. Rank, age, facial characteristics, all meant nothing. There was no identification. Everyone was covered with a thick layer of coal-dust, their eyes showing white, and whatever they touched turned black.

Richard had put down the last of the warming, soothing, coarse rum when a shout went up. Suddenly everyone was running to the port side of the ship. There were cries of 'Here she comes!' and 'The flagship!' He sprang up the mainmast ratlines with a dozen others and saw – there, scarcely a mile distant – the *Good Hope* steaming slowly round a headland, black smoke pouring from her four tall funnels, flying the white ensign and the flag of Read-Admiral Sir Christopher Cradock.

There was an echoing cheer from the big armoured cruiser, and a swarm of birds on the nearby cliff took fright and filled the air, to be joined by thousands more when the signalling guns cracked out their welcome and complement of thirteen guns to the commander-in-chief, to be answered by a seven gun 'thank you' from the *Good Hope*. The big cruiser hove to scarcely a cable's length from the *Glasgow*, there came the rattle of chains through the hawespipes and a rising brown cloud of rust before the anchors splashed into the still waters. But where was the promised battleship? Richard was not the only officer wondering what had happened and searching the sea to the south in expectation of seeing its reassuring bulk rounding the headland in its turn.

It was half an hour before the answer became clear. During that time the decks of the *Glasgow* were hosed down and officers and men alike strived to cleanse themselves of the all-penetrating coal-dust. Richard emerged from his diminutive cabin to be greeted by an AB who had been sent to look for him.

'Begging your pardon, sir, captain's compliments, sir, and would you please report to his cabin.'

William Latchmore was already there, waiting uneasily for the arrival of Captain Luce. 'I think we're wanted on board the flagship,' he said.

'But why me?' Richard asked.

'Your boss-man's in the sick-bay. Got struck by a basket of coal and hurt his leg.'

William's speculation about the purpose of this meeting was proved right when Captain Luce entered and nodded to them. 'The admiral wants to see us, gentlemen. The boat's here.'

The picket-boat was bobbing up and down against the accommodation ladder under the command of the smallest midshipman Richard had ever seen. He saluted smartly as Captain Luce sprang last on board, and with a marvellous crispness but in a voice not yet broken, ordered, 'Bear off for'd, bear off aft, slow ahead,' to his men. Then, seizing the brass steering-wheel that was rather taller than he, put it hard over and the picket-boat sped away towards the tall grey hull of the *Good Hope*. It was typical of him that Captain Luce made no remark about the age and relative inexperience of the midshipman, talking to him as if he were a mature lieutenant. As Richard studied the decks of the flagship he noted again the large number of cadets and young midshipmen among the ship's company on the one hand and the contrasting elderly appearance of the reserve ratings and officers.

A minute later, down in the admiral's cabin, Richard was also struck by the sick appearance of their C-in-C. The anxieties and privations of the last weeks had taken their toll. 'Kit' Cradock was fifty-two years old, a blunt Yorkshireman who had ridden hard to hounds all his life when ashore, and in the service had performed with supreme gallantry in numerous minor campaigns in Africa, the Near East and Far East. Here was a flag officer who did not, Richard had heard, 'suffer fools gladly'. And now, it soon became clear, he was thoroughly rattled and not well.

After greeting Captain Luce perfunctorily, Admiral Cradock turned first to William Latchmore, asking, 'Have you been picking up any signals since you left Valparaiso?'

'Yes, sir. Quite strong signals – Telefunken. Carrying the call-sign of the *Leipzig*.'

'Any other German signals?'

'No, sir. Only from merchantmen. The German merchantmen at Valparaiso were signalling day and night.'

'Damn 'em,' exclaimed Cradock. 'That's against international law.'

A hush fell over the assembled officers from the *Glasgow, Monmouth* and *Otranto*, and Cradock's chief of staff stared at the stationary fan on the ceiling. Cradock knew, and everyone present knew, that they were all flouting international law themselves by using this anchorage for warlike purposes without Chilean permission. But who was to know or do anything about it?

'That doesn't mean von Spee's not in company with the *Leipzig* and using her as his signalling-ship. I've kept wireless silence since Port Stanley, and you' – he pointed at Latchmore – 'are the only ship to transmit from now on.'

He sat down behind his desk and ordered everyone else to 'find yourselves a pew. Now,' he continued, 'you know that our orders are to search out and destroy the enemy. I have good reason to believe that von Spee has been working his way east across the Pacific, from the Marquesas to Easter Island, with our old friend *Dresden* scouting for him. If the signals Lieutenant Latchmore reports picking up were as loud as he states, then we can expect to meet the Hun at any time. I shall ask Captain Francklin to coal my flagship as soon as possible, and we shall then proceed to sea.' He turned to Captain Luce. 'And you, John, will call in at Coronel to despatch my signal and pick up any telegrams that have come from London. If we meet the enemy we shall use our best endeavours to destroy him, or at the worst to cripple him so that he will be forced to seek a dockyard for repairs – which will mean internment in a neutral port, probably Valparaiso.'

Another silence descended upon the gathering. Richard could hear the cry of gulls above the steady note of a picket-boat's engine. This isn't a conference, Richard was thinking. This is just an announcement of plans. Why wasn't anyone being consulted?

Then Captain Luce's voice broke the silence, a deep, authoritative voice, only just deferential. 'The last intelligence we picked up from Punta Arenas, sir, was that we were being reinforced by a battleship.'

'We do have a battleship, of sorts. The *Canopus*. But she arrived a week late at Port Stanley. I've ordered the *Defence* to join us from Montevideo, but it'll be a couple of weeks before she shows up. The *Canopus* has engine trouble. Her engineer commander reported she couldn't make more than twelve knots. That's no use to me. She's escorting the colliers and'll be here in a few days, if her guts don't fall out.'

In another tone of voice, which appeared to signal the end of the conference, Admiral Cradock said to Captain Luce, 'Talking of guts, John, you might pick me up some oranges when you go ashore at Coronel, say four dozen. They're good for the guts, you know.'

On this note the meeting broke-up. On the return trip to the *Glasgow* there was a middle-aged petty officer in charge of the picket-boat, Petty Officer John Taylor from Brixham, a trawlerman in peacetime. He did not look well, either, but at least he seemed cheerful – perhaps the only cheerful soul around that afternoon. Captain Luce said nothing on the way back to his ship, his mouth set tight in his determination to be discreet. But his two officers knew what he was thinking: Admiral Cradock had got no clear plan or doctrine in his head, and he was not asking anyone for one either.

Coronel is a port and market-town 300 miles south of Valparaiso with a population of some 6,000. When Richard studied it through his glasses as the *Glasgow* made her way slowly towards the harbour, he thought what a pathetically poor and ill-favoured place it looked, with unmade roads running between rows of single-storey buildings with rusting iron roofs. Pigs roamed the streets along with goats and miserable-looking sheep. Literally a pigsty of a place;

except that in England pigs would be given better accommodation. A few stone buildings in the centre appeared to mark the less poverty-stricken quarter with the town's administrative buildings, and there were offices and warehouses along the waterfront. Anchored in the harbour, or tied up alongside, were a number of merchantmen, some flying the British and German ensigns, uneasy enemies and fellow refugees from the warships of the other side which were believed to be near at hand.

Captain Luce wasted no time when they anchored, a boat putting off at once with the ship's first lieutenant and a midshipman on board. They were away for three hours, during which time a Chilean customs boat kept a watchful eye on them and an ancient gunboat appeared to work up steam in case she was called upon to bring what pressure she could to bear with her single 3-inch gun. Richard watched the local boats that soon encircled the *Glasgow*, the natives begging for escudos or trying to sell fish and trinkets. Soon tiring of this sight, he made his way to the wireless room and knocked on the door.

'Any sound from the enemy?' he asked William, who was sitting before his black Marconi set with its numerous dials and knobs.

'Listen to that. It never stops.'

Richard slipped on the earphones and was at once half-deafened by the screech of static broken intermittently by a morse message which decreased and increased in volume like the roar of waves breaking on a lee shore. Every half-minute or so it repeated what sounded like a single word.

'Is that the call-sign?' Richard asked.

'That's it. The *Leipzig* again. And very close.'

'What's she saying?'

'You'll be flattered to know it's all about us.'

'You mean she knows where we are?'

William reached over the desk beside him and took from his wireless operator rating a piece of paper. On it was written a message translated from the German.

29

Richard read: 'English four-funnel cruiser arrived Coronel at fourteen hundred. Boat has gone ashore. Ship's funnel markings white equal band on all funnels . . .'

'They don't miss much,' Richard said in astonishment. 'How did they learn all that so quickly?'

'You'll see a German steamer anchored in mid-harbour with aerials rigged between her masts. The *Göttingen*, registered in Bremen. She'll be telling the *Leipzig* everything, probably that we're having this chat now!'

'Well, let's get after this *Leipzig*,' Richard said. 'She's only got 4.1-inch guns.'

All that evening and far into the night the ether was busy with morse transmissions and replies, some in Spanish but most of them in German, like the voices of assassins conspiring before the kill. It was as if the whole German Navy was closing in to await their departure from neutral waters. But William assured Richard that the chatter involved only the *Leipzig*, the consulates at Coronel and Valparaiso and the numerous German merchantmen anchored in Chilean ports.

Late that night the shore-party returned, complete with the admiral's four dozen oranges and the vital telegrams from London. Richard slept for a few hours, taking off only his boots, and was awoken before dawn by the familiar sounds of the ship preparing for sea – the clatter of feet on steel decks, the hiss of steam, the rumble of machinery and the shouting of orders. In the confined metal shell of a small cruiser, every movement and every sound could be detected.

The captain was on the bridge, wearing a greatcoat and white scarf about his neck against the dawn chill, warming his hands on a mug of cocoa. He greeted Richard gruffly, then remarked, 'Fine time to lose your gunnery officer.'

'Is Lieutenant Phipps still sick, sir?'

'Says he can't move. The quack says his leg's broken. So it's up to you, Buller. This may be an important day.' He pointed at the choppy sea. 'And there's quite a lop on.'

'When do we expect to make the rendezvous, sir?' asked Richard. His own voice sounded so distant it might have belonged to someone else. He was bewildered by the news that as a young sub-lieutenant, he was standing in for the 'Guns'. At the same time he was quite determined not to show it.

'Soon after noon,' Captain Luce told him. 'We'll clear for action as soon as we're out of sight of these spies.' He nodded his head towards the anchored merchantmen, lights blazing, just as they shone out from the German consulate ashore. It had been a busy night for everyone.

1 November was a grey, lowering day with a heavy swell running that sent water crashing over the forecastle and spray over the *Glasgow*'s bridge as she dug in her bows. The forward 6-inch gun would be hard to work and both port and starboard number one 4-inch gun-crews would be soaked from time to time in any action. Gunnery control would not be easy under these conditions, but Richard consoled himself with the knowledge that they would be no more favourable for the enemy.

Phipps, lying on the sick-bay cot, looked up at Richard with an expression of mixed weariness and resignation on his face. 'Isn't this just my luck! For ten years I've been learning how to hit the enemy, and the first chance I get *this* happens.' He glanced at his strung-up leg in plaster and then looked up at Richard, smiling ruefully and shrugging his shoulders.

Richard said, 'I'm really very sorry. Have you got any special instructions?'

'You know we've got the best gun-crews in the Royal Navy, Richard. Your job is to keep them believing that. And tell them I'll be watching through the scuttle – every round they fire. And as for you, this may be the chance of a lifetime, good luck.'

III

Disaster off Chile

All through that morning the captain remained uncommunicative and in as dour a mood as the sea. They had been hunting the enemy for almost three months, with breaks only for coaling and taking on provisions and telegrams from London. It had been a hard and anxious time for all of them, but most of all for John Luce, who had borne the weight of responsibility alone, and with the growing uncertainty about the strength of the squadron and its leadership. Now, in this forenoon watch, up here on his bridge with the officer of the watch beside the standard compass, the signals yeoman and navigator close by the helmsman, Richard knew that his captain felt that he had never been closer to his quarry.

Just before noon the clouds broke up, the sun shafted through and they all felt its comforting warmth. At the same time, a voice from the masthead called down, 'Smoke bearing blue five-four.' Then, 'It's the *Good Hope*, sir,' news which left Richard half-relieved and half-disappointed.

A few minutes later he could make out the flagship through his glasses, identifiable by the big 9.2-inch gunforward. With visual contact established, the signal-lamps at once began flashing, the signalman on the bridge reading unerringly and at slow talking-speed the morse message *en clair*. 'F–l–a–g–t–o–g–l–a–s–g–o–w . . .'

The *Good Hope*'s flag-captain had judged the seas to be too high to lower a boat, and ordered the signals from

32

Coronel to be sent by barricoe. The signals were wrapped in oilskin, inserted into a small cask, followed by the admiral's oranges, and the bung belted well home. Two ratings then secured the waterproofing further by wrapping the cask in canvas and tacking it down.

The *Glasgow* manoeuvred close alongside the flagship. Informal signals were exchanged between officers and ratings who knew one another, and a courtesy signal was hoisted, 'Permission to pass ahead of you.' The *Glasgow* then turned eight points across the *Good Hope*'s bows, streaming the cask from her stern at the end of a grass line two hundred yards long. It was a manoeuvre that required skill at any time, and the seas were still high when the *Good Hope* collected the grass on her fo'csle and hauled in the cask. It seemed an oddly primitive method of delivering messages that had been transmitted half round the world under an ocean and across a continent by cable. But like most naval activities, it was highly practical and the only way of keeping the confidentiality of the admiral's secret orders from the eyes of the squadron and the ears of the enemy.

Two flags fluttered from the *Good Hope*'s yard-arm. 'Manoeuvre well executed,' read the yeoman of signals. Captain Luce nodded acknowledgement but the set, serious expression did not ease. The squadron was fanning out, the four ships forming a line of search fifteen miles apart, the *Monmouth* the most westerly, in the hope of sighting and destroying the elusive *Leipzig*. The mid-afternoon sun was warm, the wind astern from the south-west. William Latchmore had earlier told Richard that the signals were more frequent than ever and very close, almost on top of them. 'We *must* meet something soon,' he had said.

For a moment Richard indulged in speculation. The *Leipzig* must be expecting to meet only the *Glasgow*, for wireless silence had been strictly adhered to by the bigger ships. Instead, the German ship would face a squadron, all the ships of which were more powerful than herself.

And was that her now, the little talkative *Leipzig*? The look-out was calling down again from the masthead. 'Smoke bearing green four-five.' The yeoman beside Richard trained his telescope on the starboard bow. 'Yes, sir, I have it. And more smoke than from one ship.'

The *Glasgow* held her course, everyone on the bridge straining to identify the ships. Richard could make out a dark shape, almost hull down on the horizon. But was that a second shape? The minutes passed and the watchkeeper was swearing under his breath. 'Dammit, what's the matter with the man?'

But the look-out was doing well, waiting for certain identification. 'Two ships with four funnels, bearing green five-oh.'

So it was not the *Leipzig* alone. Then, remembering the identification silhouettes they had studied for weeks, in preparation for just this moment, Richard realized that it was not the *Leipzig* at all. The *Leipzig* had only three funnels. All von Spee's light cruisers had only three funnels. These ships bearing down on them on an opposite course were not light cruisers. They must be the two big armoured cruisers, von Spee's flagship *Scharnhorst* and her sister, the *Gneisenau*, carrying twelve 8.2-inch guns with a range far beyond their own. The crack gunnery ships in the German Navy.

Again the look-out: 'Two three-funnel ships also bearing green five-oh.' So, light cruisers in support. They had met von Spee's entire squadron. For twelve weeks dozens of men-o'-war had spanned the Pacific in search of these powerful ships. And now it was the *Glasgow* which had sighted them, still out of range of those German guns, but not for long.

The yeoman of signals was already swiftly hoisting Flag Eight at each yard-arm: 'Enemy in sight!' The most exciting signal of them all, beloved by generations of Bullers, and hoisted and kept flying permanently in the

34

hallway at Weir Park by Richard's great-great-grandfather who had originally hoisted it from the yard-arm of his two-decker at the Battle of St Vincent. And with it the most exciting sound, the bugles sounding off 'Action Stations'. To action stations. Buckling on his revolver, Richard raced up the vertical steel ladder to the foretop, a splinterproof steel cylinder with the ship's main range-finder and tight accommodation for the look-out, the gunner and his mate, and the range-taker.

For the present the distant shapes would remain distant. Captain Luce had ordered twenty knots and was closing on his flagship. The need for search formation was over. What would the admiral do? He had the margin of speed to get away south, evading this much superior force, falling back as the Admiralty must have intended on the 12-inch-gunned battleship despatched for just this situation. Only one or two knots' superior speed, but that would be enough, especially with darkness falling.

The gunner said, 'Do you think we're going to take them on, sir?' He was a carrot-haired petty officer from Wigan with a heavy Lancashire accent, stocky and tough.

'It's like the toss of a coin, Mr Barratt,' Richard replied, training the look-out's telescope on the distant shapes. There were five of them now, closer together, too, forming into line of battle. 'But I think the admiral'll take a crack at them.'

Richard could not imagine Admiral Cradock 'doing a *Goeben*'. When Richard's father had learned that his son was going to serve under his command he had said of him, 'Ah, "Kit" Cradock. Great sailor. Brave as a lion, not too much up top.' He would flinch from nothing, and listen to nothing. It was common knowledge that he had a 'brainy' flag-captain in Peter Francklin, an officer who could give sound advice. But, except for official essentials, it was also known throughout the squadron that the two officers had not spoken to one another for months.

'Have you checked the ready ammunition, Mr Barratt?'

Richard asked, knowing the answer before he received it. Eighteen rounds for the 6-inch guns, twenty-four for the 4-inch. When they had been fired, shell parties would bring in fresh supplies from the magazine hoists, but not before for safety reasons.

'The Huns have come a long way, sir,' said Barratt. 'Their bottoms will be dirty. They won't be able to make their best speed.'

Richard nodded. He did not want to deprive the chief gunner of comfort and reassurance before the action. But they had come a long way, too. All the ships on both sides had not seen a dry dock for months, steaming thousands of miles since early August. And now, quarry and pursuer, hunted and hunter, confronted one another, some four thousand men in nine men-o'-war intent on each other's destruction in these turbulent seas off this inhospitable coastline on the far side of the world. This thought passed fleetingly across Richard's consciousness, edged with a touch of irony, for, unlike the mid-Gloucestershire Hunt or a rough shoot with his father, this quarry could not only strike back, but strike back with a power greater than their own. This was going to be more like a tiger hunt with nothing better than an air-rifle.

In rapid succession the flags fluttered out from the *Good Hope*'s yard-arm, were acknowledged by the *Monmouth*, *Otranto* and *Glasgow*, and hauled down. By 5.30 p.m. the squadron was concentrated on the *Good Hope*, formed up in line ahead in descending order of gunpower: two ancient armoured cruisers dating from the last century, a modern light cruiser and an ocean liner – none built to stand in the line of battle, the last an admiral's nightmare, a huge target that could not hit back. They were on a southerly course, steaming parallel with the Germans, who were some 20,000 yards distant, brightly lit up by the low sun.

Richard climbed down to the upper deck to make a rapid final tour of the ship's guns and their crews. He was experiencing a heightened awareness brought on by the imminence of battle and a growing sense of unreality. How could he have imagined that a junior gunnery appointment could lead within a few days to this ultimate responsibility? The captain of the forward 6-inch winked solemnly at Richard as he ran his eyes over his gun. He had eighteen months' seniority over Richard but clearly felt no resentment at this odd turn of events. The officers of quarters of the 4-inch batteries and the aft 6-inch who were also senior to Richard accepted his supervision with a touch of humour. The excited anticipation of the men was reflected in their faces and their comments. 'Yes, sir. All set to give the Hun hell!' 'Will it be long before we open fire, sir?' At last, after all their years of training and drill and practice shoots, they were about to exercise their skills in earnest, in action.

Richard returned to the bridge to report to Lieutenant-Commander MacTavish. 'All closed up and ready for action, sir.'

MacTavish reported in turn to Captain Luce. 'Ready for action in all respects, sir.'

The captain nodded without removing his glasses from his eyes. If he felt any anxiety about the absence of his gunnery officer at this critical time, nothing was to be gained and much to be lost if he showed it. Luce's business was to inspire confidence and this, as always, he was doing magnificently.

'Thank you, Number One. If the admiral intends to attack, now's the time.' He lowered his glasses so that they hung by their leather strap. Whatever confidence Richard felt in him, he believed that he could see in his captain's eyes a fatal trace of non-confidence in his admiral. As a gunnery officer, Richard recognized as clearly as his captain that, until the sun set, conditions were marvellously in their favour, with the enemy gunlayers blinded by the low sun behind the British ships. But the moment it set, this advantage would be reversed, with the British ships clearly etched against the bright sky, while von Spee's squadron would be dark against the dark sea and dark coastline.

They should be closing the enemy now, forcing an early action, increasing speed to their maximum twenty knots. But they were hampered by the slow and stately 'sardine-tin', the *Otranto*. Why did not Admiral Cradock order her to fall out of line, to steam out into the Pacific where she would soon be concealed by the onset of darkness anyway? Or did the admiral not intend to seek an action now, after all? But the *Good Hope* was flying battle ensigns, so . . .

Captain Luce was clearly as puzzled as anyone by his admiral's apparent indecision. He turned to the midshipman of the watch, Arthur Richardson, and snapped, 'Present Lieutenant Latchmore with my compliments and ask him if he has picked up any signals in the last few minutes.'

The young man darted away and returned scarcely a minute later with a copy signal to a distant friendly man-o'-war. John Luce read it aloud. 'Flag to *Canopus*: I am going to attack the enemy. Timed 6.18.' He glanced at the first lieutenant. 'Well, at least we know. And we're to do the best we can without the help of her 12-inch guns.'

'We've got *Otranto*'s 4.7s,' remarked MacTavish.

'This is no time for irony, Number One.'

'No, sir.'

'But it *is* time to get to the conning-tower.' Luce led the way down to the pillbox citadel, like an enlarged foretop, with its narrow slit cut into the armour from which he would direct his ship in battle. He was followed by the navigator, MacTavish, and the midshipman. The *Good Hope* had turned four points towards the enemy at last in an attempt to close the gap, and the other ships conformed automatically.

The time had come for Richard to make his way back up to the foretop. 'Are we closing?' he asked at once when he climbed in, panting from his exertions.

'No, sir. Still 16,500 yards. The Hun just turns away to the east if it looks as if we're getting within range.'

Richard could see the twin after 6-inch guns of the *Monmouth* ahead of them fully elevated in their turret. The upper casemate guns were also at full elevation, but the crews must have been taking a soaking, and the lower 6-inch were clearly not workable. They were all old Mark VII 45-calibre weapons, built in the last century, inferior to the *Glasgow*'s more modern 6-inch.

The gunner, a wily old bird who had long since learned all there was to know about gunnery, said, 'I reckon that old von Spee's gonna keep out of our range and pepper us when 'e feels like it with his 8.2s.'

The German position and strength was a gunnery officer's dream, especially with an imminent change of light to his advantage.

'15,000,' called out the range-taker at the range-finder. And a few minutes later, '14,500.'

Richard put his mouth to the voice-pipe. 'Range closing to 14,000. 6-inch crews prepare to open fire.' He could see the forward 6-inch at full elevation, the gun-crew of eight concentrated behind the shield. Some had scarves round their heads, and under their caps, some wore rubber boots the quartermaster had bought in Valparaiso the other day, two of them were in Lammy coats, 'Little Titch' Chambers, a Geordie accustomed to the cold, stripped to the waist. The whole crew presented a picture not unlike that at Trafalgar more than a hundred years before, when eight men would work a 32-pounder on the lower deck. Able Seaman Cruikshank, McGovern and Horstman and the rest of the loading-crew could all have descended from Nelson's men, waiting as impatiently for the range to close off Cadiz on that October morning in 1805 as they were now.

'12,000.'

Richard glanced at the setting sun behind them, a huge red orb that threw a long distorted shadow of their ship across the heavy seas. It tipped the sea, fast lost its geometric symmetry as the horizon cut in deeper, and became a scarlet semi-circle. Then it was as if an electric light had been switched off, and at the same time German gunnery officers now 11,300 yards distant, activated real electric switches which closed the firing-circuits to their heavy guns.

''ere they come,' remarked the chief gunner. A trite observation but better than silence in the small foretop where no order to fire could yet be given. Deep red pinpricks of light sparkled out from the two big German ships, which had become almost invisible now, followed by rising clouds of brown smoke. The *Gneisenau* and *Scharnhorst* were firing ripple salvoes from stem to stern – the forward turret, the four beam guns, the after turret – as regular a progression of flashes as a seamstress's stitches.

Richard counted aloud – '. . . ten, eleven, twelve.' At fifteen the *Monmouth* and *Good Hope* ahead were suddenly screened by spouts of water that arose from the surface of white-torn ocean in columns as high as their mastheads. This first ranging salvo had fallen some five hundred yards short of target. The second salvo, bracketing the two armoured cruisers, exploded like whipcracks the same distance over the target.

The enemy was still just out of range to the *Glasgow*, and Richard watched this German exhibition of long-range gunnery with professional fascination. In heavy seas and high wind, the Germans had achieved a perfect straddle at maximum range. It did not even require a third salvo to convince Richard that the two British armoured cruisers were already doomed. With a sickening sense of the inevitable, which must have been shared by Admiral Cradock, his staff, and the gunnery officers of the *Good Hope* and *Monmouth*, Richard knew that the sun which had just set behind the two big ships would never shine on them again, leaving them only its afterglow as the backdrop for their destruction.

'Bloody good shooting, sir,' said the chief gunner. 'If you'll excuse my English, sir.'

'Yes,' said Richard. 'Too good.'

With the precision of a pre-set machine, the third salvo came out of the dusk sky fifteen seconds after they observed the distant pinpricks of light. Three of the shells, each weighing 320 pounds, struck home, one on the *Good Hope* and two on the *Monmouth*. The *Glasgow* was sufficiently out of line in these heavy seas for Richard to see that the *Good Hope* had been hit on the forecastle, and that where her forward heavy gun had been there was now a tangled wreckage of torn steel deck and debris, and a hole from which a dense cloud of brown smoke belched.

The *Monmouth* had also been struck – twice – on the forecastle, also causing a fire, with flames leaping twice as high as the bridge, fanned by the near-gale wind into which the cruiser was driving. None of her guns was firing, but from the flagship's remaining 9.2, the only gun left in the squadron capable of reaching the enemy, a single round was defiantly fired.

'11,500 yards,' reported the range-taker.

Richard tore his gaze from the two leading ships as another salvo crashed about them and bent to the mouthpiece. 'Range shortening, prepare to open fire.'

'11,200.'

Richard could see some of the forward 6-inch crew looking up expectantly in his direction. 'Range eleven-two, 6-inch open fire,' he ordered, voice raised in tenseness and on a higher pitch than usual. He repeated the words 'Open fire!'

Down on the forecastle and aft on the quarterdeck, the gunlayers, eyes to their telescopes, would be adjusting for direction while their mate set the range under the supervision of the officer. The layers pressed the electric firing-button and the two guns fired at maximum elevation, leaping back in their recoil and forward again on their springs. Breech swung open, emitting a swirling cloud of smoke and cordite vapour, two of the crew thrusting in the 100-pound shell, two more the propellant cartridge, two more the rammer. Within ten seconds of the first discharge, the gun fired again. It was like a sharp hammer-blow on the eardrums and the *Glasgow* gave a twitch, and another twitch as the gun aft fired.

Richard watched the shells soar up into the sky like rugger balls kicked for a distant conversion. The layers were aiming at the *Scharnhorst*, first ship in the German line, by prior instruction. But now, as a twinkling line of light flashed from the German light cruisers as well, Richard was ordered by voice-pipe from the bridge, 'Switch fire to first three-funnel ship.'

After acknowledging, Richard snapped, 'Range?'

'9,500, sir.'

Their own 4-inch guns could just make this range, which was evidently still closing, with the Germans coming in for the 'kill', their armoured cruisers' 5.9s adding to the carnage created already by their heavier guns. The *Good Hope* was in a very bad way, yawing out of line and with a fire blazing under the bridge amidships. Both big men-o'-war were like Elizabethan fire-ships driven before the wind, their flames reflected turbulently on the rollers as if the sea were ablaze, too. The *Monmouth* bravely continued to fire steady salvoes but Richard knew that they could be making no impression on the enemy. It was so dark in the east now that the gunlayers' only aiming-points were the enemies' muzzle flashes, the hulls of the German ships being indistinguishable against the seas and distant coastline. Even the range the taker was giving was mainly speculative. But Richard passed it through the voice-pipe to the officer of quarters of the port 4-inch battery, 'Nine-two-five-oh. 4-inch, open fire!'

The *Glasgow* took her first hit just as the five smaller guns blasted out, their crack sharper and even more painful to the ear than the 6-inchers'. Richard felt the ship twitch from stem to stern, like a kicked dog, then recover herself. The German shell appeared to have hit low in the hull amidships. He saw rising smoke, but there was no reduction in speed. They were receiving a lot of fire now from the German light cruisers' 4.1-inch, while every few seconds a taller waterspout indicated a near miss from the *Gneisenau* or *Scharnhorst*. The noise of bursting shell and the scream of splinters was cacophonous, drowning the sound of their own guns. Spray swept over higher than the foretop, soaking them all and forcing even the range-taker from his sights.

For a full five minutes, Richard could see nothing through his smeared glasses and could offer his gunlayers no new range. It was quite impossible to aim, range or spot. Icy water trickled down his neck, and time and again he had to duck below the foretop's screen to avoid a fresh avalanche of spray. They were hit several more times but not seriously, and not with 5.9 or 8.2 shell. One of the German light cruisers was apparently concentrating on them, but the *Glasgow* could shrug off a few 4.1s so long as she was not hit in a sensitive area like the bridge or low aft to affect the steering or propellers.

There was plenty of heavy shelling, too. Every time the *Glasgow* got off a salvo, the *Scharnhorst* or *Gneisenau* traversed her guns round to punish this little cruiser for its effrontery. But they were not hitting. Richard could hardly believe that their luck could hold for any longer, but it did. Of course, the *Monmouth* and *Good Hope* were the main targets, and they made easier targets, too, especially now that they were both blazing. And Captain Luce was zig-zagging and varying the cruiser's speed to confuse the enemy gunlayers. With every minute that passed, shooting became more difficult, even for the Germans. But it still seemed that providence was being amazingly generous to them, and harsh on the flagship and the *Monmouth*.

The dark shape of the *Otranto* was no longer astern of them. She had wisely left the line and hauled off west into the darkness, unable to contribute anything to the struggle except as a helpless target. Richard turned his glasses forward. Water from a near miss was pouring off his cap, and at first he could see nothing through the smeared glass. Then he identified the *Good Hope* by the fire amidships which illuminated her four riddled funnels. She was only a mile away on the *Glasgow*'s port bow, her guns silent, scarcely moving through the water.

Suddenly the flames arose, multiplying many times over in size and height until they seemed to consume the sky itself, the exploding ship beneath them no more than a fragment of detritus. The noise and blast together struck them like a killing punch. Richard had not believed that the end of a ship could come so instantly and completely, that it could be such an awesome spectacle. At the same time, it was beyond the capacity of the mind to comprehend that among these million fragments of steel, almost a thousand men had been killed instantly.

Men and boys. In the dying glow, the seering image still implanted on the retina of his eye, Richard remembered that diminutive midshipman gamely handling the wheel of the picket-boat, as well as the cheerful middle-aged petty officer who had been in charge on its return trip. He remembered, too, Admiral Cradock, who had been given no time even to enjoy his oranges. And the flag-captain who had not been allowed into his admiral's confidence, nor granted his friendship. The gun-crews who had suffered fifty minutes of frustration, if they had survived earlier fires and hits. The engine-room artificers and stokers who never knew what was happening above. And the hundreds more of the flagship's company, civilians in temporary uniform, most of them too young or too old for war, and certainly unprepared for it.

The *Monmouth* clung to her life for a little longer. The *Glasgow* found her rolling like a huge piece of flotsam, fires doused but with a list to port and down by the bows. Her guns were silent and there was no sign of life until a lamp signalled, 'I am badly holed, can only steam stern to sea.'

Richard returned to the bridge. Captain Luce was already there with his number one and duty midshipman, the yeoman waiting to signal the reply. 'I can't just leave them here like this. I'm going to use the torpedoes. Warn the torpedo crews.'

Only occasional gun-flashes revealed the presence of the enemy, and they came from widely scattered points of the compass. Von Spee's ships were closing in for the final kill.

MacTavish said, 'Are you sure it's worth it, sir? You know we've never been able to make our "mouldies" run straight. Is it worth another three or four hundred lives? And who's going to warn the *Canopus*, sir?'

Captain Luce was renowned for his decisiveness. But the fact that he was prepared to listen to his second-in-command indicated that, for once, he could not make up his mind – not for a few seconds. Then he suddenly turned to the yeoman. 'Tell *Monmouth* to make off as best she can,' he ordered in his clipped voice. And then lowering his tone, as if talking to himself, 'And may God help them.'

The helmsman was ordered, 'Hard a' starboard, full ahead together. Steady her on west.'

MacTavish drew out his silver case and offered a cigarette to his captain. 'Thank you, Number One.' Richard watched carefully both the hand of his captain as he put the cigarette to his lips, and the cupped hands of the second-in-command as he held a lighted match for him. He did not observe a tremor. By contrast, within seconds the steel deck was trembling as the turbines built up revolutions. Down below they would have learned that there had never before been such a need for the ship's maximum speed.

Captain Luce said to Richard, 'You can stand down your crews now, Mr Buller, if you wish.'

'Thank you, sir.' And as he complied Richard remembered, as they would remember, the statement he had made when rebuking the young midshipman, 'The Royal

45

Navy does not lose engagements at sea.'

Half an hour later, passing the W/T office, Richard heard a continuous high-pitched whine which drowned all atmospherics and any signals. He entered and saw the operator transmitting what appeared to be the same message over and over again – a call-sign followed by the body of the signal and the end-sign. At the transmitter-receiver, William Latchmore was turning the controls in a vain endeavour to douse the whine. 'The bastards!' he exclaimed when he saw Richard.

'Is that our friend von Spee?'

'I'm trying to get a warning through to the battleship but the bastards keep jamming us.'

Richard said, 'But they won't attack a battleship.'

'The skipper thinks they'll attack anything after tonight. And the *Canopus* is a very old battleship.'

It was 8.30 p.m. when Richard made his way from the W/T office. Except for the watchkeeper, there were few of the crew on deck. The aftermath of battle had left the cruiser quiet and solemn. No one was talking, and the drone of the turbines below sounded in Richard's ears like some funeral dirge in honour of the *Good Hope*'s dead. The moon had now risen over the distant Andes, flecking the wave-tops deep gold. From far aft there came the sound of hammering from a repair party shoring up a damaged deck with props.

Richard felt that he had fulfilled his unexpected responsibilities well enough and the gun-crews had performed ably under the difficult circumstances. But his thoughts of the battle were laden with a poignant sadness for the dead and shame for the defeat they had suffered. The officer commanding the forward 6-inch gun was one of those still on deck. He was Barney Miller, a bright spark in the wardroom, a small and normally eager young man. But he too seemed sunk in gloom. 'I didn't think it could happen,' he said, and repeated, 'I didn't really think it

46

could happen – not to the Royal Navy. Flagship sunk and . . .'

Richard held his arm and pointed to the north-east. Seen on land, it could have been a distant celebratory firework display. But here, at sea off Chile, only the Germans had anything to celebrate. And they were not celebrating either. They were sinking the *Monmouth*. 'Finishing her off, poor devils,' Sub-Lieutenant Miller said.

As they watched the distant flashes and needle-fine fingers of searchlight beams groping for the target, the rumble of the guns reached them across the water. The *Monmouth*'s captain would never have entertained the idea of raising the white flag, and in these cold waves there would be no survivors.

The image of death rose before Richard's eyes grotesquely – broken, freezing bodies, staring eyes, white fingers clutching emptiness before the paralysis of death, bloodstains spreading like unfolding shrouds before dissolving into the limitless volumes of the ocean.

The flashes ceased, the searchlights were doused, the deep thunder continuing for a few more seconds. The horror was overwhelming and Richard had nothing to say, absolutely nothing. Barney Miller, too, said nothing for a while. Then: 'Well, those poor devils went quickly. Don't suppose many of them even knew. Coming for a drink, Guns? Thompson'll whistle up something for us.'

Richard could see Miller's face clearly in the moonlight. It was the face of a decent young man who would no doubt have fought his gun to the end with all his crew dead about him. Not a very sensitive face, perhaps. But then who wants sensitivity and introspection in the middle of a battle in the middle of a great war?

Richard turned away, desperately needing his bunk and the solitude of his cabin. 'Maybe later, Barney,' he said.

IV

'What's the Flap, Mr Hemmings?'

Richard Buller looked up at the barrel of the 12-inch gun.
It was thirty-five feet long, and at full elevation capable of
firing a projectile weighing 850 pounds – more than twice
that of the heaviest of von Spee's shells – to a distance of
14,000 yards. He reached up a hand and patted the curve
of cold hard steel. 'We could have done with this the other
evening,' he said.

'What, an old Mark VIII! Made in 1897, the year of the
Queen's diamond jubilee. You were only just out of your
cradle.' Charlie Harris and Richard walked together side
by side to the *Canopus*'s bowsprit-cap where the Union
Jack was flying from its short staff. Harris had been
Richard's closest friend at Osborne, where for three years
they had shared the tough conditions and discipline before
advancing to Dartmouth for their final cadet's training.
Both had specialized in gunnery and could talk 'guns' for
hours on end.

'It wouldn't have mattered how old they are,' said
Richard. 'Four 12-inch guns, and von Spee would have
turned tail and shaped course in the opposite direction.
Out of sight in no time.'

'Not "no time",' the sub-lieutenant said in contradic-
tion. 'We would have given him a run for his money, too.'

'But you could only do twelve knots,' Richard protested.

'Oh no. We could log seventeen. And we did better than

48

that when we were really hurrying on the night of the fight.'

Charlie Harris then told an extraordinary story. The old *Canopus*, due for scrapping if war had not broken out, had been laid up in reserve for two years. It was a lonely life for the engineer commander, William Denbow, who had the responsibility for maintaining the ship's engines during this time, but he was rewarded when the *Canopus* was recommissioned and proved herself capable of seventeen knots, her speed when new. Her engines had clearly been maintained in tip-top order. 'I was appointed to her at this time, and almost at once we were sent out to join you,' Charlie continued. 'The engines worked splendidly and we cruised at twelve knots all the way. But at Port Stanley, Admiral Cradock was told by our captain that the engines were giving a lot of trouble and twelve knots was our maximum speed. So he left us behind as being too slow to be of any use.'

'Why did your captain make that report?' Richard asked in amazement.

It seemed that the engineer commander had not left his cabin for the entire voyage, spending much of his time writing fictitious reports to his captain detailing the faults and limitations of the *Canopus*'s engines. None of the rest of the engine-room crew knew about this and merely thought that their commander was sick. 'And so he was, it's now clear,' added Charlie. 'Mentally sick. I don't think he was scared for himself – he was scared of an action in which his beloved engines might be damaged.'

'And as a result, two of our ships are sunk and 1,500 men lost.'

The two young men looked up at the long threatening barrels of the forward 12-inch guns. Charlie said, 'He was obviously in love with his engines the same way we love our guns. Only more so!' he added bitterly.

Richard's mind went back again to the sight of that little figure at the wheel of the *Good Hope*'s picket-boat before

Coronel. 'Oh God, what a mess! And what a price to pay! Where is he now, this engineer commander?'

'He's under guard in the sick-bay. He's going to be sent home when we get to Port Stanley.'

Richard managed to throw off his sudden mood of mixed anger and bitterness. What was done, was done. And his old friend helped to cheer him up, taking him down to the wardroom before lunch and introducing him to several of the other gunnery officers.

The battleship had joined the *Glasgow* at dawn, butting into a strong south-easterly wind up the Magellan Straits, a massive bulk, aged in configuration but comforting in her size and power. Four days had passed since the battle, and a spirit of optimism had begun to creep through the *Glasgow* even before her big consort made her appearance, anchoring two cables'-length away. They were close to the low-lying Cape Virgins which marks the eastern end of the straits. Beyond was the Atlantic Ocean, grey, inhospitable, and, at present, stormlashed.

Richard was one of several officers who was granted permission to visit friends in the *Canopus*. He and Charlie had been thirteen years old when they had met on the ferry to the Isle of Wight for their first term at Osborne back in 1906. Richard had at once noted his brightness. Charlie Harris seemed to beam brightness like a lighthouse turning to offer goodwill to all. He gave out cheer when all the world was black and hostile and strange in the first days at Osborne. And ever since Richard had felt happier and better for his company. Years before, when Richard and Charlie were studying safety at sea, they were instructed in life-belts, inflatable swimming-collars and life-preservers. Charlie, Richard had reckoned, was better than a life-preserver – he was a life-improver.

The gunnery officers of the battleship were naturally keen to hear from Richard about the Coronel action. They were mostly reservists and much older than Richard, who found it a curious experience to be looked on as a blooded veteran, the source of all wisdom. They wanted to know about the accuracy and rate of fire of the German guns, the effect of 8.2-inch hits on the British armoured cruisers, the range of the 4.1 German gun, which was reputed to have a high rate of fire and high muzzle velocity. They were searching for advice, too, and Richard offered one piece: 'Don't get into the position we found ourselves in – clear for the enemy to sight, fire and spot you, while he remains invisible to you. That's a quick formula for catastrophe.'

Charlie later took Richard to the ladder to see him off. It was the middle of the afternoon watch and the gale was intensifying.

'See you in the Rose and Crown,' Richard called out to him as he descended to the picket-boat which was having a hard time lying alongside the ladder.

'In London?' Charlie asked innocently.

'No, Port Stanley, you ass.' And Richard could see the cheerful grin on his friend's face as he waved. Then he jumped into the heaving boat, and they were away.

It was the *Glasgow*'s first mail from home for eleven weeks. It arrived in the armoured cruiser *Defence* when she met the *Glasgow* in the River Plate – three sacks marked 'Royal Mail'; a familiar, comforting sight. After distribution it was as if the cruiser was overcome by an intense silence while officers and men read their letters lying in the shade on deck or below in their quarters. For the present the men were transported in their minds from the heat of this South American estuary in mid-summer, from the confinement of their damaged and rusting cruiser, from this all-masculine world of watch-keeping, stress and austerity, to their own private, distant world of family and comfortable domesticity. And, briefly, lush English green fields and woods, villages and familiar high streets replaced the reality of brown river water, distant jungle and the nearby foetid city of Montevideo.

51

It was, in fact, a letter from his father that Richard read first. It began:

17 October 1914   HMS *Incontestable*

My dear Richard,

Although you are on the other side of the world you are often in my thoughts, and I would give a year's pay to know where you are and what you are doing. Probably you are after those cursed German cruisers which are making such a nuisance of themselves – so, good hunting, and I know you will conduct yourself in the old Buller tradition if it comes to a fight.

We haven't had another scrap since that escapade in Heligoland Bight. In fact we're not even in the North Sea. The great surprise of this war so far is the submarine, and what it can do. We had three big armoured cruisers sunk in the North Sea by one German U-boat all within an hour or two, the second and third coming to the rescue of the first. That was four weeks ago but the flap's still on and the C-in-C has decided that none of the East Coast bases is safe from those underwater devils – how I'd like to get one in my sights! So we are here, in Loch na Keal, Isle of Mull. The whole Grand Fleet has been driven out of the North Sea. The enemy doesn't yet know it, but he soon will, and then the country will be open to invasion.

But it's not all bad news. The spirit of the men is high and we'll soon be back at Rosyth when the defences are complete. And we know we'll give Fritz a thrashing if he ever dares to come out.

The letter ended with family news. Harry, Richard's older brother who had never evinced the slightest interest in the Navy, had joined the Grenadier Guards, and his sister who had been such a worry with her 'votes for women'

52

suffragette work, had come to terms with reality and was training to be a nurse.

Richard read the letter through again slowly, and then opened one from his mother, written in her big rounded impatient hand, short and full of exclamation marks, gossip and the state of the dogs and Richard's hunter – 'she's pining for you and getting disgustingly fat.'

When the reading of letters was completed, the *Glasgow* seemed to shake herself back into life, and the reality of windless sweat and heat after the freezing cold of the sub-Antarctic. The bosun's mate's pipe sounded out shrilly. The buzz went round that they were shortly to raise anchor and proceed to Rio de Janeiro for repairs and refit. A few days' leave ashore at a city they knew well pleased everyone, and cheered up those few who had received no mail and were feeling dejected and neglected.

The news of the German victory at Coronel was learned first from German sources and not believed by the British Admiralty. But later confirmation arrived of the tragedy and the news had to be given to the nation. It came as a terrible blow – the first British defeat at sea for how many years? No one seemed able to remember. No mention was made of the *Glasgow* in the first announcement. Had she been sunk, too? Richard's father made urgent enquiries at the Admiralty and was about to hand over his battle-cruiser to his second-in-command in order to travel to London to console his wife when word came through in a telegram that the *Glasgow* had escaped with little damage.

Decisions to meet this sudden setback off South America were made at the Admiralty. Maximilian von Spee had to be hunted down, destroyed, revenge exacted for the humiliation of Coronel. This was essential from every point of view, to placate a disappointed and restless public, to save further disasters and paralysis of trade, and for the general good of the war effort.

The news of the Admiralty's counter-measures came as

a shock to David Beatty's Battle-Cruiser Squadron. No fewer than three great dreadnought battle-cruisers were to be taken from the command and sent to hunt von Spee. Beatty's concern at losing so many of his ships was balanced by the excitement of those who were told they were going. Captain Buller expected for a while that his would be one of the ships despatched, and that he would join the same command as his son in southern seas. But in the end it was the sister ships *Invincible* and *Inflexible* that sailed together for the South Atlantic while the even bigger 13.5-inch-gunned *Princess Royal* sailed for the Caribbean in order to cut off the German admiral if he decided to go north and head for home through the Panama Canal. So the hunt was on again.

'I'm not having you breaking your other leg, Lieutenant Phipps.' Captain Luce glanced down at the plaster encasing his gunnery officer's right leg below the knee. He had reported for duty on crutches, dressed like the other officers in white tropical kit with white cap and shoes.

'I'm very nippy on them now, sir,' Jerry Phipps protested.

'I'm not having you make an ass of yourself tumbling down the admiral's ladder. Come along, Buller. The admiral's barge is alongside.'

Richard glanced at Phipps with an apologetic smile. It had been galling enough for Phipps to have to lie in his cabin during the Coronel action, listening to his own guns and the explosion of the enemy's shells. And now he was being excluded from the crucial plans for running the enemy to earth. He saluted as best he could and hopped back a step, giving way to Richard who preceded his captain down the ladder to the barge rising and falling on the oily Atlantic rollers.

Clean and spruce, damage repaired, the *Glasgow* had arrived at the rendezvous before the reinforcements from home. Abrolhos Rocks is some five hundred miles north-east of Rio de Janeiro, a collection of small islets just outside territorial waters, offering a restricted anchorage and some protection. It is hot and steamy there, and it is one of the most inhospitable locations in the Atlantic. But suddenly, on 26 November 1914, it became a temporary base for a formidable Royal Navy squadron. On that day two great shapes loomed out of the heat haze to the north-east. Tripod masts gave the clue to their identity. They were British battle-cruisers, the *Invincible* (flagship) and *Inflexible*, sister ships each carrying twice as many 12-inch guns as the *Canopus* and easily able to outstrip any of Admiral von Spee's ships. They added the final and overwhelming measure of superiority already provided by three armoured cruisers, the light cruiser *Bristol* and the veteran *Glasgow*.

In his brief naval life Richard had never served under Admiral Sir Doveton Sturdee, who had a reputation for being a fine tactician and having a keen mind – keen enough to take him to the previous appointment of Chief of Naval War Staff at the Admiralty. In company with Luce and MacTavish, Richard now met him for the first time in the admiral's large dining cabin.

A number of officers were present from the other ships, including Admiral Stoddart and members of his staff who had been stationed in the South Atlantic in case von Spee evaded Admiral Cradock and had made for the Caribbean, South Africa, or for home. The meeting was brought to order, and the officers took their place about the long mahogany table. It was stiflingly hot in spite of the open scuttles and fans down the centre of the cabin.

Admiral Sturdee was a short, stocky man who reminded Richard of the scrum-half in the rugby team at Dartmouth. He had a broken nose, a wide expressive mouth and rather slanted eyes that appeared half-closed until they suddenly opened wide, glancing alertly from side to side.

'Gentlemen, we have come to settle a difference with our German friend, Admiral von Spee,' he began, pronouncing 'Spee' to rhyme with knee. 'He is proving a great nuisance, and we are going to put a stop to his activities.' Sturdee went on to describe the enemy's possible courses of action and what must be done to anticipate them. He did not underestimate the difficulties of finding von Spee. Spread out in search formation, with maximum visibility, the squadron would make no more than a thick pencil-line on a chart of the South Atlantic.

Admiral Sturdee ended, 'The squadron will sail on 29 November, next Sunday, for the Falkland Islands. The store-ship is due any day now and I want to complete with stores before we leave.'

Later the meeting broke up and, in the informal talk that continued among the officers, Richard again found himself in demand, the most junior officer present by a wide margin, but the only gunnery officer to have observed their quarry, and observed von Spee in action. It all seemed relaxed. But on the way back to his ship, Captain Luce confided his anxieties to Richard and his number one. 'I don't like it. I don't like it at all,' he said. 'It's my guess that von Spee will make straight for the Falkland Islands, find Port Stanley empty, blow up the docks, set fire to the supplies and the coal-store, smash the wireless station and disappear into the blue. Then we'll have lost our base and be helpless. Every day lost adds to the danger.'

Later that day a picket-boat took Captain Luce from the *Glasgow* back to the flagship. It was not only those keeping watch on board the *Glasgow* who registered this passage, and the return passage an hour later. Nothing is missed by the ship's companies of an anchored squadron, and speculation on the reasons for the visit ran rife. In the *Glasgow* it was at first said that the subject of the conversation between the admiral and Captain Luce was completely confidential. Later, and inevitably, the word got about that John Luce had had a difficult interview with Admiral Sturdee, but the C-in-C had finally agreed that the squadron would sail twenty-four hours earlier, on 28 instead of 29 November, whether or not the store-ship had arrived. So the *Glasgow*'s captain gained them a day in the hunt.

The grandly-named South Atlantic and Pacific Squadron steamed south from the coast of Brazil for eight days, the widely spread-out men-o'-war staining the sky with long, slowly-fading trails of black smoke. At one time, on the fifth day in the forenoon watch on the *Glasgow*, William Latchmore and Richard found themselves together off watch and chatting. The weather was already turning colder again and they were glad to be in the shelter of the cruiser's second funnel.

'Have you picked up anything new on that magic box of yours?' Richard asked.

'Not since early this morning. And that was no news really. Montevideo telling us that they've intercepted signals from two German armed merchantmen off Valparaiso and the Plate but have heard nothing from von Spee.'

Richard turned up his collar. Spray whipped past like hailstones as they took a green. They could see the distant flagship's bows dip into the rollers, and seconds later the water pour off her forecastle. The *Invincible* had been the wondership of her day, the first turbine-powered cruiser, the first all-big-gun battle-cruiser. She had attained over twenty-six knots on her trials at that time, and seven years ago could have destroyed or evaded any German man-o'-war.

'What happens if von Spee gets to Port Stanley first?' Richard said, answering his own question. 'If I was him I'd shell the wireless station before it could get off a warning.'

'Then von Spee helps himself to the coal he wants before burning the rest and then goes off to sink our shipping.' William pointed towards the flagship. Beyond her it was just possible to make out the *Inflexible*, tracing an identical scrawl of black against the horizon. 'Jackie Fisher can call them his "ocean greyhounds",' he said. 'But greyhounds have to be fed. If those were two of Nelson's battleships over there they could go on searching for a year without having to bother about coal. Nelson didn't have to rendezvous with colliers or find coaling-stations when he cruised up and down the Mediterranean and across the Atlantic and back looking for Admiral Villeneuve.'

Richard laughed. 'I just hope we end up with another Trafalgar.'

Port Stanley remained intact during those first tense days of December 1914 and there were, after all, no signs of von Spee. The only message received by wireless was that the whereabouts of the German squadron were not known but that the islands must expect imminent attack. The Falklanders prepared to defend themselves as best they could. They were not totally helpless. The *Canopus* had been beached and moored head and stern to cover the entrance to the harbour. Look-out stations had been sited on nearby high ground and linked by land-line to the old battleship. The ship's 12-pounder guns had also been landed and set up in protected batteries, and men not needed to man the heavy guns were formed into a defence command supported by local volunteers. Oil-barrels filled with high explosive had been strung across the outer harbour entrance to discourage close attack.

The women and children of Port Stanley were sent inland out of danger, and the town settled down to await the onslaught. On the morning of 7 December, one of the look-outs reported smoke on the horizon. The size of the cloud rapidly grew and the alarm was at once raised. Sturdee's squadron, prohibited from using W/T to warn the Falklanders of their arrival, was identified by a sharp-eyed signaller of the *Canopus*. The battle-cruisers' characteristic tripod masts provided the clue.

There was relief and rejoicing, and as the two great battle-cruisers eased into the inner harbour and secured alongside the jetty, three cheers were led by the islands' governor, William Allardyce. Shore leave was granted to some of the ships' crews, and expectations of imminent catastrophe for the Falklanders suddenly turned into celebrations.

The men swarmed into the little town, packing the two pubs and giving the stores their best day's trading since Admiral Cradock's squadron had been in port. Richard took a boat across to the *Canopus*.

'I don't know why all these ships have bothered to turn up,' Charlie greeted him. 'We could have managed on our own. We were looking forward to sinking the *Scharnhorst* and *Gneisenau* – and the rest of them, of course.'

Charlie Harris was joking but he was also confident that the battleship could have put up a good show against any bombardment by the enemy. He took Richard into Gunnery Control and showed him how the chief gunnery officer had devised a chart marking off all the area within range of the four heavy guns, both land and sea, and divided it into numbered squares so that the guns could be fired 'blind' from their concealed position which would be very difficult for the enemy to hit. Later, the *Canopus*'s captain, Heathcoat Grant, included Richard and Charlie in a small party he took for tea at the governor's house, complete with fruit cake and cucumber sandwiches. There was quite a festive air of relaxation about the town and its people now that they felt themselves secure against the enemy. Admiral von Spee, and the war, seemed a long way away to Richard as he sat in an armchair sipping a cup of hot sweet tea in the warm drawing-room just as if he were back home in England. It was not until the arrival of a messenger at the front door that the air of pleasant unreality was broken.

'Sub-Lieutenant Buller and any other officers of the *Glasgow* present please report back to the ship immediately.'

Richard thanked his host and Captain Grant, wished Charlie luck, and made his way towards the harbour, noting the sandbags around many of the buildings and the shutters across the windows to limit blast damage from shellfire.

Captain Luce addressed his officers impatiently: 'I don't like this, don't like this at all.'

The paymaster-lieutenant asked, 'What's worrying you, sir?'

'All this slackness. It's almost as if old Spee was already at the bottom. We haven't even started to coal yet. And what happens if Spee turns up when we are in the middle of it? He could just shell us at leisure. Well, the *Glasgow*'s not going to be caught with her trousers down. Number One, we'll commence coaling ship from lighters in exactly one hour.'

'Ay ay, sir.'

'And, Number One, we won't waste time when we start.'

'No, sir.'

And so it came about that by the time the two big ships and most of the other cruisers began to coal soon after midnight, the *Glasgow*'s bunkers were full again with 600 tons of best Welsh anthracite. Richard and two other officers worked the winches, hoisting ten bags of coal at a time from the lighter, swinging them across to the chutes where it was manhandled down into the bowels of the ship. Then, washed down, and with the *Glasgow*'s decks hosed clean, Richard retired to his cabin. He went to sleep with the acrid smell of coal-dust still in the air and to the sound of lighters' engines and the beat and rattle of winches now starting to fill the cavernous bunkers of the *Invincible* and *Inflexible*.

The sound which awoke him three hours later was at once urgent and mysterious. It was the crack of a signal-gun. 'I'm at Portsmouth,' was Richard's first thought. 'The C-in-C of the Channel Fleet is being saluted. Or perhaps the King himself . . .'

But the shouting that followed clashed with the expected cheering for which the Sovereign would qualify. Richard did not continue to lie in his bunk and ponder the problem. His years of training catapulted him out and he was into his shoes and coat in half a minute. He glanced at his watch. It was 7.57 a.m., 8 December. There was another crack from the ship's signal-gun. Richard raced up the ladders to the bridge. Ratings were moving at the double in all directions. Richard halted a petty officer and demanded, 'What's the flap, Mr Hemmings?'

'Enemy in sight, sir.'

Richard glanced towards the *Canopus*. A signal flying from the masthead said exactly that, 'Enemy in sight!'

On the *Glasgow*'s bridge were the captain, Jerry MacTavish, the officer-of-the-watch, the two midshipmen and William.

'Why all this gunfire?' he asked William.

'We're trying to get the buzz to the flagship. They couldn't see our flags in that cloud. The searchlight didn't raise them either.' The *Glasgow*'s anchorage was midway between the grounded *Canopus*, with only her upper works and masts showing above a peninsula, and the battle-cruisers, which were almost invisible in a cloud of coal-dust. At that moment a dim flash like the headlamp of a car in a fog showed that the *Invincible* had read and now acknowledged the signal.

Captain Luce was issuing orders in a crisp, staccato voice. 'Call for steam with the utmost despatch. Lieutenant Oates, have the bosun sound "Clear for action!" Ah, Mr Buller, you've awoken from your slumbers at last. So we may be allowed to open fire upon the enemy.'

Richard swallowed the implied reproof. 'I believe Lieutenant Phipps will be controlling the guns this time, sir.'

'Well, you'd better stand hard by him in case he skids on those wooden sticks and breaks his other leg.'

The engineer-lieutenant appeared on the bridge, panting and as dishevelled as Richard. 'I hear the enemy is in sight, sir.'

'The enemy is in sight, lieutenant. You are quite right. And I wish steam to be raised urgently.'

The *Glasgow* had been at 'two hours' notice', which meant that there was some heat in the boilers but the fires would take at best one-and-three-quarters of an hour to build up enough steam pressure for the cruiser to weigh anchor and proceed at full speed.

More news was coming in from the *Canopus*, in a rapid series of signal-lamp flashes. The yeoman read off the words with William providing confirmation. 'A four-funnelled and a two-funnelled man-o'-war in sight SE steering northwards.'

Captain Luce snapped, 'No such thing as a modern twin-funnelled Hun cruiser. Those three we saw at Coronel all had three funnels. But the *Gneisenau* had four, and that'll be her, or the *Scharnhorst*. And the other one won't be far away. Spee's got more sense than to divide his force.'

Everyone on deck who had observed the German gunnery at Coronel could imagine the devastating effect of raking fire from 8.2-inch guns on the half-ready British ships, the *Invincible* and *Inflexible*, in the middle of coaling with lighters alongside and quite unready for action. Only one ship was ready to meet the enemy, the guard-ship *Kent* which would be able to proceed out of harbour sooner than any other cruiser, and could certainly be sunk by German fire as swiftly as her sister ship *Monmouth* had been five weeks before.

You did not have to be a gunnery officer to understand the danger of their situation. If Admiral Sturdee had not taken Captain Luce's advice, von Spee would now be approaching this naval base defended by only one old battleship. Port Stanley would have been ripe for the picking. But now he could inflict an even worse blow on the British by severely damaging his hunters as well as destroying their base. No one appreciated this better than Captain Luce, the one commander who had met and fought with this enemy. Understandably, he was in a vile humour. He knew that it would not be helpful to press further the need for speed in raising steam. But he could let off his own steam, and did so in the direction of one of his junior gunnery officers.

While Admiral Sturdee's squadron struggled with the cumbersome and complex business of getting ready for sea and preparing for action, the governor of the Falkland Islands despatched an urgent wireless message to Montevideo for forwarding by cable to London. The message arrived in London in the early afternoon, was rapidly decoded and taken by messenger to the Naval War Staff office in the Admiralty. Vice-Admiral Sir Henry Oliver, who had succeeded Sturdee as chief-of-staff, immediately made his way to the office of the First Lord.

'I was working in my room when Admiral Oliver entered with the following telegram,' Winston Churchill wrote later. '"Admiral Spee arrived at daylight this morning with all his ships and is now in action with Admiral Sturdee's whole fleet, which was coaling." We had so many unpleasant surprises that these last words sent a shiver up my spine. Had we in fact been taken by surprise and, in spite of our superiority, mauled, unready at anchor?'

V

'Like a Blooming Ghost . . .'

The time was 9.20 a.m., and this morning of 8 December
1914 was crystal clear with a cloudless sky and warm sun –
a God-given day for gunnery. In the *Glasgow*, steam
pressure was steadily mounting so that soon the twelve
Yarrow small-tube boilers would be providing enough
power to drive the cruiser through the water at her
maximum speed of twenty-five knots.

The ship was cleared for action, the crews closed up to
their guns. Everyone had eaten a good breakfast, washed
and put on clean clothes, the time-proven precaution
against wound infection before battle. The captain was on
his bridge, sucking his pipe and attempting to conceal, not
very successfully, the impatience to cast off that he was
feeling.

In the foretop Richard had his eyes to the Barr and
Stroud range-finder, adjusting the knurled screws to get
the 'cut' that would accurately indicate the range of the
enemy. He could see the two ships quite clearly, the big
four-funnelled armoured cruiser and much smaller light
cruiser. The range was just over 11,500 yards, and the
ships were still steaming towards them.

The Germans could not fail to observe the enormous
cloud of smoke that still hung over the harbour, but they
might presume that it came from the coal stores, hastily
ignited in order to deny them to the enemy. If those same
Germans had been aware of the size of the force in the
harbour hidden behind this cloud and preparing to

64

confront them, they would either make off as fast as their engines would take them, or close in and bombard the seemingly helpless ships at leisure.

Richard said, 'They're well within range. Why don't they open fire?' He could see that the forward heavy turret of the armoured cruiser was trained in the direction of the wireless station on the hill behind Port Stanley, the twin guns raised to maximum elevation.

Petty Officer Barratt replied, 'They'll not want to waste their ammunition, sir. Make sure of hitting. They must have used up a good few shells at Coronel. But I reckon it's time the *Canopus* had a crack at them.'

It was as if the old battleship was taking orders from the veteran chief gunner, for at that moment there were twin, almost simultaneous cracks from beyond the spit of land that concealed the *Canopus*, chocolate-brown cordite smoke rose into the clear air and thousands of screaming seabirds flew aloft from the water or from their perches on the ships' masts and rigging. Was it Charlie Harris's forward turret or the after turret, Richard wondered, and imagined the excitement and concentration as they opened fire on the enemy after all their weeks of preparation and practice for this moment.

Richard trained his glasses on the distant ships and clearly saw the two tall waterspouts that sprang up out of the sea just short. Not bad shooting! And the Germans must at once recognize that they were up against guns heavier than their own. Still they came on, undeterred. Then the *Canopus* fired again, and this time Richard saw the shells rise into the clear morning sky from the battleship's guns speeding on their errand of destruction.

A few minutes after the second salvo landed, the look-out reported, 'Enemy altering course to east by north.' Good old *Canopus*! Maligned, mocked and despised, but when it was demanded of her, she had produced her best turn of speed. And now her guns had probably saved the squadron from bombardment when, had the Germans

65

realized it, the British squadron was at their mercy.

Jerry Phipps demanded of the chief gunner, 'Range, Mr Barratt?'

A brief pause then, '12,300 yards, sir.'

The *Glasgow*'s gunnery officer had created a sensation by ordering a winch to be rigged from the foretop to lift him the sixty feet into his battle-station. The preparations for this unorthodox operation and the sight of the burly lieutenant with his leg in splints being hauled up on ropes and pulleys had been an entertaining distraction during the tense waiting period.

'Three more ships south-east range about 18,000 yards,' the look-out called. Richard could just make out the smoke smudges on the horizon, confirming the captain's belief that all von Spee's ships were in the vicinity, no doubt with their supply ships, too.

A few minutes later, the word went round that their ship had steam up, and that they would soon be in the chase, as intent on keeping the German ships in sight as five weeks earlier they had striven to escape from them.

'Let go forward.' The order repeated, 'Let go forward.' The splash of the wire striking the water. 'All gone, sir.' 'Half ahead port. Half astern starboard.' 'Helm hard a'starboard. Slow astern starboard . . .'

The crisp voice of command and the vibration of power was followed by the first signs that they were under way, the breeze up in the foretop increasing and the slight lurch and sway as they left the protection of the harbour entrance. The *Kent* was ahead, her three tall funnels and identical silhouette evoking memories of the ill-fated *Monmouth*. She would not be able to keep up with the *Glasgow* which would be acting as scout, the only cruiser in the squadron capable of matching the speed of the *Invincible* and *Inflexible*.

Then, minutes later, with the *Glasgow* worked up to twelve knots and well clear of Cape Pembroke, Richard could see the tall tripod masts of the battle-cruisers moving against the hills behind Port Stanley. They were under way, too. Soon the enemy look-out must identify them, and von Spee would be forced to realize that, instead of making off from some inferior cruisers and from the 12-inch guns of an old beached battleship, he was about to be pursued by an enemy that was both faster and a great deal more powerful.

In the charthouses of the *Glasgow* and *Kent*, the *Invincible* and *Inflexible* and the other British cruisers, on the plotting-tables of the *Gneisenau* and *Scharnhorst* and the three accompanying light cruisers, calculations were being made with the assistance of chronometers, calipers, rulers and tables. Eleven hours of daylight remained, von Spee's theoretical maximum speed was twenty-two knots, his start fourteen miles, the maximum range of the British 12-inch guns 16,000 yards, of the German 8.2s, 14,500 yards.

But no neat calculation was possible. No one knew the real condition of the German ships, nor how much coal was in their bunkers, nor how much shell was left in their magazines after Coronel. Above all there was the weather, the first imponderable. As the *Glasgow*'s company knew better than anyone, it was rare for the weather to remain consistent for any length of time in these parts, and this promising clear morning could turn to fog and rain in half an hour, foul conditions beating up from Cape Horn. There could be an engagement by early afternoon, or the German ships could show a clean pair of heels, or be swallowed up thankfully in the mist and fog of a summer day in the sub-Antarctic. And so it was the position of the needles on the aneroid barometers that were also consulted closely for what could be the most critical calculation of them all.

But for the present, nothing could deny the *Glasgow* and the rest of the squadron the pursuit of a distant enemy. Astern, the *Invincible* and *Inflexible* were working up speed, slashes of white washing their bows and foaming in their wakes, oily black smoke pouring from their three irregularly spaced funnels, half a dozen white ensigns flying proudly, and the signal at the yard-arm of the flagship spelling out the one thrilling word – 'Chase!'

Noon. The sky still cloudless from horizon to horizon. The sun as high as it ever gets in this latitude. The sea as calm as a child's paddling-pool. Richard climbed back into the foretop, feeling better for a good lunch and two cups of tea. The gun-crews had been stood down to eat at 11.30 when the admiral recognized that an action was not imminent and signalled all ships to take lunch, in accordance with the old axiom, 'Better to fight clean and on a full belly.'

Jerry Phipps had remained aloft, eating bully beef sandwiches and drinking a mug of cocoa brought up by a steward. 'We're dropping the slow-coaches,' he told Richard. 'And about time.'

The *Glasgow* was on the *Invincible*'s port bow, three miles distant and closest to the enemy. Maximum speed of twenty-six knots had been ordered by the flagship, and already the old *Kent* was falling behind and, far astern, the armoured cruisers *Cornwall* and *Caernarvon* were losing distance, too, quite unable to match this speed. Richard put his glasses on the five black shapes to the south-east, still far out of range but formed now into the shapes of men-o'-war, their individual funnels visible, each one belching smoke as the stokers and engineroom staffs strained to get the maximum pressure and revolutions.

It was clear that Admiral Sturdee had become concerned at the slow rate they were overhauling the enemy when the weather could clamp down at any time in the afternoon, and had decided to seek action with his own big ships and the *Glasgow* alone – three against five of the enemy.

'We can manage them on our own,' said Phipps. His face, Richard noticed, was uncommonly alive with excitement, his deep blue eyes focused almost continuously on the distant enemy, reminding Richard of a jungle predator

68

mesmerizing its prey from afar. He was propped up on a
soap-box and cushion, his leg stuck out before him,
threatening to trip them up in the confined space. A few
days ago an officer had indelibly inscribed the figure of
a naked woman on his plaster while he was asleep, to
Phipps's mock fury. The drawing seemed wildly anachronistic under these conditions. 'Range?' Phipps snapped.

'17,500 yards, sir,' the rating, Wally Cornfield, at the
range-finder, called out. The *Glasgow*'s forward 6-inch
gun was fingering the sky at maximum elevation but it
would be some time before it could open fire.

Richard glanced again at their quarry: 2,500 men fleeing
for their lives, praying for the merciful cloak of fog, at the
same time steeling themselves for another fight, but this
time without the considerable weight of gunfire in their
favour as it had been at Coronel. Were the next hours to
mark the exacting of a terrible revenge for the crushing
German victory at Coronel? The expectation of renewed
battle was like the sudden heating of the blood in Richard's
veins, and he glanced at the racing *Invincible*, the 12-inch
guns elevated in the turrets for'd, aft and amidships and
trained on the enemy. But he remembered, too, the
devastating accuracy of the German gunnery and how
swiftly the 8.2s had disposed of the *Good Hope* and
Monmouth and how fortunate the *Glasgow* had been to
escape.

A muffled voice, the words almost carried away on the
wind, spoke into the voice-pipe. 'Inform your crews that
the battle-cruisers will be opening fire shortly,' Cornfield
was saying on Phipps's orders. 'Range closing rapidly now.
6-inch prepare to open fire with lyddite in thirty minutes.'

A minute later Richard saw the signal break out on the
flagship's yard-arm, 'Open fire and engage the enemy.'
And at once the *Invincible*'s fore-turret fired a single
ranging-shot – muzzle flash of piercing yellow, the instant
recoil and throwing out of evil brown cordite smoke, the
descent of the barrel to horizontal for reloading, the firing

69

of the second gun. 'Range 16,500 yards,' sang out the rating. Richard saw through his binoculars the two distant splashes, followed by two more from the *Inflexible*. They were all short, short even of the small cruiser that was trailing behind the others.

But, like pacing giant figures, the splashes crept nearer to the five bunched ships as time passed, obscuring them intermittently behind a screen of water. In addition the smoke from the *Invincible* and *Inflexible* was being blown towards the enemy, adding to the difficulties of aiming and spotting him. As he had been at Coronel, von Spee was in the better tactical position.

Straining to catch a glimpse of the effects of the now steady salvo-firing by the battle-cruisers, Richard saw the German squadron splitting up. 'I think they're scattering,' he told Phipps. The lieutenant nodded. He had his cap off and his prematurely grey hair was streaming in the wind as the *Glasgow* kept up a steady twenty-five knots, spume from her bow waves whipping across the exposed foretop.

Recognizing that sooner or later a 12-inch shell would find one of his light cruisers (and one shell would be enough) von Spee had ordered them to make off as fast as they could to the south while he fought it out with the two big enemy ships. Admiral Sturdee had provided for this contingency in his fighting instructions issued before the battle, and the *Glasgow*, *Kent* and *Cornwall* at once left station and turned to cut them off.

But before the *Glasgow* passed under the flagship's stern, Captain Luce called up to his chief gunnery officer, 'Are you within range of the German flagship?'

'Only just, sir.'

'Can you give her a few shots?'

The captain clearly wanted to make a gesture of defiance, a token of retribution for what the *Scharnhorst* had done to his consorts at Coronel.

On Phipps's instructions, Cornfield called down the

voice-pipe to the two 6-inch guns, 'Range 11,750 yards, open fire six rounds.'

Soon the enemy would be completely obscured by the bulk of the *Invincible* and the cloud of smoke streaming from her three funnels, but the two keyed-up crews for'd and aft succeeded in getting off the salvoes in rapid succession. Richard caught a whiff of cordite from the gun below them and felt the little shake of his ship, as if in ecstasy, as the guns cracked out.

The distant scattering foe then temporarily disappeared from sight. But the firing had been only an overture to action. At once the sea about them was torn asunder by exploding German heavy shells. The first return fire was as accurate as ever, straddling the *Invincible* and falling equally close to the *Glasgow*. One shell was so close that the cruiser tore through the wall of water it threw up and the crash of its explosion was followed by the scream of splinters. Like everyone in the foretop, Richard ducked down behind the screen, and when he raised his head again he found that he was soaked to the skin.

Voices were calling out. The word 'wounded' could be distinguished. Looking down over the bridge to the forecastle, Richard saw a figure lying prone on the deck with members of the 6-inch gun-crew bending over him. A first-aid party was beside the figure in less than one minute, the wounded man was rushed to the sick-bay and the gap was filled by a gunner standing by for this contingency. It might have been a peacetime exercise, carried out with the total efficiency Captain Luce always demanded. But Richard had seen the blood, had seen the face of the man contorted in agony. No, this was no exercise, this was the real thing, yet still only the preliminaries to battle – a battle the shape of which was forming before their eyes as helms were put over, ships altered course and hundreds of sweating stokers, German and British, strove to raise higher the boiler pressure of

71

their engines and the speed of their vessels.

The *Gneisenau* and *Scharnhorst*, like anxious and protective parents, were drawing the British battle-cruisers and their deadly fire away from their small charges, the three light cruisers and distant supply-ships, which had been ordered to try to escape to the south. Richard could see the three small but still distant shapes of the light cruisers, streaming smoke as they raced south. On paper, only the *Glasgow* had the speed to catch them. Much depended on the state of the ships' bottoms and when they were last cleaned, and the state of the ships' engines – even the strength and spirit of the stokers.

But the greatest imponderable of all was still the weather. For the present there was not a fleck of white against the bright blue of the Antarctic sky, and the visibility was restricted only by the curvature of the earth. Richard was not a superstitious young man but as he glanced up again at the clear blue sky he briefly pondered on the gods of war looking down on this scene stretched out over the ocean and making their decision in favour of one side or the other.

At that moment fate of quite another kind intervened in this overture to battle. Jerry Phipps seized Richard's arm and called out, 'Take a look at that!' Richard swung his glasses in the direction in which Phipps was looking, noting the stirring sight of the *Invincible* and *Inflexible* firing regular salvoes at the distant German armoured cruisers, which had turned to face them like quarries at bay, the 12-inch shell-bursts sending tall columns of water a hundred feet and more into the air. Between the two groups of protagonists there had suddenly appeared from the east a ship carrying a full spread of sail, including even stunsails, a white and graceful messenger of peace by contrast with the grey functionalism of the embattled warships. A chance in a million had brought this merchantman, on one of the world's least used sea-lanes,

72

before the barrels of a battle where never before had men fought one another at sea.

'He must be wondering what he's done to deserve this!' Richard exclaimed as he noted the details of the rig of the clipper, and watched her go about to escape the holocaust of fire.

'He'll get away all right,' Phipps said. 'And so will those Germans if we're not nippy.' The *Glasgow*'s target was the *Dresden*, the fastest and most modern of the German light cruisers. She had settled on a more easterly heading than the other two, and they seemed to be making no impression on her.

The *Glasgow* was still logging her maximum speed but the shape of the German ship seemed no larger than half an hour earlier while the wind from the north-west had the effect of building up the *Dresden*'s smoke-cloud high above her masts like a towering black mountain. Phipps had ordered a ranging-shot from the forward 6-inch gun but it had fallen far short. They appeared to be overhauling the other two German cruisers on their port bow, but the *Dresden* was slipping out of their fingers.

Far to the north-east the *Kent* and *Cornwall* appeared to be gaining no ground on the *Nürnberg* and *Leipzig*. A day which had begun early with all the advantage on the side of the enemy and later favoured the crushingly superior British, now seemed to be granting to the German light cruisers the opportunity of escaping altogether.

Far to the south, Richard could make out a faint grey line on the horizon, and the wind which had been so gentle all day was now getting up a little, flecking the wavetips with white. He had been sent down to the bridge by Phipps to hear what the captain had to say about the tactics he proposed to employ. Ten minutes earlier, the *Glasgow*'s forward 6-inch had been ordered to fire ranging-shots again, and this time had achieved two 'overs', indicating that the *Dresden* was at last in range. But cheekily, in reply, the little German cruiser had turned briefly to offer a full broadside. Her 4.1s were puny by contrast with the *Glasgow*'s heaviest guns, but as at Coronel their range proved as great – and the opening salvoes were as brilliantly accurate. The sea about the *Glasgow* had been peppered with shell-bursts, and one German shell had caught them amidships, piercing the armoured deck and exploding in the engine-room.

Captain Luce, disregarding the cramped conning-tower, had not left the bridge since the *Glasgow* had cleared Port Stanley. He stood now, a stocky, powerful figure in overcoat with the collar turned up and white silk scarf about his neck, pipe clenched between his teeth, the apotheosis of a RN captain with the decision-making responsibility of a ship and her company upon his shoulders. He now turned in acknowledgement of Richard's arrival, his sea-tanned face serious with resolve but showing a trace of anxiety, and with reason.

'Well, Buller, what does the gunnery lieutenant have to say about the situation?'

'I think he's worried about the *Dresden*'s speed, sir.'

'So am I. Tell him I'm also worried about the *Dresden*'s gunnery. If she can straddle us with her 4.1-inch, why can't we get at her with *our* 4-inch.'

The trouble with the *Glasgow*'s disposition of guns was that in a stern chase like this she could bring only a single 6-inch to bear on the enemy, unless she turned to allow the after 6-inch to bear, which would mean making the enemy a present of a mile or more in the distance between the two ships. As to the lack of range of the *Glasgow*'s secondary guns in relation to the Germans', they had learned this unfortunate fact at Coronel, and Captain Luce knew it as well as his gunnery officers.

'I'm afraid the Germans just make longer-ranging small calibre guns than we do,' said Richard.

'And not only small calibre,' the captain retorted. 'Their

74

armoured cruisers are throwing everything at our big chaps. Take a look over there.'

The ding-dong gunnery duel appeared to be at its height. The *Invincible* and *Inflexible* were almost ten miles distant by now but the ripple salvoes of mixed 6-inch and 8.2-inch guns of the *Gneisenau* and *Scharnhost* were clearly identifiable by the muzzle flashes.

'Things don't seem to be going as well as we had hoped, sir,' Richard suggested.

'I'm not worried about the admiral, Buller. He'll send those armoured cruisers to the bottom without too much difficulty. I'm worried about the *Dresden*.' He pointed his pipe at the swiftly fleeing German light cruiser, still as distant as ever. 'That hit we took just now damaged one of the boilers and I don't think we'll ever catch her now. I believe our task is to get at the *Leipzig* before she gets away, too, because she's faster than the *Cornwall*, according to the navigating officer. And I don't like the weather prospects any more, either.'

The captain ordered a three-point turn to port, which brought the *Glasgow*'s bows round to bear directly on the nearer of the other two German cruisers. 'Please present Lieutenant Phipps with my compliments and ask him to open fire with his 6-inch the moment we are in range.'

Richard saluted, turned and walked swiftly towards the ladder leading to the foretop, taking with him the scene, frozen on his mind, on the *Glasgow*'s bridge – the helmsman with his muscular gnarled hands on the spokes of the wheel, Jerry MacTavish beside Captain Luce and in earnest conversation with him, the yeoman, a tall, angular figure, no more than two paces away and with a signal rating by his side, the two young midshipmen (and what a day this was for them!) on the starboard wing peering through their glasses. And all of them, like Richard himself, keyed up for the gunnery duel that still eluded them.

At 2.45 p.m. they did not have long to wait. Richard at

the Barr and Stroud counted off the yards, and when the figure dropped to 12,000 Phipps gave the order to the forward 6-inch gun-crew to open fire. Richard felt the crack like a blow inside his ears, watched the spinning shell rise in its trajectory and fade into the distance. He counted – '12 seconds . . . 13 . . . 14.' At sixteen seconds a tall spout of water rose from the sea no more than a hundred yards from the port side of the *Leipzig*. 'Good shooting!' called out Phipps, and Cornfield spoke down the tube, 'Range correct. Right two. Commence rapid fire.'

Now the gun-crew, working like a machine turned to full speed, caught the rhythm they had practised so often, perfectly co-ordinated. Breech open, belching out the fumes from the last detonation, shot and cartridge thrown in, breech slammed shut, and almost instantaneously the crash and recoil – a scene of constant movement except for the sight-setter sitting at his sight, his mate alongside, the gunlayer pressing the trigger. Soon the ready ammunition was so depleted that more had to be brought up from the magazine, the last stage by hand as it had been in the days of Nelson and muzzle-loading cannon, the young ratings running barefoot to avoid any risk of a spark igniting their lethal loads.

The *Leipzig* was answering the fire with even swifter salvoes, at first with her after 4.1s, and then, as Richard watched her turn eight points to starboard, revealing her full silhouette, all five of her guns. Captain Luce had hoped to provoke her into making this change of course in order to give the *Cornwall* a chance to close the gap, but the price was paid in very rapid ripple-firing of great accuracy. For ten minutes the *Glasgow* was surrounded by a curtain of waterspouts, and not all of this fusillade were misses. Twice Richard felt his ship twitch sharply, sure proof that they had been hit.

Captain Luce responded by turning his own ship to starboard in order to bring his second 6-inch gun into action. Richard was now too busy to give much attention

76

to the details of the action, but he learned from a rating that they had suffered more casualties, and he could see for himself through the drifting cordite, funnel-smoke and the intermittent shroud of falling water, that they had caused a fire to break out amidships on the *Leipzig*, the flames shooting up just before the third funnel.

Then there was a temporary lull in the fierce duel, when Captain Luce completed a thirty-two-point turn in order to clear the smoke, allowing the *Glasgow* a clear view of the scene. Far away to the north, the *Scharnhorst* was no more. Richard could just make out the British battle-cruisers closing in on the *Gneisenau*, which once had four funnels but was now no more than a blazing wreck. Scarcely five miles away the *Nürnberg* was well alight too but was still giving a sturdy account of herself with her remaining guns, and the shooting was accurate, too. Captain Luce's tactics had worked. The German cruiser's turn had allowed the *Cornwall* to get within range, and her much more numerous 6-inch guns were already straddling the *Leipzig*, now a doomed ship.

They were only just in time, however. The weather had worsened during the past hour. The mist and squall clouds, once on the far horizon, had already begun to envelop the embattled ships, reducing visibility and turning the seas choppy and grey. The weather had come to the rescue of the Germans after all – but too late. The distant *Nürnberg*'s gunfire had been reduced to a defiant occasional round. The *Gneisenau* must soon succumb to the concentrated fire of the two battle-cruisers, joined now by the *Caernarvon*. Only the lucky *Dresden* had been spared, by the fates of weather and the furious activity of her stokers and engine-room crew, and had disappeared entirely into the mist and low cloud.

By 5.15 all return fire from the *Leipzig* ceased, and the weather had become so thick that, as if mercifully obscuring the horror of the sight, Richard could see only what was lit by the tortured enemy's fires against which crouched figures could be seen in silhouette, actors in the final scene of this real-life tragedy.

On receiving a message from the captain, Phipps gave the order to Richard, 'Cease fire!' Richard passed it on to the gun-crews, and at once experienced the relief as the shattering roar in his eardrums gave way to the familiar faint whirr of the *Glasgow*'s turbines and the lapping of the waves against the cruiser's hull. The warmth of the day had vanished with the sun, and the rising wind and drizzle caused all of them in the fighting-top to button tight their collars. They were approaching the stationary wreck of the *Leipzig* cautiously, at no more than five knots. The German ship was a travesty of the sleek, swift vessel which they had pursued since noon, funnels, masts and upper works reduced to a 350-foot-long wreck of twisted steel and human carnage.

But the German ensign was still flying from a mast stump, and Phipps in his cradle called out in angry frustration, 'Why don't we finish off the swine?'

Richard did not answer. He could find nothing to say in answer to this callous cry. At the same time, he understood why Captain Luce was approaching the German ship cautiously, presenting only the *Glasgow*'s bows. Below the waterline the *Leipzig* carried torpedo tubes which might still be in working order, and one 'tin fish' fired at this range could send the *Glasgow* to the bottom in minutes.

'She's like a bloomin' ghost, sir,' said an awestruck Cornfield to Richard. 'I can't believe me bloody eyes.'

By contrast another voice spoke, the cool incisive voice of the captain through the speaking-pipe. 'Reopen rapid fire, all guns.'

At every gun, where the crews had been relaxing with all eyes on the ruin they had helped to create, the men sprang back to their duties. For two more minutes the *Leipzig* was battered by hits from the two British cruisers. It was point-blank target-practice, made more terrible by the fact that they could see the effects of the fire on the clusters of survivors huddled about the shattered guns, bodies being torn apart, men rushing, arms raised, to leap into the sea.

The *Leipzig* at last began to go down at 8.30, a dying ghost in the stormy twilight, bows first, slipping slowly, inexorably, into the grey waters of the South Atlantic, her ensign still flying, the litter and men – dead and alive – spreading out from her like a stain. Through his glasses Richard could see a small group of men at the stern of the ship gathered as if for mutual comfort in the false illusion that some miracle would stay the descent of their ship at the last moment.

Faint grinding, ripping sounds came across the water, the *Leipzig*'s death rattle. Then, from much nearer, from just below, the captain's voice spoke: 'Yeoman, signal "I am sending boats to save life".' Was there anyone left to read that message of salvation – either by signal-lamp morse code, or the flutter of flags that was rapidly run up? Surely it could be only words cast over the waters to the dead?

Several of the *Glasgow*'s boats had been riddled by splinters and were unusable. Others were rapidly hoisted out by their crews, but none was in the water when the *Leipzig*'s stern, starboard propeller still turning, slipped beneath the waves, sweeping away as if by a brushstroke the handful of survivors. The scavengers were already at their ugly work. Brown giant skuas which must long have been hovering out of human sight, had appeared, shrieking in competitive anger and triumph, hell-bent on the corpses and those who had not yet given up the struggle in the icy sea and tried feebly to beat them off. They even swooped close above the boats from the *Cornwall* and *Glasgow* which were now working their way, awkwardly in the rising seas, through the litter and the bobbing heads.

Richard's last memory of that battle was of helping the officers and men detailed to bring the rescued German survivors on board. There were no more than a dozen in all, many more having died on the chill, choppy passage back and been heaved overboard to lighten the load. 'This poor bugger's dead,' said a petty officer beside Richard who glanced at the pale, soaked corpse, face yellow from the lyddite shell-bursts, ripped jumper revealing the tattooed figure of a naked woman on his chest. Once this dead sailor must have looked forward to mutual mirth with a real woman over this tattoo before clasping her nakedness to him – a dream dashed to pieces like a million more in this December twilight.

Stretcher parties were hurrying the few who were still alive to the sick-bay, each trailing drips of water and some of blood. One found the strength to raise his fist in defiance and cry out '*Heil Kaiser Wilhelm!*' The rest were silent or groaning, and their rescuers spoke little too, as if in awe at the consequences of what they had done. One rating, stepping soaked over the gunwale of his recovered launch, muttered to Richard, 'The poor buggers – oh, sir, the poor buggers!' and held the lapel of Richard's coat as if in supplication. Then, appalled at his familiarity, he said, 'Oh, sir, I'm sorry. But, oh, the poor buggers, you should have seen them in the water – all white until those bloody birds began at them. It was terrible.'

Richard held the man's shoulder for a moment. 'Get below and get some hot cocoa inside you. I expect there'll be an issue of grog soon, and that'll settle you, Jenkins.'

11 p.m. The *Glasgow* on a northerly heading for Port Stanley, speed twelve knots, tracing a reverse course over the route they had taken that morning (it seemed like a week ago!) on their long pursuit. Richard Buller, dead tired like all the ship's company, dropped in to the wardroom before turning in. There were four officers there, drinking pink gins, and they had had a few already. One of them saw Richard at the door and called out, 'Come and join us, Rich. We're having a bit of a celebration.'

Richard nodded and smiled, but was already regretting his decision.

Phipps was among them, his dud leg up on a chair. 'Well, we did for the swine, didn't we?' he said convivially. 'Pretty good shooting. Tore 'em to bits. Revenge for Coronel at last.'

Richard took a glass from Thompson and raised it. 'Yes, quite a day,' he said uncertainly.

'D'you know, one of those Huns we picked up was shouting away in the sick-bay about his "*Vaterland*" and "*Got* save the *Kaiser*" and how we had tricked them and in a fair fight they'd have sent us to the bottom.' It was Barney Miller talking, indignantly and somewhat drunkenly. 'I'd have put the lot back in the sea if I'd had my way.'

There seemed to be general agreement that this would have been the right thing to do. Richard left as soon as he could, feeling wretched and appalled at the attitude of his fellow officers – men he had lived, worked and played with for so many months, men he liked, and men with whom he had shared the dangers of combat, the shame of defeat and now the triumph of victory. What had come over these normally decent young officers – these old friends? What was it that Portia had said in *The Merchant of Venice*? Richard's mother used to read Shakespeare aloud to them on wet Saturday afternoons . . . 'The quality of mercy is not strain'd.' Then who had said, 'Humble and merciful in victory . . .'?

There was little humility or mercy among those officers, anyway for the time being with their judgement blurred by gin. Richard remembered the aftermath of Coronel, and how low and bitter he had felt. Now, when he should have been elated by the great victory they had scored, he felt almost as wretched, sickened by the loss of life and the sufferings of the survivors.

He found his cabin and collapsed, utterly weary, onto

81

his bunk. 'I'm not a fighting Buller at all,' he kept telling himself before sleep overwhelmed him. 'My father never felt like this, or his father – what's so different, what's wrong with me?'

When dawn broke on the morning of 9 December, Richard Buller, on watch on the *Glasgow*'s bridge, was feeling better, the introspection and worry of the previous evening forgotten in the clear Atlantic air and in the company of his steady, admirable captain. Captain Luce had slept for a couple of hours – no more – on the bunk rigged up for him aft of the bridge. He was unshaven, but fresh and alert and eager to be after the *Dresden* as soon as they had put ashore their prisoners, coaled and consulted with the commander-in-chief.

'Well, Richard, it has been a great victory and no mistake. And it'll help silence all this criticism of the Navy back home. Four out of five German ships sunk, and the *Bristol* has signalled that she has destroyed the supply ships. Now we're going after the *Dresden*. And you mark my words, we're going to get her.' Captain Luce tapped out his pipe into an empty tobacco-tin and began at once to refill it from a leather pouch.

Richard asked, 'Have we lost many men, sir?'

'I'm sorry to say we had a man killed – one of the forward 6-inch gun-crew, Able Seaman Maitland. The *Kent* lost four men sinking the *Nürnberg*, and I believe the *Inflexible* lost a man, too. And that's all. Yes, a great victory,' Luce repeated. 'There's been nothing like it since Trafalgar. I only wish poor old Kit Cradock could have seen how we avenged the loss of his flagship.' He smiled at Richard and added, 'And your father'll be pleased, too. One more engagement to notch up for the Bullers.'

The Falkland Islands were in sight, faint low smudges on the northern horizon. The whole of Port Stanley would be out to greet them, secure now in the knowledge that they were free from the risk of a German attack. Only the

Kent and *Cornwall* were in sight, steaming to port and starboard of the *Glasgow* as if escorting the veteran and battle-scarred smaller consort back to harbour. The big armoured cruiser captains and engine-room staff had good reason to be proud of themselves for both these old ships had achieved speeds well above their supposed maximum, which had enabled them to catch the nominally faster modern German cruisers. And, as Richard was qualified to recognize, they all had good reason to be proud of their gunnery which had first overwhelmed and then sunk the *Nürnberg* and *Leipzig*.

The *Bristol* had radioed that she was already in Port Stanley harbour, and soon the *Invincible* and *Inflexible* would appear from the south along with the *Caernarvon*, ensigns streaming in triumph.

Von Spee had committed only one mistake in all his months of ranging about the Pacific causing fear and chaos wherever he sailed: one mistake only, and that against the advice of his staff. He had decided to attack the Falkland Islands, believing them to be free of enemy ships. But no one could deny the British squadron its great victory. Back at the Buller ancestral home in Gloucestershire there was a plaque beneath a portrait of Captain Alastair Buller (1710–77). It read, 'May my sons and their sons and all Bullers who follow them to sea be favoured by God with the good fortune and the victories with which He has chosen to bless me, His most Humble and Grateful servant.' It was this captain's prize money which had founded the fortune and estate of the Buller family, and he had reason to be grateful. As Richard saluted his captain and descended the ladder from the *Glasgow*'s bridge to carry out routine early gun inspection, he recalled this message, supposed to have been uttered by his ancestor on his deathbed at Weir Park 137 years before.

The *Glasgow*'s two midshipmen, Arthur Richardson and John Letchworth, emerged from the doorway off the upper deck as he passed, and they stood respectfully aside and saluted him. Richard paused and asked them if they were feeling cheerful after the events of the previous day.

'Yes, sir. We gave them a real drubbing, didn't we?'

'More cheerful than you were back in October?'

'Yes, sir,' said Letchworth, smiling cheekily. 'We remembered what you said – "The Royal Navy does not lose engagements at sea."'

'Or if it does,' said Richard with an answering smile, 'it soon bites back with a vengeance. Carry on, gentlemen.'

Captain John Luce's prediction was realized. The *Glasgow* did go after the swift and elusive *Dresden*, and, though it took many weeks, located her at last at the remote island of Más Afuera off the Chilean coast where, again with the help of the *Kent*, she was so battered by shellfire while at anchor that her Captain surrendered in order to save loss of life. The date was 14 March 1915. But Richard Buller was not present at this second victory. He was by this time far away on the other side of the world witnessing the progress of a very different battle.

VI

The Dangerous Brief

The tradition of victory in sea engagements which the Bullers had sustained since the first of the Dutch Wars (1652–4) was maintained by Richard Buller at the Battle of the Falkland Islands, and again by his father a few weeks later at another clash with the enemy, this time in the North Sea, the expected arena in the war against Germany and her allies. After a series of successful raids by German raiders against England's east coast, bombarding ports and causing severe loss of life, Admiral Sir David Beatty's Battle-Cruiser Squadron at last succeeded in intercepting them as they fled for home on 24 January 1915. The battle-cruiser commanded by Captain Archibald Buller took a leading role in the destruction of one of the four German heavy ships.

For his part in this action, Archy Buller was later to be appointed a Companion of the Most Honourable Order of the Bath. Richard had been at sea, on his way home to take up a new appointment, when the Battle of the Dogger Bank had been fought, but he was back in England for the investiture at which his father was to receive his honour and the family celebration which followed. Richard himself had been on the list for a DSC for his part in the *Glasgow*'s action but his name, along with many others, had been crossed off the list put forward by Admiral Sturdee. This was the legacy of a personal feud which had cast a shadow over the Royal Navy in the ten years leading up to the outbreak of war in August 1914.

Many years earlier, the two most colourful and popular senior officers in the Royal Navy had been friends working for the reform of a service which had fallen into reactionary ways in the nineteenth century following the Battle of Trafalgar and the death of Nelson. While the Navy was never seriously challenged in numbers, with its numerous bases all over the world it maintained the *pax Britannica* and the solidarity of the Empire. But the lack of any action, combined with arrogance, self-satisfaction and too much concern for tradition, had turned the fine fighting fleet of 1805 into something resembling a shambling, dim monster, eyes half-closed, teeth and claws blunted from disuse.

Towards the end of the century reformers like Admirals Sir Frederick Richards and Sir George Tryon were beginning to make some progress. Among other younger officers who recognized that all was not well with the service they loved were Lord Charles Beresford and Sir John Fisher. These two men came from quite different backgrounds, Beresford being an Anglo-Irish aristocrat, the possessor of vast estates and wealth. He was swashbuckling, fearless, a disciplinarian but beloved by all who served under him. Jackie Fisher had come into the Navy with no advantages except a keen brain, abiding ambition, charm and a belief that to achieve anything worth while one had to be 'ruthless, relentless and remorseless', as he liked to think of himself. Both men would have made as good actors as admirals.

As the years passed and Fisher and Beresford were promoted ever higher, rivalry and a division of views on how the Navy should be reformed set in between these two officers. Both attracted loyal followers, and when in 1904 Fisher succeeded to the highest post in the Navy as First Sea Lord ahead of Beresford, something close to civil war broke out in the Navy. It continued until Fisher resigned five years later after bringing about a revolution in the ships and fighting efficiency of the service in the teeth of the opposition of his rival. The Royal Navy of 1914 was essentially the Navy of Jackie Fisher – its ships, its men, its inspiration.

'There is no doubt whatever', said Winston Churchill, First Lord of the Admiralty and civil head of the Navy at the outbreak of the war, 'that Fisher was right in nine-tenths of what he fought for.' Then, after citing his wonderful achievements, Churchill added, 'But the Navy was not a pleasant place while this was going on.' Archy Buller, one of the few senior officers who had succeeded in keeping free of this feud, agreed entirely with Churchill, though his twin elder brothers, both captains of Grand Fleet battleships in 1914, remained admirers of Beresford and kept clear of what was called 'the Fishpond', or Fisher disciples.

At the outbreak of war with Germany, Fisher and Beresford were in retirement, with Churchill still civil head of the Navy. Then, as a result of public concern at the poor early performance of the Navy and suspicion of the German-born First Sea Lord, Admiral Prince Louis of Battenberg, Fisher had been brought back at the age of seventy-three. Archy Buller was delighted; but his old friend and one-time shipmate King George V was not pleased. The Fisher-Beresford feud had even split the Royal Family, the late Edward VII being a stout Fisher admirer, his son a Beresford man. The King said that he viewed Fisher's reappointment as First Sea Lord 'with some reluctance and misgivings . . . I cannot help feeling', he continued, 'that his presence at the Admiralty will not inspire the Navy with that confidence which ought to exist.'

Fisher's arrival at the Admiralty for his second term of office as First Sea Lord coincided with the disaster of Coronel. It was he who at once set about correcting the dangerous situation, collecting and despatching the overwhelmingly superior squadron which – thanks to Captain Luce of the *Glasgow* – had arrived in the nick of time to catch

Admiral von Spee. Immediately he heard of the Falklands victory, Churchill wrote generously to Fisher, 'This was your show and your luck. Your *flair* was quite true. Let us have some more victories together and confound all our foes abroad – and (don't forget) – at home.'

Fisher was less pleased. He was an unforgiving man. 'Never forget a friend. Never forgive an enemy,' he was fond of quoting. Sturdee had been one of his foes at home – a Beresford man to the heart. In Fisher's eyes, Sturdee had failed in his task. Given a force overwhelmingly superior to von Spee's he had let one of the enemy escape. 'He should have collared the lot! Damned incompetence!' he cried out. He wanted to keep Sturdee in the South Atlantic until he had tracked down and destroyed the *Dresden*. But Churchill overruled him. He wanted the big battle-cruisers safely back with the Grand Fleet. And he wanted to enjoy the political and public accolades that would be his when Admiral Sturdee arrived home.

When Admiral Sturdee did arrive triumphantly in London, Fisher did not even want to see him, and when presented with the recommended honours and awards list, he slashed his pen through it arbitrarily as a gesture of disapproval of the victors. Archy Buller heard of this through a clerk at the Admiralty who was an old friend. 'That's rotten luck, young fellow,' his father said in commiseration to Richard when he met him on his return to London. But Richard Buller was philosophical. 'What's a bit of ribbon?' he said, glancing with a mischievous expression at his father's two rows of them.

Cut off for so long from news of the war in Europe, Richard since his return had been learning rapidly about the disasters and triumphs, of the loss from striking a single mine of the new super-dreadnought *Audacious*, of the early successes of the submarines, both German (the U-boats) and British, and how fear of enemy torpedoes and mines had driven the Grand Fleet to seek safe bases on the west coast of Scotland and Ireland, far from the scene of likely action.

But the latest and most important news had come, not from home waters, but from the Eastern Mediterranean, and the attack by the Royal Navy, assisted by some French ships, on the Dardanelles in an attempt to force a passage through to the Black Sea. According to the newspapers the greatest bombardment in naval history had shattered the defending forts, and success was near.

But on that evening in early March, Buller father and son, now walking from Whitehall across St James's Park to dine at one of Buller's clubs, the Athenaeum, were to learn more of these operations. The willow trees beside the lake were already turning green, the ducks were showing signs of liveliness, the daffodils were in full bloom and there was a feel of early spring in the air. They talked briefly of family affairs, of the loss of servants both at the Clarges Street town house and at Wyston Court in Gloucestershire, of Richard's sister Lucy who was about to leave for France as a trained nurse, and of Richard's elder brother Harry. Harry, who had shown an early disinclination to go to sea, to the amazement and even horror of the male members of the Buller family, had left Harrow to go 'into the City' where, by the outbreak of the war, he was starting to make a fortune. But he had at once joined the Grenadier Guards and within three months was in France.

'You've got a few days to spare – why don't you go over and see him? Get a taste of the land war,' suggested his father. Richard had received his appointment as second-in-command of a destroyer attached to the Grand Fleet, and promotion to full lieutenant, which at twenty-one was a reflection of the Admiralty's approval of his performance as number two gunnery officer to Jerry Phipps in the *Glasgow*, even if he had been deprived of his DSC.

The land war was trench warfare, barbed-wire and shell-holes, corpses half-submerged in the mud of Flanders.

Richard had seen many pictures of the fighting in France, had read the dreadful casualty lists in the newspapers, had heard from friends who had returned, wounded, several maimed for life. From the Swiss border in the south to the Channel ports in the north, the fighting had raged since last August, and had settled down to static bloody warfare.

Now, hearing his father's suggestion, Richard felt a recurrence of fear – fear not for himself but fear of the horror he had experienced at the Falklands battle. He had been prepared and trained for war since the age of twelve – prepared for it in every department but one, and that was the reality of death and injury and the effect it might have upon him. Why had he been afflicted in this way when no one else appeared to be? And why did he resent so strongly the way others experienced no sense of revulsion, treating the death and suffering of the enemy with jocular callousness?

Perhaps this war would cure him, or at least give him the answer. It was certainly not a subject he could ever discuss with anyone, least of all his father, to whom he now replied, 'Yes, I'd like that. A good idea, Papa.'

They marched rapidly up the steps to the Athenaeum's front doors. Archy Buller was forty-nine and therefore near the top of the captain's list, awaiting promotion to flag rank. He was a heavy figure now but still strong and fit, steady brown eyes set wide apart, face hardened and lined, like the limestone of his native Gloucestershire, after thirty-five years at sea, with the long deep scar on his cheek from the Battle of Colenso, the large Buller nose 'like the prow of a three-decker' as his father-in-law had once described it, hair receding and turning grey. His younger son was lighter-boned and took more after his mother, light brown hair cut a shade too long, fine blue eyes, a somewhat feminine neck, and now striding loose-limbed beside his father like a colt held back from his natural pace.

The porter saluted them. 'Good evening, sir. And your

son, sir. What a pleasant surprise! And promotion for him.' Turning to Richard. 'Perhaps I may congratulate you, sir?'

Richard laughed. 'Thank you, Squires. It's very good to see you.'

They were about to pass through the big glass door when the porter said quickly to Buller. 'Ah, excuse me, sir. Admiral Fisher, sir.'

Both Bullers turned and at once recognized the figure of the First Sea Lord in black overcoat, black boots and bowler-hat walking alone across the pavement to the bottom of the steps. To Archy Buller the dark complexion, wide mouth, heavy cheekbones and narrow eyes were familiar, as was the voice when he called out in recognition, 'Ah, Captain Buller – hero of the hour, eh?' Richard, however, had seen him only once or twice when he had been a cadet at Osborne Naval College, and once when he had visited Clarges Street after some crisis at the Admiralty.

After the two Bullers had followed the admiral into the great hall of the Athenaeum and were handing their coats to the liveried servants, Fisher turned his protruding eyes on Richard. 'This your boy, Archy?' he asked. 'In the *Glasgow*, weren't you? You did well. Should have caught the *Dresden*, though. Damned ineptitude on your admiral's part. I suppose if I'd given him the whole Grand Fleet, he'd have let one ship slip away – eh, Buller?'

'Well, sir, we only collared one out of four at the Dogger Bank, and that seems to have been hailed as a great victory. So perhaps four out of five at the Falklands wasn't too bad.'

They were at the door of the dining-room where the head waiter stood ready to receive them and to conduct Fisher to his usual solitary table. The admiral responded to Archy Buller's plea fiercely, his brows knitted, his eyes flashing. 'Admiral Sturdee's failure was criminal ineptitude, Buller. He was five knots faster and five times more

91

powerful. Like the word of God, Sturdee was "quick, and powerful, and sharper than any two-edged sword" – IV, 12, *The Epistle of Paul to the Hebrews*, as you will recall, Buller. Yet he took all day to sink von Spee, and let one of his ships escape.'

Admiral Fisher shook his fist and repeated, like the crack of a 12-pounder, 'Criminal ineptitude!' Then his face suddenly cleared, assumed a smiling expression, and he said, 'Join me for a brandy and cigar after dinner, Buller. And bring along this boy of yours if he can keep a secret.' At that moment it appeared as if hate could never enter the heart of this man.

Father and son ate well. Buller had always been a good trencherman and he drank the lion's share of the two bottles of 1900 Smith-Haut-Lafite they had with their veal cutlets. For an hour they talked 'Navy', and anyone overhearing them would recognize at once the harmony between father and son and their engrossed interest in their chosen career. It had been so since Richard had first become aware of the existence of the sea and ships and had learned from his father and grandfather – old George Buller whose father had served under Nelson – of that first wonder of the world, Britain's Royal Navy.

Richard had seen out of the corner of his eye a waiter bring to Admiral Fisher's table the daily and evening newspapers and the service magazines, the *Naval and Military Gazette, Journal of the* RUSI and others, and had once or twice stolen a glance at the solitary, impressive figure, the most famous sailor alive, turning the pages over rapidly or reading intently some item that had caught his eye. Richard's father also revealed that Fisher was never far from his thoughts when he said, 'The flagship has made a signal, Richard, though you may not have read it.' And indeed, Richard saw that Admiral Fisher had pulled himself to his feet and with a word of thanks to his waiter set course for the smoking-room, where the two Bullers were quick to join him.

Fisher's first words as the three men sat down in a quiet corner of the vast room, in which the few members present were fast asleep, surprised Richard but were in fact characteristic of the admiral: 'Well, Buller, how's that beautiful wife of yours. I've been madly in love with her since I first set eyes on her many years ago. My beloved Queen Alexandra agrees with me. "Who's that handsome woman, Jackie?" she once asked me at a soirée. "Is that Clemmie Buller – mad Lord Huntley's daughter? A comely figure, eh Jackie?"'

Fisher did not wait for an answer to his question but steamed on as swiftly as one of his battle-cruisers. 'Buller, I am going to ask a very great kindness of you. Remember I Corinthians XIII, 4: "Charity suffereth long, and is kind." I want you to give up your command.'

Richard felt his father stiffen beside him, and thought, 'What a thing to ask, his beloved battle-cruiser in the middle of a great war!' Fisher held up his hand. 'Do not fear, you shall have back the *Incontestable*. But the Navy and the nation need you again in a special capacity.' He leaned forward in his chair and half-whispered eagerly, 'You are needed as the most experienced serving gunnery officer in the Fleet. Against my advice and judgement, we have, as you know, embarked on a massive enterprise in distant waters. It has involved a bombardment the like of which has not been seen since Vesuvius erupted in AD 79. I want you to observe these operations from one of the vessels taking part just as you observed the Battle of Tsu-Shima from that Japanese cruiser in '05.'

The report made after Tsu-Shima by Buller and his fellow gunnery officer, Rod Maclewin, had convinced Fisher that the heaviest guns must be fitted to the dreadnought battle-cruisers then under consideration, thus stealing a march on the Germans. With the charm and generosity of language Fisher had always been able to deploy rapidly he continued. 'You may have saved our country last time, Archy. I do not wish to prejudge your report, but this time you may save our lords and masters of the War Cabinet, who know as much of naval warfare as the Spaniards at Trafalgar, from further bombardment follies far from the main theatre—' and he beat his fist on the table so that the coffee-cups rattled and a septuagenarian by the fire opened one eye and glared in their direction – 'the main theatre, which is the ONLY theatre, AND THAT IS THE NORTH SEA WHERE THE GERMAN NAVY DAILY THREATENS US!

'This Dardanelles nonsense *must cease*. It is a folly of the first order, the madcap enterprise of Churchill and Kitchener who have duped the Prime Minister and the War Cabinet. I have told them that it is madness, that if they need a diversion to break the stalemate in France, they should land an army on the German Pomeranian coast and march on Berlin. I am preparing the vessels for this landing now – every shipyard is bending its energies:

> For their work continueth,
> And their work continueth,
> Broad and deep continueth,
> Greater than their knowing.

You recall, of course, that great song by the great Kipling.

'Soon I shall have an Armada to finish the war in a few days – the Grenadiers and the Royal Marines marching down the Unter den Linden, the Kaiser cowering, *pleading for mercy*!'

His voice dropped, and he said crisply to Buller, 'Captain Parsons in the appointments branch will give you sailing instructions tomorrow. I will see you when you return – if the enemy does not drown you.' He was on his feet and glanced fleetingly at Richard. 'And what about you, young man? What are you going to do to help smash the Kaiser?'

'Admiral Beatty's destroyers, sir,' he answered.

'Ha!' exclaimed Fisher with infinite satisfaction. 'You

won't be able to keep up with my New Testament ships. 30,000 tons, thirty-three knots, only twenty-one-feet draught to cover the German landing. 15-inch guns and no more armour than a sardine-tin. Who wants armour when you can outpace the enemy and blow him to bits when he can't even *reach you*? I've told Jellicoe he can have them in twelve months from now. Meanwhile, do your best with what you've got.'

With a last beatific smile, Admiral Fisher turned and made off, his voice fading: 'Got to get to bed to face Winston's pile of rubbish at 7 a.m. . . .'

'What does he mean by that?' Richard asked his father when they were alone.

'He and Churchill love one another but they're like a match and a dreadnought's magazine. One day the match will be struck, mark my words. Already they are a sore trial to one another. Churchill will just be starting dinner now, and he'll wine and dine in amusing company until midnight. Then he'll start on his papers in bed, his "pile of rubbish" as Admiral Fisher called it, and work through till four, when a messenger will take them to the Admiralty for Admiral Fisher, who goes to bed after saying his prayers at about 10.30 and gets up at 5.30, prays in Westminster Abbey and walks to the Admiralty.'

'How do you know all this, Father?'

'Everyone who's watching for signals knows it. Already things don't sound too good at the Admiralty. What I don't know is when I'm going. And what I do know is that I've lost my ship – a fine ship and the best company of men in the Battle-Cruiser Squadron.'

On the train to Cirencester the next afternoon Archy Buller read, for a short time, the war news intently. The news from the Dardanelles was optimistic and spoke of an imminent breakthrough by the Royal Navy. There was no hint of Admiral Fisher's despondency and pessimism in the reports from Admiral Carden, which spoke of the vast damage done by the early bombardments, and of the crushing of Turkish forts.

Buller remembered an aphorism he had heard a wise politician utter at the time of the Boer War – 'The first casualty in war is truth' – and reflected on the difficulty of reviving truth, or even discovering it; which was a task upon which he was about to embark.

The news from France, where only recently Paris itself seemed likely to fall to the Germans, was equally reassuring. The French were holding their line, and the small British Army was daily growing in strength. Buller had had a good lunch at the Marlborough, with a bottle of Bollinger to wash it down, and by Reading he was asleep, to awake only to the sound of the porters calling, 'Cirencester – Cirencester. Change here for Chedworth and Cheltenham.'

'Well, Mills, I'm glad you've managed to keep clear of the war, it's good to see you,' Buller greeted his coachman, who took the luggage from the porter.

'It's not for want of trying, sir,' said Mills, portly but still nimble on his feet. 'I went to the recruiting-office but they said I was too old.'

'And how is her Ladyship?'

'She was out hunting again yesterday, and very fit she seemed, sir. Though she's worried about fodder for all the hunters, sir. They say it's all wanted for the horses in France. This war's a terrible business, sir.'

It was a crisp early March morning and there were still traces of frost under the cedar trees on the lawns to the front of Wyston Court, and Buller reflected briefly on the perfect proportions of his Queen Anne manor-house, the fine state of the trees, and the pleasure of arriving home in the old family coach, drawn by Bessie and Belinda, rather than the Rolls-Royce which had been stored away as a measure of fuel economy.

Buller also reflected wonderingly on how Clemmie always seemed to assume (quite unintentionally, he knew) a graceful attitude of welcome for his return, whether from London after a short time, or from being away at sea, sometimes for years. And there she was, in a wide-brimmed hat and long blue-grey tweed coat edged with fur and clutching a bunch of hothouse lilies. She was about to enter the front door, and turned at the sound of the hooves and wheels on gravel.

Lady Clementine Buller looked her age, which was fifty at her next birthday, but no more – a fine, well set-up figure of a woman, as she was usually described by admiring men, and there were plenty of these. Her hair, drawn back into a tight bun, had once been the colour of a field of Gloucestershire corn and now matched the Cotswold grey walls that bounded the fields of the Home Farm. Her eyes, Buller had always observed, had not changed since he had proposed to her – large and kind yet shrewd, clear-brown, missing little that went on about her. Although born with wealth, privilege and a title, life had not flowed as gently as the young River Thames which rose from a spring little more than a mile from Wyston Court. Aside from the numerous infidelities in their marriage, on both sides, Clemmie had fallen seriously in love at a time when she thought she had lost Buller for ever, and for three years had suffered cruelly.

Of her children, both Harry and Lucy had been the cause of much anxiety. But whatever tragedies there might be in store for Archy Buller's family, at sea or in France, the war had brought solidarity of purpose to them as it had to millions of families throughout the land; and Lucy was now doing her duty for her country like most other young people.

Clemmie handed her basket to one of the gardener's boys and embraced her husband. 'How long, darling?'

'Until breakfast tomorrow.'

'Oh, is that all? It's not fair. Jackie might have allowed me one full day with you.'

'I'm sorry – it's really very urgent.'

They walked in through the front door, and Buller handed his hat and coat to the butler, greeting him cheerfully, 'Well, Gutteridge, you're keeping the home fires burning for us?'

When they were alone, Clemmie said, 'Are you allowed to tell me where you're going?'

'Of course I can, though it's a secret to anyone else. The old boy's sending me out to the Dardanelles. He's dead against the whole enterprise and wants proof that the bombardment's a fiasco, and why, so that he can get all the battleships back home for his own enterprise in the North Sea.'

'Archy, are you going spying again?' asked Clemmie in some concern, recalling with horror Buller's earlier cloak-and-dagger operation which had so nearly cost him his life and brought about the rift that had so nearly broken their marriage.

'No, not spying *exactly*,' Buller said. 'But I daresay Churchill and Kitchener won't know I'm being sent out there, and certainly won't be told why.'

'And if you come back with a report that doesn't support Jackie Fisher?'

'He won't be pleased.'

'And if your report says he's right to damn the whole business?'

'Then Winston won't be pleased.'

Clemmie laughed, but there was a trace of bitterness in her voice. 'Not good for your promotion chances, Archy. Either way it doesn't look as if you'll ever be able to say "I am the Ruler of the Queen's Navee!" Archy Buller, they're making a monkey out of you.'

'No, my dear, I don't think so. I have never believed that if you report the truth that it can be damaging to you. And promotion to flag rank, however desirable, is not an important consideration when the nation's at war.'

Clemmie put her arms round Buller and kissed him.

'Darling, I do love you when you're being pompous. Just take care of yourself, that's all.'

And they went to bed early and made love with all the zeal and enthusiasm of their early married days.

VII

The Bombardment

Some two thousand miles of ocean separate the continent of America from the continent of Europe. Between Turkey in Asia and Europe there are scarcely two thousand yards of water. From the exit from the Black Sea at the Bosporus and the exit from the Mediterranean at Cape Helles there are two narrow channels which widen into a small inland sea, the Sea of Marmora. It is as if one giant force of nature had endeavoured to tear Europe apart from Asia, and a counterforce had shouted 'No!' and held on so tenaciously that the division scarcely succeeded.

Xerxes once built a bridge of boats across these southern narrows – the Dardanelles – and his army marched over it from Asia to Europe on its conquering way. Byron, in 1810, was not the only man to swim the Hellespont; officers of the frigate *Salsette* also succeeded in making the crossing in the same year, and others are supposed to have made it from time to time. The distance is no obstacle. The dangers are from the four- to five-knot current that sweeps down from the Black Sea, and the coldness of the water, especially in winter.

It was this channel, the Dardanelles, which the Royal Navy, assisted by units of the French Navy, had been ordered to force. Once the battleships had reached the Sea of Marmora, claimed the planners of this enterprise, Constantinople would be at their mercy and the way would be open to the Black Sea ports of Russia, the enemy divided, Turkey cut off from her allies, her 'big brothers', Austria–Hungary and Germany.

Archy Buller had sailed up the Dardanelles to Constantinople in peacetime when serving in the Mediterranean, and had last viewed the Mediterranean entrance, between Cape Helles and Kum Kale, when serving in the battleship *Victoria* back in the summer of 1893. From the deck of a ship in the Aegean lying offshore, this division between Asia and Europe appears to be no more than a narrow gorge cutting through the drab grey hills covered in rough scrub and rocky outcrops.

Buller was piped on board the battleship HMS *Incomparable*, hove to eight miles south-west of Cape Helles, shortly before noon on 14 March 1915, to be greeted by his fellow-captain and old friend and shipmate, Mark Holly. Holly was a tall (six feet seven inches), narrow-faced, plain but ever-cheerful man who had been gangling and clumsy as a cadet back in the *Britannia* days when he had fallen out of the rigging so often he had finally been forbidden the ratlines altogether. An object of amused affection among young women, Holly had taken life's rebuffs philosophically. In his late thirties he had married a somewhat grasping and shrewish widow who, it was believed, had been attracted more to the brewery fortune Holly had inherited than by his happy and tolerant nature. He shamelessly admired Buller and was now delighted that he was to have his company on board his old battleship in the role of 'special observer'.

The two old friends paced the quarterdeck together, Buller noting with some wonder the number of men-o'-war of all kinds gathered here off the Gallipoli peninsula, from the latest super-dreadnought, HMS *Queen Elizabeth*, and the battle-cruiser *Inflexible* back from the Falkland Islands, to a number of older battleships like the *Incomparable*, cruisers, destroyers, the seaplane carrier *Ark Royal* and dozens of little North Sea trawlers.

'What sort of passage did you have, Buller?' Holly asked.

'A day and a night in the train to Marseilles, then a French cruiser which logged an average twenty-five knots the whole way. The Admiralty told me I wouldn't be wasting time *en route* – and they were right. How are things going, Mark?' Buller asked.

'Come down to my cabin and I'll explain.'

And the two captains, Holly so tall and thin but by no means devoid of dignity and style, and the heavily built Buller, himself over six feet, descended the wide steps, all gleaming brass and polished teak, to Holly's quarters aft.

A large-scale chart was spread out on the round mahogany table that occupied the centre of Holly's day-cabin. Holly pointed out the known searchlight and gun emplacements on both shores, some of them small calibre artillery pieces, the heavy batteries concentrated mainly at the Narrows. 'What are not marked', explained Holly, 'are the mobile batteries, which may appear anywhere and are devilishly cleverly camouflaged. Mostly howitzers. Then there are the mines and torpedoes. If they see us coming up, they let loose mines which float down with the current. There are also secured minefields.'

Buller took his leather cigar-case from his pocket, selected one and completed the ritual of rubbing it between his fingers to check the aroma, snipping off the end and lighting it. A thick cloud of Corona-Corona smoke arose in the air. His brain was a sound but not a swift-moving machine, and, having long ago recognized this fact, he liked to consider any situation for a while before commenting. At length he said, 'But Holly, old man, there's enough weight of shell to blow the whole peninsula to pieces – enough to blast the Narrows wider,' he added with a laugh. 'Twenty-odd battleships, including the newest and most powerful in the world. And you're held up by a few Turkish pea-shooters! It's amazing.'

'It's uncommonly more difficult than you imagine, Buller,' Holly said, placing his index finger on the centre of the peninsula. 'Gallipoli's like an unsinkable battleship, bristling with guns. We've got to hit those guns, and they make a small target. A near miss is no good. But for the Turkish gunners they've got ships hundreds of feet long to fire at and whatever they hit does damage. Moreover, we're firing from a moving and not altogether steady platform, but they lay their sights on us from a static base.'

Holly ordered a bottle of Veuve Clicquot, which was brought in and opened by his steward. 'An '89 – your favourite, I seem to recall,' Holly said. He raised his glass. 'Here's to the damnation of the Sultan – and all his gunners. We're going in at five p.m. so you'll be able to see what we're up against.'

HMS *Incomparable* was fifteen years old, 13,000 tons and built to a design which had been little changed until the advent of the *Dreadnought* six years later. She showed in profile two tall funnels amidships, a mainmast and foremast embracing conning-tower, fighting-top, a bridge and searchlight platform. Heavy armour plate protected the sides of the ship amidships over the engine rooms, and most heavily protected of all were the turrets housing the four 12-inch guns, two of them forward and two aft. Smaller guns ranged from 6-inch to quick-firing Maxims. Her triple-expansion steam-engines, fired by coal, could push this 400-foot-long man-o'-war through the sea at eighteen knots.

Like most of the battleships on this operation, the *Incomparable* could never serve in the line of battle in a modern engagement. She had neither the speed nor the gunpower, but she still packed a heavy punch with her 12-inch guns and Buller thought she was ideal for shore bombardment. Her gunnery officer, Commander Martin Hoskins, agreed with this and was proud of what they had so far achieved since the first bombardment of 18 February. 'We silenced the outer forts then,' he told Buller, 'and we can destroy the Hamidieh fort up at the Narrows if we can get close enough. But the mines are the very devil and we're not allowed to fire enough shells.'

Four battleships, including the *Incomparable* and a French pre-dreadnought, closed the Dardanelles late in the afternoon, spread wide apart, with the *Queen Elizabeth* taking up station two miles astern, her 15-inch guns being able to range more distantly than the other battleships'. It was a clear, beautiful late afternoon, with the low sun behind them so that its glare would make sighting more difficult for the Turkish gunners. A Sopwith 'Baby' seaplane took off from the water beside the *Ark Royal*, climbing slowly in circles to some 2,000 feet. Hoskins had told Buller that the observer had a wireless set with which he could transmit by morse reports on the *Queen Elizabeth*'s shooting, the first time this had ever been done at sea. Before entering the closed world of the ship's conning-tower, Buller saw the frail-looking little plane steering towards the enemy coast and heard the high-pitched whine of its little motor. It looked uncommonly vulnerable, and Buller remarked, 'You'd think a shell passing anywhere near would swat it out of the sky.'

Picture now Archy Buller in the *Incomparable*'s conning-tower. He has his Barr and Stroud glasses to his eyes, peering keenly through the narrow slit in the all-round 8-inch armour, and a notebook is strung round his neck by a length of string. This is his world, the world of gunnery, in which he has been a specialist since young manhood, when the Navy's guns were still muzzle-loaders as in Nelson's time, when gunnery practice took place at little more than 1,000 yards.

In these cramped quarters, there is, besides Buller, the captain, his commander and first lieutenant, his warrant officer gunner and his number two, the signal officer, the helmsman at the wheel and a boy to run messages in case of damage to the ship's communications system. There is little room to move, and everyone wants a view of the target, the forts on the Gallipoli side of the Dardanelles.

The first ship to open fire is the *Queen Elizabeth*, the percussive sound of her 15-inch guns penetrating the conning-tower like a punch at the eardrums. Buller notes the time and the number of shells in the salvo. Her targets are the big forts at Kalid Bahr on the west side of the Narrows. Buller waits for twenty seconds, trains his glasses on the approximate distant position but sees no evidence of the shells exploding.

At five p.m. precisely, Commander Hoskins gives the order for the *Incomparable*'s two forward guns to open fire. The guns, at eight degrees elevation and trained in their turrets in the direction of the olive-drab hills of the peninsula, fire in turn – starboard first, then port – two successive crashes causing the great ship to shake like a dog from water.

After the third salvo, Buller taps Holly on the shoulder and says, 'I'm going out. I can't see anything from here.'

Holly answers laconically, 'I can't stop you. You always were mad and I'll tell them so at the court of inquiry into your death.'

Buller climbs down to the deserted bridge and takes a stool onto the starboard wing where he has a clear all-round view of the action, which now intensifies as the Turkish forts at Cape Helles, which had already been knocked out several times but now were reactivated, open up with a brisk fire on the four battleships. The water about the slow-moving *Incomparable* is rapidly turned into a sea of waterspouts.

With the fatalistic attitude he assumes when under fire – 'If the shell has your name on it it will get you anyway' – Buller gets on with his task of notetaking, calculating the calibre of the enemy shells by the height and volume of the bursts and, when he can see through the curtains of water, the accuracy of the battleships' fire. As they approach within 5,000 yards of the entrance to the Dardanelles he can see their 12-inch shells tearing into the rock and scrub on the side of the hills about the Turkish gun emplacements. Smoke and spouts of red earth and dust, corresponding to the waterspouts surrounding the ships, rise into the air. 'Excellent shooting,' Buller writes. And adds, when he observes the muzzle flashes of the Turkish guns apparently undiminished, 'but enemy fire unaffected.'

Distantly, far up the peninsula, Buller catches glimpses of the *Queen Elizabeth*'s shooting, the enormous explosions of the bigger shells – 1,920 pounds in weight against the 12-inch guns' 850 pounds – clearly distinguishable. And yet these bursts appear to be far inland from the target, and all are falling on the same spot. 'Consistently poor shooting' Buller notes of the biggest ship's effort. 'Fort believed untouched.'

Just as he completes this critical note, a near miss on the port side amidships sends a torrent of water showering down on him, soaking him through and wrenching the notebook from his hands as he sprawls to the deck. Buller gets up, curses out loud, recovers his hat and notebook. At that moment, the ship is struck aft by a heavy shell. Buller sees it land, sees the flash of its explosion and the sudden belch of smoke and debris from the quarterdeck, hears the scream of steel fragments racing past him. Almost at once there is another, smaller explosion on the port side amidships, followed by the rattle of more steel splinters against the funnels and superstructure.

'For God's sake get under cover!' a voice shouts from above. He catches a glimpse of Holly at the entrance to the conning-tower, waving his arms. 'We're in action and getting hit in case you've missed the show,' he calls.

Buller waves back cheerfully and reinstalls himself on

his stool. As if in undeserved reward for his bravado, the enemy fire begins to flag, and at the same time he notices that the *Incomparable*, in unison with the other three battleships, is turning through sixteen points and beginning to retire. After half an hour the bombardment is over, no ships sunk, little evident damage done to the Turkish forts.

Buller called it 'a feel for the positive'. He had long ago made up his mind that commanders either had this feel for the positive, or a feel for the negative. There was nothing in between, in his judgement. Buller had also developed over his long years of service in the Royal Navy an unerring eye for discerning instantly which of these instincts a commander possessed. He had never before met Admiral Sackville Carden, who commanded this fleet and was seven years older than Buller.

The moment Carden entered Holly's cabin, accompanied by his flag captain and members of his staff and with Holly at his side, Buller knew that the commander-in-chief was a negative man. Although a tall and impressive-looking admiral of fifty-seven, there hung about him, like a grey cloak over his shoulders, an air of pessimism and evidence of intolerable strain. He certainly showed no great pleasure when he was introduced to Buller.

'Ah, Captain Buller, I have only recently learned of your arrival here. The Admiralty did not have the courtesy to inform me of your appointment until I enquired of them by telegram yesterday.'

'I am sorry to hear that, sir,' Buller replied, determined to go no further in the way of an apology for a situation for which he was not responsible.

'You've come to report on the progress and effect of the bombardments?'

'That's correct, sir.'

'And you are a great supporter of Admiral Fisher, I understand.'

107

Buller felt the first flash of anger, and dowsed it at once, only too aware of the damage his quick temper had created in the past. 'I hope, sir, that I am a supporter of all superior officers under whom I serve – including, sir, yourself, if I may say so.' There was no warmth in his voice, but no trace of truculence either.

Carden grunted. 'Well, I am glad to hear that, Captain Buller. I understand that Admiral Fisher is lukewarm in his support of these operations, that he wishes the *Queen Elizabeth* and the battle-cruisers back with the Grand Fleet. To force the Dardanelles we require the whole-hearted support of all, from the First Sea Lord down. The bombardments are not having the success we hoped for. We are having to ration our ammunition, spotting from the air is proving a failure, our minesweepers are inadequate in numbers and are unable to withstand the fire from the shore batteries.'

Admiral Carden sat down at the table, his staff about him. 'I am visiting a number of my battleships tonight to meet my captains individually and to learn their views.' This statement seemed to be addressed to all the officers in the cabin. He now looked at Buller and addressed him again. 'Due to a number of factors, including deprival of sufficient shells, I am having grave doubts about whether we can force the Dardanelles alone. I am beginning to believe it can be accomplished only by military support – by a landing by a large force, and a co-ordinated attack against the forts.'

Yes, Buller was thinking, a feel for the negative if not for defeatism. And when there is defeatism at the top it comes down through the commands and ranks with the speed and inexorability of a mountain torrent . . .

From the bridge of the *Incomparable*, late on the following afternoon, Buller and Holly watched the minesweepers assemble and prepare for a night assault on the Turkish minefields, the real barrier to the Dardanelles.

'It's a rum thought that they were looking for fish instead of mines a few months ago,' Holly remarked. These North Sea fishing-trawlers had been commandeered for this minesweeping task and the men asked to sign on as crew in this new wartime role. Moreover, it had proved to be a tougher and altogether more dangerous role than anyone had expected. Equipped with minesweeping gear in place of their trawls, these defenceless fishing-boats had been savagely mauled by the guns while struggling against the rapid current that swept down the Dardanelles. Boats had been sunk and many fishermen killed and wounded in daylight efforts to clear the mines. Now the minesweepers were to go in under cover of darkness, with a battleship to back them up and shoot out any searchlights that threatened to illuminate them.

'It's also a rum thought,' said Buller, 'that we're forced to use a few fishing-boats to make things safe for a battleship.' The trawlers could be seen at that moment close to the *Queen Elizabeth*, like ants scurrying past a recumbent bull. A signal-lamp from the battleship flashed out the message, 'Good luck!', and Holly asked the signals officer of the watch to repeat the message. Other ships flashed out their own message. 'They'll need it all,' said Holly, 'judging by what happened last time.'

From the *Incomparable* two hours later the first rumble of gunfire could be heard – the deep boom of 14-inch artillery, the sharper crack of the lighter batteries and the howitzers, and, faintly during intermittent lulls, the rattle of quick-firers sounding like the tearing of calico. Yellow-white pencil-thin beams swinging from side to side low on the horizon pointed to the failure of efforts to shoot out the searchlights, and underlined the ordeal of the gallant little trawlers.

The full horror of that minesweeping operation was known only to those who took part and survived. For others there were statistics – the fact that three of the twenty trawlers taking part had been sunk, five others damaged beyond repair, and only two had been able to get out their sweeps before being forced to flee from the hail of shell and bullet fire. The casualties were fearful.

Buller was in his cabin writing up his report on the bombardment when Holly came in. There was driving rain and a bitter wind on deck and the *Incomparable*'s captain was dripping wet and blue in the face from the cold. He shook out his heavy waterproof coat and hung his hat behind the door.

'The news is *not* good,' he told Buller emphatically; and he recounted in detail the report he had received on the night's abortive efforts, while Buller poured him out a stiff brandy. Holly sat down, sipped it gratefully and hoisted his long legs onto the table. 'And we've lost our C-in-C.'

'Do you mean he's drowned?' Buller asked incredulously.

'No, resigned. Resigned through ill-health, says the official report. De Robeck is taking over, and he's convened a conference at midday on his flagship.'

Admiral John de Robeck was a year older than Buller and had been a 'Four' in the *Britannia* training-ship when Buller had first arrived as a 'New'. Buller had always liked and admired this bachelor officer to whom the service was his whole life. He was quite fearless, straight and just, and though a firm disciplinarian was also a kind and understanding man who fully deserved his high rank, and now his new and appallingly heavy responsibility.

At a conference with his staff and senior officers on board his flagship later that day, de Robeck called Buller over before the meeting began and spoke to him with characteristic openness. 'I know you're here on a difficult errand, Buller,' he said generously, 'between the devil and the deep blue sea, as you might say. And so are we. But we're going to succeed, you mark my words. You hold back your report until after the 18th – the day after tomorrow. You're going to see some sparks flying then.'

The admiral smiled and indicated to his chief of staff that the meeting should open.

It was a sight that Buller, and everyone else who witnessed it, would never forget: sixteen battleships assembling on the morning of 18 March, hell-bent on forcing their way through the narrow gorge of the Dardanelles against all the shellfire, the minefields and torpedoes that would be used against them. Their destination was the great Moslem capital of Constantinople, their spirit inspired with all the fire and courage of a twelfth-century crusader, John de Robeck the modern Richard the Lionheart.

This time there were to be no half-measures, no tentative or brief attacks by a few ships, their shell expenditure rationed. This was to be the great culminating attack that must and would succeed in accordance with the old traditions of the Royal Navy.

The vanguard of the attack, the spearhead, seen distantly to the north-east from the bridge of the *Incomparable* as six smudges almost on the horizon, were the *Queen Elizabeth*, the battle-cruiser *Inflexible* and the *Lord Nelson* and *Agamemnon*, the last a well-named ship to be going into battle so close to the Trojan plain. They were flanked by two more battleships, and were followed by four French battleships, their silhouettes clearer against the distant hills of Gallipoli, the black smoke from their funnels drifting away slowly in the light wind.

The *Incomparable* was in the third line of attack, with 13,000-ton battleships on both sides, decks cleared for action, all top hamper sent down, boats protected from light shellfire and splinters by hundreds of hammocks. For a moment Buller imagined himself a Turkish gunner, glass trained on this approaching armada with its almost limitless power for destruction. Holly had prevailed upon him to keep within the protection of the conning-tower armour this time. 'They'll be firing point-blank and every

111

inch of my ship's going to be hit by something today,' he had said. 'You stand less chance out in the open than Nelson at Trafalgar. And you're not even an admiral yet,' he had added with mock provocation.

Shortly before eleven a.m. the *Queen Elizabeth* and her consorts closed up and entered in stately line-abreast the Dardanelles between Cape Helles and Kum Kale. At the same moment the Turkish batteries opened up at short range, and were answered a dozen times over in sound and weight of shell by the 15-inch and 12-inch guns of the ships. Almost before the sound of the bombardment reached the *Incomparable*, gouts of smoke and dust arose from the entrance to the strait, and rapidly increased in height and volume.

In the conning-tower Holly and his navigating officer stood close behind the helmsman, a middle-aged petty officer of long experience. Once or twice the navigating officer issued an order for more or fewer revolutions or for a slight turn to port or starboard, watched intently, checking their relative position with the ships on either side and then putting his glasses to his eyes to observe the advancing formation of French ships ahead. Buller envied his old friend the sense of power and responsibility he was at this moment wielding, and remembered a similar moment back in January when his battle-cruiser was about to open fire, and at the same time suffer the fire of the enemy.

By 11.45 the noise was thunderous and communication could be made only by cupped hands to the ear of the listener. Buller's pen was swiftly writing the details of what he was witnessing, no longer frustrated at his own inactivity.

Who had written of 'The fog of war . . .'? Well, here it was multiplied many times above what he had seen at the Battle of Dogger Bank, many times worse than he could ever imagine. The French battleships with their two

112

flanking ships had disappeared into the smoke like cabs into a London peasouper, identifiable only by the muzzle flashes of their guns as they opened salvo-firing at point-blank range. Minutes later the *Incomparable* opened up with her secondary armament of 6-inch guns at almost nil elevation so close were their targets. The ship shivered slightly, as a horse shakes off flies on a hot day, and then, a minute later, the concussion of the heavy guns opening fire was like a series of blows.

Now they were in the Dardanelles proper, committed to the run up the channel, land close on either side, high land to starboard, the Asian side, lower to port until the hills began to rise towards Achi Baba. Through his glasses Buller could make out what was left of the battery and searchlight station on Cape Helles, surrounded by the pockmarks of recent shellholes. The *Incomparable*'s heavy guns were firing ahead at the big forts towards the Narrows, her secondary guns at the lighter batteries. Nothing living, no gun battery, it seemed, could survive under this massive bombardment now that sixteen battleships were committed to the cause of Turkish destruction.

For a minute or two heavy Turkish shells fell close alongside in the water, sending up waterspouts higher than the *Incomparable*'s mainmast. But the 15-inch and 12-inch shells of the leading ships were clearly taking their toll on the Chanak and Killid Bahr batteries, and only the smaller calibre Turkish guns were making themselves felt. All the big ships were hit time and again and the sound of flying splinters and larger fragments of steel was continuous. But the battleship's rate of return fire was unaffected; nor were any of the other ships in trouble as far as the smoke and dust clouds allowed Buller to observe. One by one the batteries were succumbing to the weight of fire. They were already three miles up the Dardanelles and the *Queen Elizabeth* was at least three more miles ahead.

Holly moved to a position beside Buller and bent down

113

to shout in his ear, 'We're giving them a licking this time. They won't need your report back in London!'

Buller smiled back but said nothing. They still had to get past the Narrows, and after that there was the long pull through unknown waters up to the Sea of Marmora. But at that moment, with the Turkish return fire reduced to isolated and almost random shots, it really seemed as if they might be in Constantinople that evening. And that, according to the planners, must mean the end of Turkey's part in the war, to the relief of Russia in particular, allowing her to concentrate all her armies on throwing back the Germans and Austrians.

It was 1.45 p.m. The bombardment from the three lines of battleships, inching their way up the narrowing channel, continued relentlessly. Not a single heavy Turkish shell had been fired for several minutes, the gunners put to flight or the guns themselves knocked from their mountings.

Above the sound of their own salvoes, reduced now to two rounds a minute from the 6-inch and a shot every two minutes from the big guns, Buller heard the voice of the first lieutenant. 'The captain suggests we adjourn to the bridge.'

They did so at once, thankful to leave behind the restricted space, heavy with cordite fumes, of the conning-tower. Holly had been right. Plating, ventilators, case-mates, turrets, ladders were all pockmarked with shell splinters or dented and twisted by direct hits from small calibre shells. The cutter and launch and three of the boats on the starboard side had been so badly holed, in spite of their protective hammocks, that they would never float. The *Incomparable* looked a shambles, but her fighting efficiency was intact and she had lived up to her name of ironclad.

'It'll be out with the paintpots when this lot is over, sir,' remarked a young lieutenant to Buller.

'The "chippies" will be busy, too.'

'Here come the 'sweepers, sir.'

From the port wing of the bridge Buller could see six of the little vessels struggling against the current, a mile distant. At the same moment fresh fire broke out from the shore and from behind a hill. They were Turkish howitzers firing blind, probably directed by concealed spotters; and if so, they were doing their job well. Their target was the trawlers, which at once broke their tidy formation. The howitzer fire increased, and there was nothing effective with which the battleships could reply. The smaller guns reopened fire, aiming over the low hill, but their trajectory must take the shells far beyond the invisible Turkish guns.

Now the howitzer fire increased to a storm. The shells were clearly visible at the top of their trajectory, hovering, it seemed, in the afternoon sun, before descending onto the hapless boats. But this was not the worst event in the sudden reversal of the attackers' fortunes. A mere six cables ahead, the French battleship *Bouvet*, armed with 12-inch and 10.8-inch guns, exploded – torn apart, a ship of 12,000 tons one second, a white and scarlet flash blasting debris high into the air the next. Her back was not just broken, it had been severed so that the bows and stern slipped down into the water separately but simultaneously amidst a tumult of bubbles and top hamper. There were countless heads in the water, like the sudden surfacing of a giant school of penguins. But few of these sailors, even those who could swim, could survive long in these icy waters.

The *Incomparable*'s commander was calling out, 'Lower the boats! Lower the boats!' The cry was taken up by several petty officers, and boat parties were doubling to the less damaged boats. The first boat was swung out on its davits, Holly was leaning over the extreme end of the starboard bridge wing, his first lieutenant was shouting something through a megaphone, the signals officer was talking urgently to his yeoman and a rating was in the act of hoisting a signal to the flagship; the helmsman was at the wheel, quite still, his hands on the spokes as if paralysed, the number two port 6-inch gun had just fired, a distant voice from the stern of the ship was calling, 'Hoist out the nets!' Buller had his glasses on the turbulence and litter, all that survived of the French battleship: all these sights and sounds were frozen on Buller's consciousness, fixed for all time in a single rendering like a painting seen daily since childhood, when the *Incomparable* suffered a similar explosion to the *Bouvet*'s.

A giant sledgehammer struck the ship, a flaming torch as high as the Eiffel Tower was ignited under it, a sound that must destroy the eardrums blasted out, shattering the sky as the explosion tore apart plating and boilers, decks of teak and heavy steel. Buller saw the foremast, snapped and falling, bringing down searchlights and quick-firers and men caught like flies in the spider's web of descending rigging and wireless aerials. He saw Holly walking from starboard to port across the bridge at its already steep angle, megaphone to his mouth and shouting (firmly, authoritatively, not a touch of panic or haste), 'Abandon ship! Take it steady. But abandon ship!' He did not see Buller until almost a minute later.

It was the sounds during that minute that were recorded so fully in Buller's memory, the sounds of a great ship breaking up, in ceaseless progression like a tower crumbling, swift stage by swift stage, under the impact of explosion. Torpedo flats, mess-decks, stores and bunkers, turret trunks, passages, flats, shafts, stairways, cabins and hatches – all the intricate complexity of a great man-o'-war, all the equipment and plating, crankshafts and pistons and boilers and condensers, broken or thrown together in the anarchic confusion that accompanies the death of a ship, and the death of the men who man her, trapped behind bulkheads and jammed doorways, thrown by

116

sudden angles that no storm could cause, swept into fires, swept down stairways, catapulted into corners and crannies untouched since the ship was built. And with this tossing and crushing and clawing and burning came their last cries, some cut short by water or fire or impact, others agonizingly prolonged, the distraught chorus rising up the ventilating shafts from below like a giant trumpet chorus of suffering.

These were the sounds that held Buller and the lucky few – perhaps a hundred of the ship's company of 600 – who were above decks when the mine struck the *Incomparable* just abaft the second funnel-trunk and the 6-inch shell-room. The only mercy permitted to the stricken vessel and the men below was the swiftness of the sinking. Few could have lived down there for more than a minute. Within two minutes the sea was rising like a tidal race across the tilted decks of the battleship, carrying everything unsecured and every man with it, brushing them away like debris in a typhoon.

Suddenly the bridge was empty of all personnel – all but Holly, the ship's commander and Buller. The commander scrambled down the side of the superstructure, disappearing from sight at once, as Buller made his way to Holly's side, holding a stanchion. His hat was gone, and now he struggled out of his overcoat.

Holly was holding a life-preserver and awkwardly pushing it at Buller while he held onto the compass binnacle with the other arm. 'Well, this is a rather beastly business,' he said, with just a faint trace of the smile that Buller knew so well. 'All my poor men!' And now the smile was gone. Perhaps Buller was mistaken and it had been only a grimace of suffering. Buller felt it all right, this suffering. But no fear for himself. More a repeated stabbing of anguish for the dimensions of this disaster, like the pulse of a festering wound.

But this was all in seconds, or fractions of seconds, as

swift as the swiftest of deaths below.

'What are you doing?' shouted Buller. Holly was pressing the life-preserver into his chest.

'Put this on. That is your captain's order. Put it on, Archy Buller.'

It was not the order that compelled Buller to obey. It was being called Archy for the first time since they had known one another, and that was more than thirty-five years ago. Oh, what an age since . . .

'NO!' Buller was shouting. But Holly was forcing it on him, over his head.

'I can swim, I'll be all right,' Holly was saying. 'I'll be last off but I'll be all right. Always swum well.'

Buller's inability to swim was notorious among his friends, especially since his survival of the *Victoria* disaster back in '93. Any further struggle between the two men ceased when the ship gave a convulsive lurch – surely the death throes, surely the end. And only two and a half minutes had passed since the protruding lead horn of that Turkish mine had been crushed by the *Incomparable*'s plating five feet below the waterline and set off the explosion.

Buller was thrown against the side of the bridge and knocked half-unconscious. It was the end. For one instant in a flash of semi-consciousness, he knew it was death which had overcome him, and it was no surprise. How could it be anything but inevitable? He had pushed his luck often enough, hadn't he? Fate had been generous enough, hadn't she? 'Egad, you've done well with lady luck!' as his old father would have said. Yes, no doubt of it.

The peace that had descended upon him like a warm cloak was swiftly shattered, as if this cloak had been rudely snatched and he was thrust naked into an Arctic gale. The water was cruelly cold, cutting deep to the bones, paralysing the lungs. At first Buller could think of nothing but the agony of the cold. Then, like the opening of doors to a crowded room, he heard a sound, a chorus of sound, a sound of wailing. It was the lament of many men struggling in the water knowing that, having escaped from their ship, they had only minutes of survival left to them, knowing that this cold was a lethal cold. Isolated words sprang from the chorus. Buller could hear one voice crying repeatedly, 'Jack – oh Jack!' and another, 'Throw it 'ere!' and a third simply, 'Oh God – save me . . . !'

Buller felt the numbness creeping up from his feet and kicked out violently to revive his circulation. The life-preserver kept his head above water and he could see other heads about him, some clutching spars, three men on a small carley float helping a fourth out of the water. But there were not many and the voices and cries were fading like the sound of a fast retreating crowd.

The deep boom of another exploding mine set off vibrations through the water, but Buller could not see which ship had caught it this time. In fact he could see very little, as if the cold was affecting even his sight. This cold was consuming him, eating through his body, leaving him nothing but a brain that was slowing up, second by second. Buller could feel its increasing inadequacy, knew that the time for rational thought was running out. Just as all about him, men were slipping under, surrendering to the cold, so his capacity for taking action was disappearing.

The next minutes were remembered like a series of glass-plate negatives from the old Soho camera he had used when, years ago, he had been seized with an enthusiasm for photography: misty, dim, hazy outlines, and dusk light overall. Hands reaching down over the gunwale of a launch, the tall spout of an exploding shell beyond; a big ship with three irregularly spaced funnels slipping by, forecastle awash; a battleship in its death throes, listing, drifting onto the Gallipoli shore; the face of a rating, with a scar on his chin, leaning close over him, with an intent expression, pulling off his shoes; another face beside him, blue and white from the cold, eyes closed, lips apart.

Later there was a mug at his lips, two mugs in turn, one pouring rum, the second scalding hot cocoa. He felt the roughness of blankets next to his skin and hands were massaging his feet. Down here, in the battleship's sick-bay, no one knew his rank or name, and Buller felt the peace of anonymity as if he were just one of the dead, for later identification.

Holly had gone down with his ship, as Buller knew he would; gone down along with 487 of his men, his body no doubt swept to the Aegean to join the countless numbers of Greeks and Trojans, Romans and Egyptians, who had fought their triremes in these waters. So Holly had gone, childless, leaving a widow who might not mourn too deeply and would certainly enjoy the inheritance. Poor old Mark Holly, who had never had an ungenerous thought in his life and had never made an enemy. He had at least been saved the grief at the loss of his men and his ship he would have suffered if he had survived.

Besides the *Bouvet* and the *Incomparable*, two more battleships had been lost on that deadly Turkish minefield, and the battle-cruiser *Inflexible* had limped away, as Buller had seen her, to beach herself. At the very doors of victory, with not a single heavy gun to bar the passage to Constantinople, Admiral de Robeck had had to call off the attack and bring his ships back down the Dardanelles.

In London, Churchill read aloud a series of telegrams from Admirals Carden and de Robeck to the War Council detailing the losses of battleships in the failed attempt to 'rush' the Dardanelles. He later added that he had information that the Turks were short of ammunition and mines. This was in fact the case. Almost all the Turkish batteries had exhausted their ammunition and if Admiral de Robeck had continued the attack regardless of his losses he would almost certainly have broken through to Constantinople.

But Archy Buller could not have known this. In a borrowed cabin on board the *Queen Elizabeth*, in a borrowed uniform, he spent the whole of 19 March redrafting his report, based now only on the memory of what he had observed since he had arrived. He wrote clearly, concisely, and totally without prejudice, giving examples with details and times. At eight o'clock in the evening, with a bottle of Mumm's Extra Dry half-consumed in front of him, he read it through carefully and signed at the bottom of the last page in his sloping emphatic hand, 'Archibald Buller, Captain, RN'.

VIII

The Morning of the Guns

At 7.30 a.m., just eight days before the attack on the Dardanelles, there had been a bombardment of the German positions before Neuve Chapelle on the Western Front. As the Gallipoli bombardment was the heaviest ever undertaken by the Royal Navy, the British Army's shelling was the heaviest in their history. Nearly seventy heavy guns had opened up on 10 March and had fired continuously for thirty-five minutes, blasting the German trenches and forward batteries, opening the way for the infantry to go in.

Richard Buller arrived at Harry's regiment on this section of the Western Front soon after lunch on the afternoon of 9 March, quite ignorant of the fact that the British IV Corps and the Indian Corps were about to launch the biggest British offensive of the war so far in less than twenty-four hours. He came up the road from Bethune in a motorcycle despatch rider's sidecar. It was raining, the road, which had been shelled and repaired frequently over the past months, was atrociously bumpy and Richard had long since decided that war at sea was to be preferred to war on land.

It was all very much as he had imagined it. The rumble of guns like distant thunder became louder with every mile along which they bumped and slithered. They passed through villages which had been in German hands the previous autumn, their buildings shattered by shellfire, roofs fallen in, walls collapsed and revealing bright peeling wallpaper and broken, once-prized furniture; a church with its spire pierced again and again leaning more heavily than the tower of Pisa. A few French families still survived in makeshift homes of scavenged timber and bricks, a tethered pig or cow near by. Woodland was like carelessly scythed weeds, trees splintered and white-scarred. Fields were pockmarked by shell-holes, glinting with mud, their hedges devastated.

And everywhere – men. Soldiers marching, rifles over their shoulders, in platoons or companies, tight-bunched and singing in open lorries; men escorting prisoners, bringing back wounded; men in ambulances and wagons, men riding horses, service corpsmen leading horses, staff officers in cars, other like himself in sidecars. And all wet and hunched up against the driving rain.

At a crossroads a mile from Richard's destination, a stray German shell had hit a loaded wagon, its contents and its dead driver spilled over onto the road, the horses dead, except one wounded and struggling hopelessly to get on its feet. Other men had stopped to deal with the disaster, and Richard saw an infantryman putting his revolver to the wounded horse's head.

Soon Richard caught the stench of battle, the mixed smell of men and horses, of cordite and smoke, and – sweet and appalling – of men long since dead. The driver of his motorcycle was asking the way, and all Richard wanted, suddenly and urgently, was a way out of this vista of war. But there was no turning back now. He was as committed to visiting his brother's regiment as the *Glasgow* had been committed to meeting von Spee.

They came on the first units of 25th Infantry Brigade in a hamlet less than a mile from enemy-held Neuve Chapelle. They were bivouacked in a farmyard, some in camouflaged tents, others under makeshift shelters. There was the smell of cooking, and smoke and steam rose into

123

the rain-sodden sky. They were all awaiting their turn to take over the front-line trenches two hundred yards farther forward. A German medium-calibre shell landed a short distance down the road, sending up a gout of dust and smoke. No one bothered to turn his head.

Richard got out of the sidecar, spilling out the pool of rainwater which had collected in his lap. A corporal indicated the direction of HQ and Richard made his way towards a badly-smashed farmhouse. Richard had not seen his brother since the early days of the war when he had sailed out to the South Atlantic to rejoin the *Glasgow*. He was amazed, and amused, by the transformation.

Harry Buller had always been a careful and conventional dresser, departing for his office in the City every morning in a black suit, stiff winged collar, spats and black boots, and carrying a tightly-rolled umbrella. Harry had always taken himself seriously and suffered teasing from Lucy and Richard with evident pain. Now Richard found him one among five fellow officers, crouched round a small portable stove drinking mugs of tea. His uniform was mud-stained and creased, his boots heavy with clay, his cap on a box beside him. He was laughing at a joke and was about to embark on a story of his own when he caught sight of his younger brother. He got to his feet, arms stretched wide in a gesture of greeting Richard had never seen his brother assume before.

Harry Buller, unlike Richard, was a real chip off the old block, with the heavy Buller nose, Archy Buller's eyes and muscular hands, dark hair slicked down in the fashion of the day. There was a relaxed air about his brother which Richard found novel and welcome, as if the need for restraint and respectability had been left behind in Throgmorton Street. Whatever else the war might do to Harry Buller, it was making him jollier company, Richard thought, as he embraced him, noting the day's growth of beard and a broad grin he had seldom seen since Harry had decided to become a businessman.

Now Richard was introduced to Harry's fellow officers and given a mug of tea by a steward. He might have been received with some reservation as a 'softie sailor' untouched by war if Harry had not explained Richard's part in the battles of Coronel and the Falkland Islands. Now everyone appeared keen to hear about his adventures, which Richard disposed of as soon as he decently could. Then Harry said, 'You've arrived at a good moment.'

'He may not think that tomorrow,' interrupted a red-haired lieutenant with a laugh.

'We're having a bit of a push tomorrow,' Harry explained. 'In fact quite a big push, as you'll hear, and maybe see.'

'We're pushing the Hun/To Kingdom come . . .,' someone sang, and was promptly pushed off his chair.

'We do have a few scores to settle, Rich,' Harry remarked, the light tone no longer so evident in his voice. 'They're a lot of butchers out there.'

'Animals. Pigs for pig-sticking,' said the red-haired officer. 'The men are all sharpening their bayonets like razors tonight, you mark my words.'

For several minutes the bloodthirsty talk continued, with tales of first-aid men carrying white flags being shot to pieces as they searched for wounded in no man's land. Richard felt the old sickness returning and prayed that they would soon stop. Relief came at length when Harry got up and suggested that he should show Richard the plan.

A map had been pinned on a folding card-table in the adjutant's office. It was on a very large scale and showed the contour lines and the position of all the German network of trenches, correct to within a few yards. 'We've never made an attack as well-informed as this before,' Harry said, pointing out with a stick the exact direction his platoon would be following from the road running south-

125

east to La Bassée, and the likely danger-points. 'As the barrage of shells moves forward, we'll follow, and with luck we'll just be walking over German corpses.'

Harry explained how the map had been built up from aerial photographs, the first time this had ever been done, and how the attack had been worked out in greater detail than ever before. 'You won't be able to take part, of course, Rich. But you'll be able to see quite a bit from HQ. I'll introduce you to the brigade major. He'll look after you.'

Richard wondered again at the change in his elder brother. War had made him into quite a different person, open and unguarded in manner, light in style, and yet clearly as determined to succeed in this business of war as the ultra-careful City man Harold Buller Esq had once been to succeed in the business of making money. Yet he appeared to be taking much less seriously the task of killing Germans than he had applied to the harmless task of judging the movements of Consols. Certainly Richard had been taken by surprise, and while appalled at the levity in the tone of the conversation of Harry and his friends when talking about fighting and killing the enemy, he had to admit life with this new Harry was rather more fun.

As a gunnery officer Richard was accustomed to the sound of artillery fire. In his time he had been behind the breech of every calibre of naval gun, from the old 8 cwt 3-inch to the latest Mark XII 12-inch. He had once been on board the *Dreadnought* when she had fired a full broadside of eight 12-inch. The ship had reeled under the recoil impact and the air had been torn apart by the devastating din. But the sound had been no more than a whisper compared with that of the artillery barrage which broke the silence of this March dawn at 7.30, painting the sky yellow like a continuous flash of lightning, setting the earth trembling, scattering startled birds, stirring the air with the massed onrush of shells.

126

Richard stood at the smashed window of a cottage which offered him a clear view across a muddy country road and fields towards a wood and rising ground to the east. Over there and just out of sight was the town of Neuve Chapelle, the first objective of the attack. For the first time since he had arrived in France, there was no one in sight – not a blue-smocked French farm worker, not a private, non-commissioned officer, or officer. Nothing moved, neither farm animal nor vehicle. It was as if, in this corner of the world, everything had surrendered and vanished, giving up the sky and the earth to the thunder and destruction of the guns.

For thirty-five minutes there was no relief from this cacophony of sound. Richard once or twice lowered his hands from his ears to put his glasses to his eyes. But the pain was unbearable and he had to do what he could to shut it off as he observed the ever-growing cloud beyond the woods and to left and right as far as he could see.

Then, at exactly five minutes past eight, the gunfire rapidly died away. For perhaps thirty seconds there was silence, the stunned silence of a man made unconscious, followed by the faint growing of a new and muted sound, the sound of many voices, harsh and animal-like. And with the sound there came movement, faint and fleeting and ominous – the movement of figures stirring and moving across the landscape. Through his glasses Richard could see that they were khaki-clad figures, moving fast and at a crouch, rifles held low, bayonets fixed, flitting from side to side, disappearing and appearing again between scrub and hedges and into the woods.

Like a harsh counter to the chorus of voices there came the crack of rifle-fire and the staccato rattle of machine-gun fire. The wave of infantrymen disappeared from sight. Richard saw no one fall but he knew that out there men of 25th Infantry Brigade were being struck down, a Mauser bullet fatally in the head or chest, or into thigh or leg, transforming them from fit, hurrying young men into corpses or cripples. At close quarters as they stormed the German trenches, there would be the flash and thrust of bayonets – 'pigs for pig-sticking', as that lieutenant had said last night.

A voice spoke beside him and as he turned Richard realized that he had been shaking and that the reason why he held his glasses in his hand was that he knew they would be unsteady at his eyes. 'That looks like a good start.' It was the brigade major, a middle-aged bespectacled officer to whom Richard had been introduced the previous evening. He was Geoffrey Stanford, a veteran of twenty years in the regiment who had been wounded out in South Africa and seconded to regimental clerical duties, a man trained and practised in war for all his adult life. 'Yes, a satisfactory beginning,' he repeated in his military clipped voice, a soldier through and through who had been working twenty hours a day to prepare this offensive. 'I'm going forward with my number one to recce the gains we've made. Want to come, young feller?'

They left the damaged cottage and with two other HQ staff made their way across an orchard enclosure, Major Stanford limping heavily but still moving fast. A field telephone message had informed HQ that the forward troops were in the outskirts of the town and meeting little resistance. The British guns had reopened fire, less intensely and laying down a carpet ahead of the predicted advance line of the infantrymen. The air was full of smoke and the sounds of distant shouts and sporadic rifle and machine-gun fire. To the noise of battle was added the litter and aftermath. They crossed the first British trenches and scarcely two hundred yards beyond, the German trenches, savaged by shellfire, barbed-wire entanglements torn apart. And here Richard saw the first corpses, hammered into distorted shapes by the ferocious explosion of British shells, spread out into a mixed frieze of shapes across the mud and water-filled shell-holes, spiked helmets of the II *Jäger*, rifles and fragments of clothing and limbs scattered about them.

There were wounded, too, British and German, driven into neutrality, lying mute, most of them silent, some moaning, awaiting their turn for attention from the medical corpsmen working across the battlefield like harvest-time gleaners. Richard forced himself to look at the wounded as he passed them, giving a cheering word where there was a response – 'They'll be along soon . . .' – terrified of revealing his horror and revulsion to these army officers and thus making a laughing-stock of himself and his service.

'Y'know, young feller, it's a splendid victory. That's what it is, a splendid victory.' Major Stanford cracked his stick against his calf-length leather boots, mud-spattered from the walk. The first houses of Neuve Chapelle were not three hundred yards distant, some mere shells, others holed, a few untouched. There were late snowdrops and crocuses in bloom in the gardens and a Frenchman stood at the back door of his house, staring at them without friendliness or hostility. One hour ago he had been under German rule, now the British occupied his town. He was still there when they passed close by, a dog at his feet.

In the town, people were emerging from their houses or the ruins that were once their houses, stunned and only half-comprehending. But some enterprising Frenchman had already raised the tricolour above the Mairie in the central square. Liberation had come unexpectedly and more swiftly than any of them could have dreamed.

German artillery had opened up, the c-r-u-m-p of exploding shells echoing in the narrow streets of the town and sending the citizens back into the cellars from which they had just emerged. A breathless messenger, ordered to halt by Major Stanford, said, 'Yes, sir, we're on the other side of the Bidault road and still advancing.' 'Yes, as I said, a splendid victory,' the major again cracked his stick against his leather boot.

Already the first prisoners were trickling back, dazed and miserable, some bandaged or with an arm in a sling or limping from a leg wound. Richard saw one party of a dozen huddled against a wall, guarded by a private and a corporal with fixed bayonets. The Germans clearly expected to be shot.

Richard did not see his brother for the next twenty-four hours but was assured by the major that they would hear if he had been killed or wounded. He spent the first night and most of the following day at Brigade HQ, which had been set up in the Mairie in Neuve Chapelle, several times venturing as close to the front line as he was allowed and helping out with odd tasks. By the evening of 10 March the excitement caused by the successful advance had been dissipated. 'Why didn't we exploit our advantage?' 'We had them cooked and then we let the Hun settle down and dig himself in.' 'Why didn't the guns keep up the barrage?' 'No one's telling anyone anything!' These were the questions and exclamations of dismay that Richard heard on that first evening. And no one had the answers, except that the guns had run short of shells. At nine o'clock three officers asked Richard if he would like to make up a four at bridge, just as if they had completed dinner in Mayfair. It seemed typical of the sense of resignation.

The next day the Germans struck back. They had had time to bring up reinforcements, including numerous batteries of heavy guns and howitzers. And now the British had a taste of what they had given to the Germans the day before. The ground shook under the impact of 75mm and 105mm howitzer shells and the air was thick with lethal, screaming shrapnel. The casualties mounted, and from the glassless windows of HQ, Richard counted the Red Cross wagons crossing the square and making their way to the forward casualty clearing-station.

Shortly before two in the afternoon Richard saw the brigade major leave by the front door of the Mairie and limp fast towards an officer of the Middlesex Regiment who was walking north-east across the square, heading for the front. Richard heard him call out a name, and then heard a sharp crack and saw Major Stanford stumble, fall and lie inert on the cobblestones. There had been rumours of German snipers in the town, and now one of them had struck.

There were already half a dozen men round Stanford when Richard reached him, and more were scanning the buildings searching for a sign of the sniper. The major had been struck in the thigh of his already damaged leg. He was obviously in great pain but Richard heard him say between groans, 'Well, the Huns have finished off what the Boers started.'

They got him into the Mairie on a stretcher, where the brigadier himself appeared, concerned at the loss of such a valuable and experienced officer. Richard heard him say, 'You'll be properly looked after, Geoffrey. I'll see to that personally.' He glanced about the room and caught sight of Richard. 'You're not doing anything useful, young man. I want you to act as escort to my major.'

Richard saluted. 'Yes, sir.'

'I'll hold you personally responsible for his well-being and safety.'

Richard just had time to put together a few belongings and scribble a note to Harry. The brigadier's Crossley motor was waiting outside. The front passenger seat had been removed, the stretcher fitted in neatly, and Richard sat beside Stanford's head in the back seat. The driver drove fast across the square, which was clear now of civilians and soldiers alike after the sniper's attack, and headed the Crossley in the direction of Amiens.

The medical officer had given the major something to

make him sleep, and for an hour he lay still beside Richard, eyes shut. A chill drizzle blew in through the screenless side of the motor, and Richard huddled in his seat feeling cold as well as useless. He had decided that he would be thankful to get up to Rosyth to join his destroyers to fight the sort of war he understood. Here, on the Western Front, lives were being thrown away without any evident benefit to the cause. It seemed a futile and sad business.

After negotiating some particularly rough *pavé* which shook the car badly, Richard heard the major say, 'They'll still be there when I get back.'

Richard turned, startled by the sound of his voice, and presumed that the officer was delirious. 'They won't have moved more than half a mile back or forward.' Richard saw now that his eyes were open and that he was in fact talking coherently. Richard said, 'I don't think you'll be back at HQ for a while yet.'

'It doesn't matter when,' Stanford continued. 'In a year's time, probably two years. The Brigade'll still be there. The way this war's going, one month the Germans will have a push, win a few hundred yards, lose a few thousand men, then we'll have a push and the same thing'll happen.' His grey eyes were on Richard, and he was smiling. 'It'll probably go on till there's no more men left to fight.'

Struck by the world-weary cynicism of this old soldier, Richard did not know how to respond. At length he said, 'Surely not, sir. I mean, that was an awfully successful attack we made yesterday.'

'Until the Germans decided to stop us.' The voice sounded suddenly weary and Richard saw that he had closed his eyes again.

Lucy exclaimed, 'Richard! Are you all right?'

Richard looked up at the sound of his sister's voice. She was in the reception area of the big hospital, looking very fetching in her smart white starched uniform. Under the steady eyes of the staff nurse, she did not embrace him, nor even offer her hand. But she was clearly delighted to see him, and to recognize that he was unharmed and only acting as escort.

Richard spoke to the staff nurse. 'Brigadier Lord Sutcliffe asked me to ensure as well as I could that his major got here safely and received the best attention.'

The staff nurse replied sharply. 'You may tell the brigadier that everyone here in Amiens gets the same attention, whatever their rank – in the Army or the peerage. And that attention is always the best.'

Richard felt himself blushing and at once apologized. 'Nurse Buller,' said the staff nurse in a voice which had clearly spoken with this degree of authority for many years, 'will you take this wounded major to Ward 14. The doctor will be along in a few moments to make an examination.'

Richard had never felt so redundant in his life. It was clear that the hospital was superbly run; his duty, if such it could be called, was over. All that remained was to get a message back to the brigadier to inform him that his major was safely and comfortably installed in hospital – in the best of hands, including his own sister's.

It was late in the evening before Lucy came off duty looking tired but cheerful. As Richard saw her coming down the corridor, smiling and apologizing for keeping him waiting, he recognized in her another member of the Buller family who had already been radically changed by the war. While a student at Lady Margaret Hall, Lucy had picked up radical ideas about the role of women in society, had become an ardent suffragette and brought shame on the family name by appearing on public platforms, brushing with the police and finally ending up in prison.

But the war had changed all that, as it had changed so many things – and so many people. The idea that Lucy would become a nurse, conforming to the authoritarian regime, at the beck and call of sisters and matron and calling doctors 'sir', would have been inconceivable a few months ago. But the common cause of defeating the Germans had finished all those prejudices.

At twenty-five, Lucy had her mother's fine looks – light brown hair, an English countrywoman's colour, soft skin and brown eyes. A dozen young men a year had fallen in love with her, but her 'great cause' (as she used to call it) had left all this fund of love unrequited. Richard guessed that this might not be the case in the future as she put her arms round his neck and embraced him with unusual warmth.

'How lovely to see you, Rich! What are you doing here? I thought you were with the Fleet.'

'Not until next week. I came over here to see Harry. And now I've got you as a bonus – isn't that jolly?'

After some difficulty, Richard obtained permission to take Lucy out to dinner in Amiens, and Lucy herself brought along a friend. 'Do you mind terribly? She's leaving for London tomorrow to go on a course and we were going to have a last meal and a gossip before you turned up.'

Richard had to admit to feeling rather pleased with himself walking into the bright lights of the town with his pretty sister on one arm and Lucy's fellow nurse on the other arm. The mud and blood, the wire and trenches and noise of the front line seemed a million rather than fifty miles distant. Lucy's friend was Helena Cochrane, the only daughter of a diplomat and his wife who were in Hong Kong. Richard took at once to her dark good looks and her lively personality. She was neither as tall nor as impressive a figure as Lucy, who had the Buller bearing and stature, but she had a dash and glitter about her which appealed to Richard, who found himself talking to her as freely as she talked to him, quite without reserve or shyness.

134

They dined at the Etoile in the Rue de la Gare. The availability and quality of French food appeared unaffected by the war, and they had lobster and partridge, fresh hothouse peaches and Chablis and Beaune to wash it down. It was not only a memorable meal for the cuisine. By common but unspoken consent, the subject of the war never crossed their lips for the two hours they sat at their corner-table. Richard asked nothing about the girls' hospital life, and the battles of Coronel and the Falkland Islands might never have taken place. Lucy spoke in passing of the new lives of all her old suffragette friends, Richard of Harry but not of the battle of Neuve Chapelle, Helena of her unchaperoned voyage to Europe and her fellow passengers whom she recalled in amusing detail, spiced with anecdotes. They talked of people they had known, of shows and exhibitions they had seen in London before the war had enveloped them, of village personalities in Gloucestershire, of colonial characters in the Far East.

All through that evening Richard was struck by the sharp mind of Lucy's friend, her observations that were shrewd and amusing but never unkind; and by her large dark brown eyes that glanced about the restaurant observing all that was going on, then back towards Lucy as she talked, smiling at a story she was telling, turning to Richard as if to indicate 'You have a nice sister – I like her.'

They returned to the hospital at ten p.m. Richard intended to spend the night at an hotel and to go on to Rouen to look at the sights there the next day. But the duty officer told Lucy that there was a telegram for a naval officer with the same name as hers, and handed it to her as they came in: 'Lieutenant R. Buller RN, c/o Lieutenant H. Buller, Grenadier Guards . . .' followed by a military post office number.

Richard glanced at the yellow envelope, at least relieved that it could not be bad news of his brother, tore it open and read the movement order telling him to report to his ship without delay and giving him travelling instructions. So he had only been play-acting all evening – play-acting with a cast that included these two attractive girls, and now the curtain had come down and he must walk off-stage into the real world again, the world of war and danger and death. He was half-pleased at this abrupt end to unreality and the evident urgent need for his services, half disappointed at the loss of his last few days of leave.

He checked his watch. 'If there's a train to Dieppe tonight I must take it,' he said. 'The one a.m. destroyer to Newhaven means I can catch the midday train from London to Scotland.'

Helena took the telegram from him and read it. 'Well, I am just as important and needed for the war as you are,' she said lightly. 'I'm on His Majesty's Service, too, so I shall come on your destroyer.'

Richard laughed, now only half-surprised by the unexpected from her. 'We can try.'

'I'm glad you're on my side. Fancy, we'll have breakfast on the train to London. That *will* be jolly.'

The hospital duty officer told them that there was a train in half an hour. A wheezing De Dion cab was summoned to the door. 'Look after my major for me.' 'Give my love to London.' Helena's luggage went onto the cab's roof. Soon she was settling down into a corner seat of the train while the great locomotive drew out of Amiens, heading north for the Channel port. 'There,' she said with infinite satisfaction. 'The evening's only just begun.'

As Richard suspected, it was not at all difficult to persuade the destroyer's commander to allow Helena, in her beguiling nurse's uniform and pleading the urgency of her mission, to travel to Newhaven in his ship. Better still, he even cleared his cabin for her. But for the first hour of

136

the three-hour passage Helena preferred to remain on deck with Richard watching the darkened little ship speeding through the water. It was a cold but fine clear night and they were protected from the spray by a canvas screen.

Now, in this setting, with a 20-inch searchlight on one side and a long, sinister torpedo-tube on the other, with the steady rumble of the 25,000-horsepower turbines below, and the hints of danger on the horizon – intermittent flashes, the swiftly moving arc of a searchlight beam – it was no longer possible to insulate themselves from the war.

'Will your ship be like this? Just as fast and *dangerous*?' she asked emphasizing the last word with some relish.

He told her that it was a sister ship, that she could do thirty-four knots. It was just possible to make out the silhouette of the 4-inch quick-firer aft. 'There are two of them, Mark XIVs with a 31-pound shell. Twelve rounds a minute with a good crew.'

He had fired her interest, and Helena, always hungry for knowledge, wanted to know everything about the ship and its armament. At length Richard laughed. 'You'll have me shot if I go on like this,' he said.

Undeterred, Helena asked, 'What's it like to fire your gun at an enemy ship?' Richard had noticed several times during this long night that she might suddenly introduce a seemingly naïve question and hang on eagerly for the response. Now he paused, torn between cliché and a thoughtful answer. 'I suppose it's like any other job which needs all your attention. You're concerned with doing it well, using your skill. Like one of your surgeons when he's operating.'

'Not the same thing, not the same thing at all. I've seen plenty of operations, and now I'm going to Guy's Hospital for a course as a theatre nurse. But that's saving life, not trying to take it.'

These words made him uneasy, and Richard wished she

137

had not spoken them. She seemed to sense his discomfort and added, 'I know you've got this job of work to do and I'm sure you're terribly good at it. But how do you *feel*?'

Helena was going too deep too soon. Richard was not ready for this kind of conversation, which was brushing too close to his innermost, disturbing thoughts. So he resorted to the banal and declared roundly, 'You feel good if you win. And rotten if you don't.'

Her hand was on his sleeve and he turned, at once conscious of her in a way that had been undefined all evening, the moment made half-unreal, too, by her presence in this masculine place of guns and torpedoes and purposeful preparedness for combat. There was even just a trace of perfume, only hinted at like a whiff of balsam from a poplar, before it was swept away on the thirty-knot Channel wind.

'I'm going down to my snug little cabin now. Will you show me the way?'

He helped her down the ladder to the diminutive main deck, warning her of steel protruberances and other hazards along the narrow passageway, through water-tight doors, to the captain's cabin. A dim light revealed the bunk and locker. She affected mock disappointment. 'Oh, no hammock! I did so want to sling my hammock. Goodnight, my kind sailor.'

The destroyer drove on through the night, trailing a faintly phosphorescent wake, bow waves white and high against the bows, stem like an arrow flying towards its target. Richard greeted the officer of the watch on the bridge, a lieutenant he had known six years ago at Osborne.

'Do you ever have any trouble on this run?' he asked.

'No, we're too fast for the U-boats. But we picked up what was left of the crew of a tramp the other night. Not very nice, the poor devils. I like thirty knots and something to fight back with. I'd really like to get one of those cowardly swine.'

138

IX

Buller Speaks Out

Admiral Fisher waved Archy Buller's clipped sheets of paper in his face. He was, Buller recognized, working himself into a frenzy. 'This report you have just given me – I'll tell you what it says. It says ships can never succeed against forts, as even the great and good Lord Nelson had to discover at the cost of an arm. It says that mines pose a deadly threat to the battleship, as the Russians and Japanese discovered ten years ago even before the underwater mine was perfected. It says "So what happens if the Fleet does get through the Dardanelles?" And then answers the question, "It cannot survive without supplies and support – fuel and ammunition." It says in addition that, in any case, the attacks have been ill-conducted by craven, indecisive and useless commanders who should have been on the scrap-heap before this war started, officers who have neither colour nor positivity. You will recall, Buller, Revelations III, 16. I'm an Old Testament man, myself, but there is good sense in the new, I concede that:

> I know thy works, that thou art neither cold nor hot:
> I would thou were cold or hot.
> So then because thou art lukewarm, and neither cold
> nor hot, I will spew thee out of my mouth.'

The old admiral now beat his desk with Buller's report,

and ended with a characteristic flourish. 'I would spew out these antediluvian, lukewarm admirals. And the ignorant soldiers like Kitchener and politicians like Churchill who send them on lunatic errands in distant waters when the *one and only decisive theatre is the North Sea*. A failure in the Dardanelles would be nothing. A failure in the North Sea would be ruin. But the Dardanelles is draining our strength in the North Sea and the German admirals are rubbing their hands with *glee!*'

Fisher looked at Buller as if recognizing his presence and identity for the first time. Then he smiled his seraphic smile. 'Am I not right about your report, Buller? Tell me what else is in it.' And he handed it back with a flourish.

Buller had no need to look at it. He knew it almost by heart – the references to the failure to acknowledge the usefulness of the *Ark Royal*'s seaplanes and the ignoring of their spotting reports, especially by the *Queen Elizabeth* which wasted tons of its ammunition because the gunnery officers did not trust these newfangled flying machines nor those who flew them; the failure to use the modern destroyers available for mine-sweeping; the failure to appreciate the danger from German U-boats said to be *en route* to the Aegean; the difficulty of knocking out unseen batteries; and numerous other points which he now incisively recounted to the First Sea Lord.

'Just as I expected,' declared Admiral Fisher in tones of complete satisfaction. 'You have done well. Your father would be proud of you if he were alive. Now, with this report, I have the 15-inch ammunition I need to blast my opponents and bring home my ships. The detonation will be heard all over Whitehall, like the great Matthew Arnold's "troubled sound of storms that rage outside".'

Feeling relieved and thoroughly pleased with himself, Archy Buller made his way from Admiral Fisher's office on the first floor of the Admiralty, passed the time of day with the Royal Marines watchman on duty in the yard, remembering his name and asking after his children, and strode across Horse Guards Parade towards the Marlborough Club. He was in a mood to celebrate and the Marlborough was a more suitable place to do so than the Athenaeum. It would be just like the old peacetime days – a bottle of Veuve Clicquot, port over the backgammon-table, and perhaps a visit to the Hon Mrs Fitzpatrick in Belgravia later in the afternoon. For many years she had always welcomed Archy Buller; their understanding and mutual enjoyment in and out of bed were a total pleasure. A task fulfilled satisfactorily, Buller found, always led him towards Belgravia when he was in London. Then three days' leave before he rejoined his ship . . .

Alas for Captain Archibald Buller! His wife's anxieties about his role in the Dardanelles appeared, over the following days, to be justified. Buller had understood all along that if his report was critical of the concept of the operation it would not please Winston Churchill, its prime mover. What came as a shock was that his criticism of the manner of the attack would become so widely known in the Admiralty, penetrating every department and office, causing rancour and resentment, opening up wounds sustained in the old bitter Fisher–Beresford feud. The fact that the report was confidential stemmed the flow of its contents only momentarily. Admiral Fisher was not an enthusiast for confidentiality when he caught the heady scent of victory over his opponents. To Buller the negation of his belief that the truth could never damage came as a shock and disillusionment to him.

In the eyes of Churchill, and the majority of the members of the Naval War Staff, and most of those working in the multitudinous departments under the various Sea Lords, Buller was suddenly identified with those who had had doubts that the Fleet could force the Dardanelles and opposed withdrawing valuable ships from home waters for this purpose. Overnight, he had become a Fisher man. And how was Buller to know that the power of Jackie Fisher, whose strength and influence had been omnipotent only months earlier, was now on the wane? Had he known, he would no doubt have still spoken the truth about what he had seen, for Buller was a man whose integrity was like the steel of a dreadnought's framing, and he had no time for the intrigues and petty feuds of naval politics.

The first evidence that Buller was to be treated like a twig on the sacrificial fire, ignited by the continuing failure of the Fleet off Gallipoli, appeared in a telegram delivered to Wyston Court where he had intended to take his leave before returning to his ship. It was from the office of Winston Churchill's naval secretary and requested his presence at the First Lord's office the next day.

The telegram did not take him totally by surprise. He tried, without success, to reassure Clemmie that this was no more than he expected, and that he would certainly be questioned closely about some of his statements and conclusions. But on the following morning in the Admiralty he did take the precaution of calling first at the Department of Naval Intelligence. The Director, Captain Reginald Hall, was an old friend and had been captain of the battle-cruiser *Queen Mary* when Buller had commanded the *Incontestable*. He was an unusually bright officer who had also run a very happy ship. Now he was involved in the grey world of ciphers and codes, crackling wireless signals from the other side of the North Sea, and their interpretation – in short a place where confidences were *not* broken.

Captain Hall took a great deal of finding. The existence of his department was no secret, but its exact whereabouts appeared to be unknown. For almost an hour Buller pursued a wild goose chase up and down corridors and stairs until at length he seized a telephone and informed the switchboard officer that he had an urgent message for

Captain Hall from the First Sea Lord and had to deliver it personally. A hastily-summoned messenger took Buller through a number of double-locked doors into a wing of the Admiralty building which he had not known existed.

The Director of Naval Intelligence, whose department had led the Battle-Cruiser Squadron, including Buller's ship, onto the enemy at the Battle of the Dogger Bank (though Buller was not privy to this secret), was an officer of below average height, almost totally bald, with wide-set grey eyes, a wide mouth and strong jaw-line. The derivation of his nickname was obvious from one glance at those eyes. Buller greeted him: 'Well, "Blinker", it's very good indeed to see you. How's the spy-catching business?'

Captain Hall sat Buller down in a leather armchair and offered him a cigar. 'Oh, we're trawling them like herrings and eating them for breakfast,' he answered with a deep laugh. 'And what about the Dardanelles? I hear you took a swim, and lost a chum.'

'That about sums it up. An awful business. Poor old Holly. He was a great sport to the end, and he saved my life.'

Hall commiserated with him. 'Yes, a bad business. The old man's not pleased at losing all those ships. He told me he's going to resign unless the *Queen Elizabeth* is brought home and not another ship goes out to that graveyard, as he described it. But he told me he's pleased with you.'

'But what about Churchill and the politicians? They're not going to be best pleased.'

Captain Hall's eyes blinked faster than ever: they always did when there was a problem on hand. For the present he appeared not to have the answer and merely glanced at the clock on the wall. 'You're due at the First Lord's office in eight minutes, Buller. You'd better be on your way.'

'How do you know that?' Buller asked in astonishment.

'Oh, we get to know most things here. It's our business, y'know.'

143

Churchill kept him waiting for almost an hour, which Buller regarded as ominous. And all his worst fears were realized. Buller, like most naval officers, instinctively distrusted politicians, regarding them as devious and motivated for their own gain rather than for the benefit of the nation. Now his mind went back to 1912 when he had first met Churchill who had come to inspect his ship when she was completing her fitting-out on the Tyne. He recalled the full, round face, the clever, darting eyes, the receding hair, the full lips wrapped round the big Havana-Havana, the unusual air of good living for a man not yet forty. He recalled too, the deep patrician voice, as rapid speaking in observation as interrogation. Buller also remembered how this statesman had crossed the floor in the House of Commons back in 1904 and came to be regarded as a traitor by every Conservative in the land. He was not much liked or admired in the Navy either, although any well-informed officer must give him credit for the many reforms he had carried out and for creating a much-needed Naval Staff.

Churchill was talking to a young woman stenographer when Buller was admitted to his office. He completed his conversation at leisure before he turned his attention to Buller, who recognized a copy of his report on the desk.

'Captain Buller, our tracks cross again.' Churchill held out a pudgy hand and shook Buller's hand with a weak perfunctory grip, sitting down again at once and staring at him. He was wearing a dark, double-breasted suit, white wing-collar with polka-dot dark blue bow-tie. A cigar smoked unheeded for the moment on an ashtray by his right hand. 'You have had an eventful war. And so, I see, has your son, with two major battles in one month. And you have a new and much-deserved decoration upon your manly chest.'

Churchill smiled briefly, his cheeks formed into chubbiness like a little boy's. But almost at once his voice became grave. 'To sink the *Blücher* was a fine deed. To try to sink our efforts to breach the Dardanelles was less laudable. I have read your report and regard it as irresponsible.'

He paused, and Buller wondered for a nonplussed moment if he was being teased. But no. There was no laughter there. The man meant it. And then Buller felt the dread tremors of anger coursing through his veins, unwanted adrenalin. 'Irresponsible, sir? That is a strong word.' He was containing the urge to release the rapidly building rage.

'I regard it as not only irresponsible but treasonable in time of war to give comfort to our enemies, to undermine the confidence in our country's leaders and fighting men alike. What you have written here' – and he raised and dropped the papers onto his desk, the draught causing the cigar ash to fall – 'indicates that our naval operations were ill-conceived as well as poorly carried out. You offend, sir, against all principles of conduct and behaviour of an officer and a gentleman. This report will be consigned to the furnace, and you will learn where you shall be consigned.'

It was useless to stem the tide. The fury which had been Buller's undoing when he was a young man, and, thank God, he would say, less frequently as a senior officer, now spilt over. He stood up and barked at this politician, whom he despised, as if he were a first-year cadet at Osborne.

'Mr Churchill, what I have written in that report is the truth as I have seen it, and if you are capable of listening to reason you should take heed of it.' He was trembling, he could feel it. He was trembling as if in the throes of some fearful fever, but his eloquence thrived. 'You are squandering lives out there. But for a loyal friend who drowned I should have lost mine. I have survived to tell the truth, while your reputation will sink in those Dardanelles waters. It will sink like the great ships that went down before my eyes, and will go down as I saw hundreds of my shipmates and young sailors drown in this hopeless, ill-conceived operation.'

Buller could have continued in this vein but Churchill was barking back at him, his voice high-pitched with rage as great as his own. 'Last time we met, Captain Buller, I recall that you had recently returned from an expedition involving deception and outright spying, again at the behest of the First Sea Lord. I see it is becoming a habit. It is not an activity we can tolerate in time of war . . .'

It was as well that there was a broad desk between the two men or (Buller reckoned afterwards) he might have struck the civil head of the Royal Navy. All his life he had been trained in the art of the offensive, never in the art of the defensive. To explain to this man – this politician – that he had been acting under orders and these required him to do his duty and not to question these orders was a consideration as distant as the Dardanelles themselves. 'Never complain, never explain,' he had often heard Jackie Fisher himself say. He was going to do neither now.

Standing to his full height of over six feet, a formidable figure breathing rage and aggression, Buller uttered these words, breaking Churchill's diatribe: 'You, sir, are a disgrace to your office and to the Crown, the Navy and the country we have served for all our lives. Good-day to you, sir.' And Archy Buller turned, strode to the door without a backward glance, opened it, and derived a certain satisfaction in closing the heavy, polished mahogany door neither too softly to indicate a sudden obsequiousness, nor with a power and sound to suggest that he did not have himself under proper control. Just c-l-i-c-k.

Once outside in the corridor, the self-imposed discipline continued to rule him. Steadily he walked to the head of the stairs, firmly he walked down them, and crisply did he respond to the salute from the watchman – though no conversation this time, for he did not yet trust his voice.

It was a day for the Athenaeum. Yes, definitely not the Marlborough. A modest luncheon. A conscientious read of the service weeklies – not the political weeklies, oh no, not them! But already his mind was racing speculatively ahead, thrusting aside the regrets just as his dear old *Incontestable* thrust her stem into gale-driven rollers. No regrets for the end of his career, for his ship's company, for his reputation in the eyes of many of his contemporaries, whose minds would be poisoned by those who were now hell-bent on discrediting him because he had the effrontery to question the policies of those running the war.

Nothing could save him, not even the First Sea Lord himself. It was no longer a question of failing to hoist his flag. He would be out of the service altogether. And so the tide of planning began to flow again as he entered St James's Park. Daffodils over, the first spring tulips a dazzle of colour by the lake-shore. He would sign on in an infantry regiment as a private. Boys were putting up their ages to get into the Army; he would put his down. He could pass as a thirty-nine-year-old. He was fit and strong and an exceptional shot.

'Good morning, Squires. Yes, a fine spring day.'

His voice was all right. For the present he was still a senior Captain RN, receiving his customary salute from the Athenaeum's porter. For a little while the play would continue, even though his part was as hollow as if he were playing charades with the children all those long years ago at Wyston Court.

'Yes, my darling, it is as bad as bad can be. And I lost my temper. Was that not foolish? No, I must not come down to the country yet though I ache to be with you. Yes, I feel like a naughty little boy who needs consolation . . . Clemmie, darling, you are such a brick. I don't know how I could get on without you . . . I fear I have disgraced the name of Buller in the annals of the Royal Navy . . . No, I

147

am *not* being pompous.' And he laughed down the telephone now, feeling that the world, after all, though still reeling might also perhaps be staggering to its feet. The telephone trunk-line to Cirencester was never good. After a while the crackling interference became so intrusive that it was not worth going on. So he said 'Good-bye, my darling,' and hung up the receiver.

In the afternoon Buller went alone to a matinée. In the early evening he returned to Clarges Street, changed into a dinner-jacket and walked back to the Athenaeum where he drank a glass of sherry, ate a light meal with a half-bottle of wine, and made up a four of bridge at one shilling a hundred with some distant and somewhat staid acquaintances. There was no message for him, and none when he went home, surprising Randolph by the early hour of his return and his totally sober condition.

It was not until breakfast the next morning, when Buller was wondering what on earth he was to do with himself, that a messenger arrived. The note was from 'Blinker' Hall: 'Buller, old man, come and take luncheon with me at the In-and-Out. I wish to have words.'

Buller preferred the raffishness of the Marlborough and the staid traditionalism of the Athenaeum to the austerity of the Army and Navy Club, nicknamed the 'In-and-Out' for the prominent notices on its two drive entrances in Piccadilly, but on this April morning these prejudices did not figure in his thoughts. The enormity of his misdemeanour in Churchill's office still lay heavily on Buller's mind, but it was a hot weight, warmed by the still smouldering anger at his treatment and what he considered to be the perfidy of this politician. In company with these considerations remained the certain knowledge that his naval career was finished. And for a Buller that was indeed a cataclysmic thought.

The chillness of the dining-room at the In-and-Out

matched Buller's mood. But at least Hall's greeting was cheerful. 'I hear you gave the old man a piece of your mind,' he said, laughing as the waiter set Buller into his chair.

'I expect our exchange of fire was heard all over the Admiralty – or at least the echo of it. Admiral Buller died in action yesterday, before he had even hoisted his flag.'

'Blinker' nodded and blinked his eyes like a ship's semaphore with an urgent signal. 'No, my bookmaker is not giving you even odds to command the Grand Fleet. But there are consolations.'

'And what may they be?' Buller asked.

'I think you may have contributed towards the decision not to use the Navy again alone at Gallipoli. And that will save many hundreds, perhaps thousands of lives. The First Lord is furious, but de Robeck has said, in effect, enough is enough, and that he's not going to waste any more battleships.' Captain Hall dug his way decisively into the roast beef, then held up his fork to emphasize his point. 'Captain Richmond, the only man with any brains on the Naval War Staff and the only officer except you who does not mince his words ever, says that Churchill was already losing the Dardanelles battle of words before the circulation of your report by Jackie.'

'I don't understand. He said it was to be burnt.'

'No, too late. Like sinking the U-boat after it has fired its torpedo at the flagship. Bearing your signature, it is being read. And being read, it is sowing doubts about the whole enterprise. Anyway, the War Council has made the decision that future assaults must be accompanied by mass landing of troops on the peninsula – in fact a combined attack, which it always should have been and would have been if Kitchener had agreed to release a division of troops. Fisher is preening himself and saying "I told you so" to all and sundry, and issuing an ultimatum – "If I'm asked for as much as a length of rope or a sailor's hat badge for this madcap scheme, I shall resign".'

Buller listened to all this highly confidential and messy political inside talk with increasing distaste, his mind going back to Holly on the steeply-angled bridge of his sinking battleship, and the hundreds of heads bobbing in the fast-flowing icy water before disappearing from sight. He recalled the cries of agony and anguish from those trapped below in the *Incomparable*. At length, pushing his plate to one side, he said, 'I feel no pride or shame in what I did, Blinker. I simply did what I was told to do, as you and I have done all our service lives. If it has led to my downfall, then I won't be the first naval officer to experience bad luck. One of my best friends, Mark Holly, paid a higher price the other day for doing *his* duty.'

Buller scooped out a sizeable helping of Stilton and helped himself to the proffered biscuits. No personal crisis was to be allowed to interfere with his appetite. 'In the past,' he continued, 'when I have been low or in trouble, I have always declared that there is only one correction, and that is to go back to sea. And now, this time, I shall be deprived even of that consolation.'

Captain Hall looked quizzically across the table at him, a faint smile on his lips. 'I am not sure about that.' He looked round to satisfy himself that no one was in earshot. 'I have a suggestion to make.'

X

The Dangerous Decoy

On the afternoon of 27 May 1915 a small and exceedingly
dirty tramp steamer worked her way slowly round Penlee
Point leading into Cawsand Bay and the entrance to the
Hamoaze and Devonport dockyard. She was 3,248 tons,
with a single small smokestack, the usual mast fore and aft
with derricks for loading and unloading her mixed cargo
from her holds. Except for her ridiculously pretentious
name, *Duchess of Marlborough*, she might have been any
one of the many hundreds of similar steamers that sailed
under the red ensign, through fair weather and foul, up
and down the coasts of Britain, sometimes crossing the
Channel to Cherbourg or Brest or the smaller ports on the
north and west coasts of France. She would have a crew of
about twenty-five, half of whom would be stokers or
engine-room artificers, a skipper and mate and the usual
assortment of officers and deck-hands.

Buller watched her make her laborious way up the
Hamoaze until she tied up to the jetty. Beside the sleek
destroyers, a couple of light cruisers and three pre-
dreadnought battleships which were anchored in the river,
the *Duchess of Marlborough* appeared a sorry anachronism.
He recalled the last time he had seen the *Incontestable*
anchored in Cromarty alongside the *Queen Mary* and
Princess Royal and the other great ships of the Battle-
Cruiser Squadron, and spoke to the lieutenant-commander
at his side. 'I suppose you might call this a bit of a come-
down, Rod.'

They laughed, the middle-aged lieutenant-commander and the middle-aged captain RN who had known each other since boyhood.

Rod said, 'Can you see the admiral superintendent's face when we say we don't require any paint or brass polish? "Get this old tub out of my dockyard!" he'll shout.'

'"Is this a man-o'-war of the Royal Navy, or something that escaped from the scrapyard?"' Buller mimicked the voice of the admiral.

'Special Duties' was all that Buller had first been told about the new job he had been offered by the Naval Secretary in London. There had been not a word, not a hint, as to how or why Buller had not been obliged to resign his commission. Nor had it been indicated by the elderly rear-admiral in charge that this was the only appointment open to him, though Buller understood this completely, and also understood that 'Blinker' Hall had been at his Machiavellian work behind the scenes. He was quite sure that neither Churchill nor any of the Commissioners of the Admiralty, nor of the War Council, knew what was going on. Captain Archibald Buller had simply disappeared without trace from the records at the Admiralty, and no doubt the thoughts of those responsible for his downfall from grace, for at that time they already had far too many problems on their mind. Buller doubted even Jack Fisher knew. For Fisher himself had resigned in a characteristic flurry of publicity and acrimony on 15 May, and, it was said, had disappeared to his own 'wilderness' somewhere in Scotland. With him Fisher took more than the wisdom and experience of sixty years in the Royal Navy. He took with him Churchill. For the First Lord could not survive the double-linked scandal of Fisher's resignation and the cause of it – the Navy's failure to force the Dardanelles. Within days the Prime Minister had been obliged to form a coalition government. Such was the price of the Gallipoli adventure, for which

Churchill was to be held responsible, and in which Buller himself had played his own small part.

His new part, his new role in the war at sea, began the moment he stepped off the gangway onto the far from clean and by no means rust-free steel deck of the *Duchess of Marlborough*. 'I think you'll find this very much a "please yourself" job,' the captain in charge of special duties had told him. 'It'll be a test of your ingenuity and your tolerance because no one'll know quite what you're up to. However, when you want something, or if you get into trouble, you'll have to produce this.' And the captain, ten years junior to Buller, had handed him a stiff manila envelope containing a letter, signed by the Chief of Naval War Staff, requesting the fullest co-operation of 'to whom it may concern on behalf of Captain Archibald Buller CB DSO RN in the important and confidential work to which he has been assigned'.

The proof of the effectiveness of this letter could be seen (if a number of heavy covering tarpaulins were raised) in a corner of the shed at Number 3 dock: two 12-pounder quick-firers, a Maxim gun and two Lewis guns. 'Guns are no good unless I get the right man to look after them,' Buller had said. 'And whom do you want for gunnery officer?' he was asked. 'The best damn gunnery officer in the Fleet, and an old friend of mine.'

The master of the *Duchess of Marlborough* stepped forward to greet them and to hand over his vessel. He was dressed in rubber boots, turned over at the top, a pair of baggy trousers streaked with oil, the double-breasted jacket of a once-prized suit with papers and a rag sticking out of the pockets, a grimy scarf and battered peaked cap. He had a pipe clenched between his teeth, and it remained there as he said cheerfully to Buller, 'I can't think what the Navy wants with this old tub. But they're welcome. She'll do nine knots on a good day when number two boiler's not leaking.'

*   *   *

Rod Maclewin had been known as 'Gramps' in the Battle-Cruiser Squadron. At fifty-three he was not only, by Buller's definition, 'the best damn gunnery officer in the Fleet'; he was also the oldest gunnery officer. Coming up from the lower deck, Rod had risen to the appointment of gunnery officer of the *Incontestable* by a combination of skill, energy and (important in the Royal Navy) a talent to please. The Battle of the Dogger Bank had enhanced Rod's reputation even further and brought him a decoration – a DSO to match Buller's.

Rod's home background and upbringing were in complete contrast with Buller's. Fatherless from infancy, Rod had first been driven into the Royal Navy as a boy as a result of family poverty and the lack of work in Newcastle in the 1870s. His friendship with the wealthy, high-born Archy Buller had been forged during the heat of battle in Egypt in 1884, and they had served together for much of their careers ever since. Gunnery was the professional bond. But of much greater importance in their long friendship was their mutual understanding and the mutual respect and ready acceptance of one another's weaknesses. Rod could no more put down a couple of bottles of champagne over dinner than he could bring himself to practise the infidelities in his married life for which Buller was renowned. Rod did not call the King 'Georgie' in private, but was sometimes teased by Buller for his rather prim ways and also admired for his limitless courage. It was, perhaps, an odd and surprising friendship. Even their physical differences were almost comically in contrast, Rod being a mere five foot six, with a wiry frame, and a 'displacement' (as he termed it) of 145 lbs.

The strength of their friendship was confirmed once again on that day in May when Rod, summoned from the *Incontestable* up at Cromarty, agreed in London to resign his appointment as gunnery officer of a great battle-cruiser with 12-inch guns and, instead, serve in a converted tramp steamer whose biggest guns would be 12-pounders. 'You may not see action again with the Grand Fleet,' Buller had said. 'And you may not see it in my new ship. But if you do, it should be quite lively work!'

Lively work? Down at Devonport dockyard, concealed by high canvas screens for security, the work was hectic as well as lively, as Rod supervised the fitting of the guns to the decks, one on the forecastle, the other abaft the funnel, of the *Duchess of Marlborough*. The decks had to be strengthened to cope with the weight and firing stresses and provision made for the installation of magazines below decks with sketchy protection of inch-thick steel plate. The Lewis guns were concealed in cawls at the extremities of the bridge wings; and the heavy Maxim gun mounted on a raised structure abaft the mainmast. Concealed behind the rust and sea-salt stained sides of the bridge were vertical sheets of bullet-proof armour plate.

The men of Devonport dockyard were accustomed to a wide range of work, especially since the start of the war, and Buller let it be known that his ship was a new type of escort vessel, the need for which was widely known in the relentless battle with the German U-boats. But for the last stage of the fitting out of his ship, Buller dismissed the civilian dockyard men and used his own crew, supervised by the ship's carpenter.

Buller and Rod worked with the 'chippy' for long hours in Buller's cabin devising the best form of camouflage for the guns – 'The art of deception,' as Buller called it. 'We are a sea wolf in dirty sheep's clothing,' he began the first of these meetings. 'The Hun is a wily bird, a wily eagle, suspicious of every quarry he attacks. We must practise the art of deception to the finest degree.'

In these early months of the U-boat war, German submarines normally sank ships with their guns, approaching them submerged or on the surface, giving warning of their intention to attack, and as soon as the crew had taken to the boats, sinking the ship with a few rounds of shell or high explosive charges secured to the ship's side. They carried too few torpedoes and did not squander them on merchantmen, reserving them for their big prey – warships.

It was Captain Richmond at the Admiralty who had devised the Q-ship, the code word given to men-o'-war disguised as innocent tramp steamers, and it had fallen to Buller to test out this officer's idea for the first time. 'When the Hun opens fire,' Richmond had said, 'abandon ship – all but the hidden gun-crews – then wait until you can see the whites of their eyes before you drop your camouflage and blow him out of the water . . .'

That, in essence, was the tidy and ingenious theory, but Buller knew from the start that it was not going to be as simple as that, and that it was also going to be a highly hazardous business, dependent for success on 'the art of deception'. And so, as the days went by, the ship's company built a chicken-coop round the Maxim gun, with open slatted sides of lengths of timber they scrounged from the wood-store. With the help of the admiral superintendent, a dozen hens and a cock were acquired and installed inside. Fitted round the after 12-pounder was a simulated steering engine-house of wooden planks, well weathered by age, with three sides hinged like shutters to fall outwards when a connected wire released all three holding-pins simultaneously. A steam pipe in the roof puffed real steam originating under pressure in the engine-room and travelling along a series of tubes.

After the first week, the ship's complement of officers was completed with the arrival of a young lieutenant, Sandy Marchant. Marchant was an executive lieutenant, a friend of Rod's who had applied to the new captain of the *Incontestable* to join him on special duties. Sandy Marchant, of solid professional stock and roughly midway between Buller and Rod in the social scale, had joined the Royal Navy by the new direct entry method straight from school instead of, like his two fellow officers, at the age of twelve. There was no seafaring tradition in his family. He had simply taken against the idea of spending his life in an office and opted instead for the sea and adventure. He was twenty years younger than Buller and Rod, rather nondescript in appearance – brown hair thinning in front, and amiable face with, like Rod, a broken nose (from rugby) and sparkling grey eyes that seemed forever to be darting about seeking fun and action.

Buller had taken to him at once, immediately after asking him if he knew what he was in for. 'Oh, no, of course not, sir. I put in for the appointment because I guessed it might mean something jolly might happen. And I knew that Rod has a good nose for excitement.'

'Things have tended to happen when Rod and I are serving in the same ship,' Buller conceded, and at once qualified this statement. 'But there have also been long years when we've had to be content with routine – like everyone in a peacetime Navy. And nothing may happen on this little jaunt either, let me warn you.' He went on to explain the functions of HMS *Duchess of Marlborough*. 'All play-acting and deceit,' he concluded. 'And you're in charge of the wardrobe.'

'The wardrobe, sir?'

'Yes, your first job is dresser.'

When Buller explained further, Sandy burst into peals of laughter and proclaimed himself 'C-in-C slops'. 'As our Frog allies would say, "*Ce n'est pas magnifique mais c'est la guerre.*"' Rod agreed to accompany him into the city, and the following morning the lieutenant-commander RN and lieutenant RN called at a number of second-hand clothes shops where normally ratings would not have been seen, and returned before noon in a taxicab loaded down with sacks of assorted and not at all clean jackets, trousers and caps that officers and the crew of a seedy tramp steamer might wear.

157

Buller ordered a kit inspection and the mixed assortment of clothing, much of it torn or patched, was spread out on the forecastle of the ship. It was viewed with mixed horror and hilarity by the ship's company, and Buller ordered a laundry for four bells at the end of the first dog-watch after, as he said, 'you've all made your choice of uniform'. He then turned to Sandy and demanded to know what the objects were lined up by the port rails – an old accordion, a barrel of rum and a parrot in a cage.

'They're the "props", sir,' Sandy replied blandly. 'For the panic party, sir. I thought you would like it as realistic as possible.' He walked over and picked up the parrot cage, holding it before Buller and speaking to the parrot: 'And what have you to say, Pol?'

'Damn the Huns, and good-day to you, sir.' Polly's voice, loud and clear, was heard by all the crew. When the laughter had died Buller took the cage by the hook and asked the parrot, 'And what else do you have to say, Pol?'

'Damn the Huns, and good-day to you, sir,' the parrot repeated.

'That's his total repertoire, I am afraid,' said Sandy. 'But you must admit that his heart's in the right place.'

A volunteer was found who could play the accordion and a Scots able seaman said he would be in charge of the rum, though when Sandy told him that the barrel was empty he withdrew his offer amid boos from his mates.

Buller and Rod encouraged the light-hearted approach to the job ahead of them, within the confines of naval discipline, and Sandy Marchant was the ideal number one to help make the *Duchess of Marlborough* a happy ship even before she sailed on her maiden voyage. But the serious side could scarcely be ignored when, on the tenth day after Buller assumed command, the problem had to be faced of concealing the forward gun. This 12-pounder was an 18 cwt weapon with a long barrel, the gun most likely to make any killing-shot against the hull of a submarine, and the most difficult to hide. A number of suggestions were made and Buller welcomed ideas from all ranks. But it was Rod who came up with the answer after a delivery of stores by a large naval truck.

'A deck-house is out of the question,' he said to Buller and Sandy over tea in the diminutive cabin adapted as a ward-room. 'There's no possible reason for building a deck-house forward and it would be immediately suspect as the place most likely to conceal a gun. So what about deck cargo?'

'That would be just as suspicious,' Buller objected.

'It depends what it is. If it was something unusual the Huns might look at it twice, might even not believe their eyes. But they wouldn't be likely to believe that it concealed a gun.'

Sandy asked, 'And what have you in mind, Rod? Waxwork dummies?'

'A truck.'

'Your mind needs a refit – like this ship,' pronounced Buller.

But in the end Buller was convinced, and after facing a flat refusal from the admiral superintendent for one of the dockyard trucks, Buller went out, camouflaged in the old trousers and patched blazer he had chosen from the slops stock, and succeeded in finding an old Scammel the owner was prepared to sell. The engine had not worked for some time so it was towed to the dockyard by a pair of dray horses, and the crew at once began to adapt it for its new role.

Two days later Captain Richmond arrived at Devonport from the Admiralty to inspect his brain-child. The captain's ingenuity and cleverness were matched by the intensity and seriousness of his manner. By this time the *Duchess of Marlborough* was bristling with innovations and tricks of deception, including a device which hurled time-fused 125-pound bombs into the sea in the suspected vicinity of a submerged U-boat. Richmond noted and approved of everything, including the accordion and parrot for the panic party, but never smiled once, even when he was shown the big Scammel truck on the forecastle.

'This is my department, sir,' Rod said proudly, and showed Richmond how they had hollowed out the main body, including the drive-shaft and rear axle, leaving only the wooden sides and rear which were hinged at the base to fall outwards when quick-release pins were removed to expose the gun and allow it a good arc of fire on either beam. Captain Richmond made one or two practical suggestions to speed up, when the moment of crisis arrived, the transformation of the *Duchess of Marlborough* from an innocent and vulnerable tramp steamer to a lethal man-o'-war. 'A few seconds may decide whether you can damage your target fatally or give the U-boat time to crash-dive and get away,' he told Buller and his two senior officers. 'And once bitten twice shy, remember. If he does get away the whole German U-boat service will know about our little tricks in no time.'

Before he left to return to London, Captain Richmond asked Buller if he could address the ship's company. This he did, with Buller and Rod standing beside him, from the unusual vantage-point of the open cab of the old truck. He told them that they were now actors as well as sailors but that strict discipline was even more important in this Q-ship, whether they were to be one of the 'panic party' to abandon ship or one of those left behind in concealment to await their chance.

'This is a very serious business,' he declared in his crisp voice, the tone severe. 'Last month we lost thirty-seven ships – all sunk by U-boats. 126,000 tons, and the lost of vitally needed raw materials and food-stuffs for our country. Like any hunting, you may not catch the scent for a long time – perhaps a very long time. So you'll have to be patient, too.' His voice very slightly mellowed and Buller thought he discerned an effort to smile as Richmond ended, 'So on behalf of their Lordships at the Admiralty, who are taking a keen interest in your enterprise, I wish you good luck.'

Buller led the ship's company with 'Three cheers', the sailors raising their motley hats and caps in the traditional way, and then escorted Captain Richmond back to the admiral superintendent's office.

'When do you hope to sail?' Richmond asked Buller before they parted.

'Tomorrow at noon. The tide's right then, and we've had reports of a U-boat operating off Bantry Bay.'

The *Duchess of Marlborough* slipped down the Hamoaze, which was crowded with men-o'-war, at one p.m. on the afternoon of 14 June. She looked no cleaner than when her ex-skipper had brought her up the river two weeks earlier. There were large areas of rust near her bows and round her counter, the paint on her single funnel was as chipped as before.

It was Make and Mend on board the last ship they passed, a grey-painted armoured cruiser, the sun winking from the brass on rails and gangways, bridgework and the tompions of her 9.2 and 6-inch guns. The men looked up from their work as the *Duchess of Marlborough* slowly passed a cable-length away, smoke pouring blackly from her funnel. They noted her name and her rig, and that the 'c' and one of the 's's' of 'Duchess' painted on either side of her bows was missing. The ship's master and mate and the helmsman on the bridge looked a slack trio, the master in an old cap worn back to front and chewing on a pipe as he glanced up without apparent interest at the glistening anchored man-o'-war his ship passed. One or two of those who watched the tramp pass by remarked on her deck

161

cargo and one wag cracked that even Father Neptune had a motor these days.

The *Duchess of Marlborough* headed for the open sea, and the seamen of the armoured cruiser returned to their needles and thread utterly ignorant of the fact that concealed within that old truck and within the hen-coop and the steering engine-house were weapons in immaculate condition and well-greased, with ready ammunition in lockers, and gun-crews of the highest calibre in the Royal Navy to man them.

As the sun went down over the English Channel that evening the first-ever U-boat hunter Q-ship was off the Lizard, whose lighthouse winked conspiratorially. In the wireless cabin, the ship's 'sparks' was decoding a message in morse from 'Blinker' Hall's Intelligence Department telling of the sinking of a large British merchantman in the Bay of Biscay.

When Buller read this report on the bridge he remarked to Rod at his side, 'I just hope it's our turn next.' And he added, 'And how good it is to feel a rolling deck under your feet and smell the clean sea instead of the reek of Whitehall political intrigue.'

'And I'll second that,' said Rod earnestly.

XI

The Terrors of the Night

Yes, of course I am dreaming – a dying dream they call it. Once, after awakening from a childhood nightmare, Richard had been told by his fat, darling nursemaid that nightmares happened all through life, until the very end when you had nothing but lovely dreams as a farewell gift from God. That moment, it seemed, had come. Richard tried again to focus his eyes, but all he could make out was the faint outline of the face, a pair of wide-set large brown eyes and a mouth, gently smiling. This picture, this woman's portrait, faded into the mist and came back again only slowly.

It was the eyes that told him whose face it was. Yes, his nursemaid had been right. It was a lovely dying dream, the face of the last woman he had spoken to. Richard's brain was starting to work again, laboriously and unreliably, but was slowly recalling images: of Helena Cochrane at Victoria Station after their arrival from Newhaven, Helena destined for Guy's Hospital, Richard to catch the noon train north to Scotland and his ship.

A troop train was about to leave. At every window the head and shoulders of a soldier, sometimes two soldiers, leaning out to kiss held-up babies or wives or girl-friends. Some of the soldiers were still on the platform, heavily loaded with packs, kitbags, Lee-Enfield rifles, but still contriving to embrace their women. A guard blowing his whistle, the hiss of escaping steam from the big locomotive, voices crying.

Richard and Helena paused to gaze at this panorama of anxiety and grief. Helena said, 'I've never seen so much kissing in all my life. *Everybody*'s kissing!'

'Except us,' said Richard, and then even more recklessly put his arms round her. To his amazement, she responded at once, pressing her lips hard against his. They broke apart and smiled at one another, oblivious to the scene beside them, the train moving slowly, a hundred cries of 'Good luck!' and 'Good-bye!'

Richard said, 'I must run. Make sure they treat you kindly – and write to me.'

It was said of Victoria Station: 'Ten thousand tear-stained farewells a day!' And the parting of Helena Cochrane and Richard Buller was no different from those they had just witnessed except that they climbed into different cabs, one destined north for King's Cross Station, the other for Guy's Hospital.

And now Richard was focusing more clearly. Yes, it was not only the eyes he recognized, it was the smile he had seen on her face after they had kissed that told him who she was. His brain was certainly working better, too, and he wanted to talk. He even tried to, but heard only a husky sound like the first stroke of a saw on hard wood and then a woman's voice saying, 'Don't try to talk. Just rest – you're going to be all right.'

They were logging twenty-four knots and it was blowing half a gale. It was pitch dark and the flotilla was station-keeping in close formation by no more than a single dimmed stern light on each destroyer. They had seen no sun, nor stars, nor land for forty-eight hours and even their dead-reckoning position must be only approximate by now. Richard had been on watch on the bridge for three

164

and a half hours, feet set wide apart, clutching the bridge-rail with both hands except when drinking the frequent mugs of cocoa that sustained his strength.

Once again the *Arrow* flung herself out of the water as far aft as the bridge and then crashed down onto the sea like a rearing horse. But, as her commander had said when Richard left port in her for his first patrol, 'She's a proper little lady – a proper little ballerina and she never misses a step.' On top of the swell the sea was short and choppy but almost no green seas came aboard as she cut through the water in a continuous shower of spray. Lifelines had been rigged fore and aft before the storm had set in hard, and Richard watched a rating in oilskins hooked to them working his way aft gingerly.

After a particularly heavy jump, the compass from time to time turned completely upside-down and jammed itself. The helmsman could not take his hands off the wheel for a moment so Richard set it right for him, and he could see the helmsman's grin by the faint glow from the compass.

Shortly before the end of the watch the commander joined them on the bridge from the chart-house where he had been resting. Richard only felt his presence until he put a hand on his arm and shouted in his ear, 'Will you double the look-outs, things may be livening up.'

'How's that, sir?'

'We've just taken in a W/T message. German scouting force, destroyers and a light cruiser or two. Probably trying to get a nibble at the Dutch convoy.'

Holland, as a neutral country in the European war, was open to sea traffic from Britain and Germany. Frequent convoys crossed the North Sea from British to Dutch ports to pick up the much-needed rich farm products of that country. U-boats often attacked these convoys, and the Germans sometimes sent surface men-o'-war too, which led to swift brushes and running fights. This North Sea sweep by the flotilla had been planned to continue far enough south to pick up any stray German raiders that might be heading for these convoys. Now it seemed that the *Arrow* and her consorts might soon catch the scent.

The flotilla leader, three cable lengths ahead, was flashing a message, the longs and shorts punching the darkness with swift bright pinpricks, too fast for Richard to read. But beside him the signalman read the message as if it were a newspaper headline: 'Starboard four points in succession. Increase speed to twenty-six knots. Enemy believed close.'

Richard raised the voice-pipe linking the bridge to the destroyer's two 4-inch and two 12-pounders and called down the warning. Confirmation of receipt of message came back almost instantly from the four guns.

They were no longer heading into the wind and the seas and the *Arrow* began rolling badly as she settled on her new course.

It was unmistakably Helena's voice. She was saying, 'There's no need to speak. You don't have to say a word if you don't feel like it.' But Richard could hear his own voice. It sounded distant and echoing, like the signals in 'Sparks' Latchmore's wireless office before Coronel, fading and regaining volume unpredictably. 'It was so dark all you could see was the wake of the ship ahead. A pitch-black night. How the devil did they see us?' he asked, his voice shrill with anguish.

Then he felt her hand on his arm . . .

The *Arrow*'s commander had a hand on Richard's arm as if about to say something when a brilliant yellow light suddenly illuminated the destroyer. For a fraction of a second it might have been a paralysing death-ray so fierce, blinding and all-revealing was the point-blank searchlight beam. The spell was broken by smothering shell-fire that seemed to come tearing and crashing in on them from

166

every quarter, the chorus of accompanying sound ranging from the thud-thud-thud of heavy quick-firers to the tearing screech of machine-guns and lethal whistle of shell splinters.

Not a shot, not a bullet, seemed to miss the little *Arrow*, which flinched and shuddered as if struck repeatedly by massive steam-hammers. Richard's response was as swift and instinctive as a kicked dog's – 'Open rapid fire, all guns!' he bawled down the speaking-tube. Both 4-inch gunlayers beat him to it. Already the pungent stench of spent cordite swept over the bridge from the forward quick-firer, and seconds later another note was struck in the cacophony of sound that had broken out as swiftly as the searchlights had turned a dense black night into midday summer sun – the high-pitched hiss of released compressed air as the destroyer's 21-inch torpedoes were fired.

A stab of agony in Richard's right shoulder. A simultaneous cry from the helmsman, as if in echoing sympathy. But for the helmsman it was a death cry, his body hurled to the rear of the bridge, crashing against the searchlight platform. Richard saw through his own sudden pain that his body appeared to be almost severed in two, collapsing head to feet in a bundle on the steel deck.

But what about the wheel? Who was going to steer the *Arrow* now in this wild confusion of fast-moving ships?

'The helmsman was one of the first to be hit. Not very nice, I can tell you. Blood everywhere. Oh, dear God, it was terrible. Cut in half by a splinter. When I was a boy I read all the time about sea battles. I had a book called *Our Gallant Sailors*. St Vincent, the Nile, Trafalgar. Cannonballs were always knocking off heads, chain-shot "cutting the man in twain". It all sounded so clean and tidy. Funny even. "Look," I would say to Nina my nursemaid, "it says here 'the master gunner was cut in twain'. That means cut in two!" Once she took the book away from me and said it would give me nightmares.'

There was a smile again on the face above him, and he heard her voice: 'Don't tire yourself out telling me all that now. There'll be plenty of time later.'

But he had to go on talking, just as he had to save the ship from disaster. The helmsman dead, the wheel spinning. He reached forward violently, arms outstretched, feeling the agony in his right shoulder. But there were firm hands on his arms . . .

Richard reached out for the wheel, encumbered by his headphones, handicapped with only a single working arm. And still the *Arrow* tore on through the heavy seas, the searchlight only intermittent and flickering, shell splashes to port and starboard and ahead, splinters humming through the air. A gout of white flame arose somewhere out there in the insane confusion of brilliance and black of the battle's heat. Some unfortunate ship – British or German, who could tell – had had her cordite cartridges on deck for ready use ignited by a hit. The *Arrow*'s after 20-inch searchlight, miraculously untouched, stabbed out and struck a twin-funnel German destroyer no more than three hundred yards distant, and the starboard midships gun opened fire almost simultaneously.

Richard felt a surge of pride at the speed of the gunnery. But he felt also a pulsating pain and a warm dampness creeping swiftly down his back. He knew that his injury was serious, that he was good for little more, as the pain began to numb his mind. A rating was at his side, holding him, calling out something that he could not understand. Someone must have successfully reached the wheel and was putting the helm hard over, the *Arrow* heeling deeply. There came a shout from somewhere forward, 'Get out the collision mat!' Another voice – it was the commander's this time – shouted 'Clear the forecastle!'

The shuddering crash, the sound of tearing metal like a sawmill in the hands of a madman, the sudden grotesque tilt of the little ship, the equally sudden deceleration. The blow to Richard's head when he struck a steel bridge stanchion, completed the loss of consciousness which the pain and bleeding was drawing over him as all-enveloping as a blanket over the body of a dead man. Something cruelly large and heavy fell across his right leg. But Richard cared no more than if he had been that nearby corpse.

The gentle voice was saying, 'They want you to go back to sleep for a while. Just to rest. You'll feel better when you wake up.' No, there was nothing more to worry about. Even the knowledge that he now knew the ultimate secret, the secret of what it was like to die, touched no chord of wonder in him.

And now the darkness, which had once held such expectation of terror and promise of noise, was serenely silent . . .

The battle was disappearing, fading into the night like an express train; the *Arrow*, her forepart stove in and crumpled back almost to the bridge, wallowed alone on the turbulent sea, the cacophony of the last minutes yielding to the sound of men's voices, some in pain, more on urgent and purposeful business – the business of saving this ship and those in her who were still alive.

Richard Buller knew nothing of this, the damage to his ship, of crushed bulkheads, scattered stores and chains, a 4-inch gun thrown like a twig twenty yards into the sea, complete with mounting, of gushing oil-fuel carrying a dozen bodies of his shipmates to far astern of the scene of the ferocious battle. Nor did he know of his own injuries – the shattered femur and clavicle, the fractured skull, the ruptured brachial artery from which his life blood was fast flowing.

An able seaman called George Emery, born and brought up in Brixham (a Devon man through and through), lifted Richard to a slumped sitting position five minutes after the collision. There was a great deal of blood washing about the bridge, and there was no way of telling how much was from the dead helmsman, from one of the searchlight crew who had fallen onto the bridge with the shock of the collision, or from Richard. But he succeeded in cutting off Richard's lamming-coat and jacket and, holding a rag to the splinter wound, managed to staunch the flow of blood until the medical party arrived. George Emery saved Richard's life, for a delay of another few minutes would have led to a fatal loss of blood.

The destroyer *Mason* took two hours to get a wire tow across to the *Arrow*. Time and again men on the deck of the *Mason*, which frequently disappeared from sight in the trough of a wave, attempted to throw a heaving line to the crippled destroyer, and each time it fell short, struck a rising wave or was hurled back by the wind into their faces.

A murky dawn was breaking when the *Mason* began to lower a whaler. It was a desperate undertaking, and every foot by which the boat was lowered, its crew clinging to the gunwales, oars shipped, the greater was the arc through which it swung with the violent movements of the ship, one moment far out from her side and threatened by the top of a roller, the next moment lurching back to crash against the destroyer's side-plating.

Then, with superb timing, she was set free on the back of a breaking sea to the cry of, 'Let go! Out pins!', and was swept along the length of the ship like a twig in a mill-race. It appeared to be impossible for a few oars to affect the progress of the little whaler in seas as violent as these, but by degrees the gap closed between it and the crippled

Arrow and the line carried by the whaler was hauled onboard.

As if to signal the miracle, a low, wet sun broke through as first the coir hawser and then the towing-wire were hauled onto the stern of the *Arrow* and safely shackled. Now, stern first, with the constant danger of the towing-wire being carried away under the fearful pressures and counter-pressures, with bulkheads and collision mats bulging and under threat of giving way, the *Arrow* was brought onto a westerly heading. If the half-gale turned into a full gale, she was certainly doomed. If the seas remained as high as they were, at three to four knots it would take twenty hours to reach the safety of Harwich, with the first five hours or so at risk of attack by superior German forces.

In the event the wind dropped, a comforting pair of light cruisers made their appearance as escort, and at five p.m. a tug came along to relieve the *Mason* of her burden, and brought the wrecked *Arrow* into a berth at midnight. Eighteen of her crew of seventy-two had died in the action. Another three had died of their wounds in the sick-bay, and fifteen more were seriously wounded.

Richard Buller, only intermittently conscious, was among those brought ashore on a stretcher and tucked into the hospital train which had been shunted alongside the dock and with stunning efficiency was ready to leave within minutes of the last casualty's arrival.

In all the London teaching hospitals several wards had been set aside at the beginning of the war for naval casualties in the event of a major clash at sea. At Guy's Hospital, Helena Cochrane was on early day duty in Ward 47, which had received some earlier casualties from the brush off the Dutch coast. Richard was not brought to this ward but to Ward 49.

Word that several more seriously wounded officers and

petty officers had arrived spread rapidly through all the naval wards. Out of curiosity and with no sense of alarm, Helena walked along the corridor during a lull in her work and glanced at the typed list of newly-arrived patients on the notice-board. For security reasons, the names of ships had been omitted. But there, at the bottom of the list of names was Lieutenant R. Buller RN.

The administrative machinery for the notification of casualties was now well run-in. The war was already ten months old and tens of thousands of soldiers and sailors and merchant seamen had been wounded or killed, or made prisoner or were missing. At the same time as Helena had read that Richard was in Guy's Hospital and in a bed only yards away, Clemmie Buller as her son's next of kin picked up the buff telegram envelope from the silver tray brought into the breakfast-room by the butler.

Aware that her elder son was in the thick of the fighting in France (and believing by now that her husband was immune to enemy fire and fatal accident alike), her alarmed mind raced ahead to the conclusion that Harry had been killed in the trenches. Richard's name after the 'regret to inform you . . .' came therefore as a singular shock, a shock that was eased by the almost simultaneous discovery that he was seriously wounded and not dead. To her own later astonishment she realized that her hand holding the telegram was shaking and that the tears were coursing down her cheeks. Clemmie Buller had been through many trials and anxious periods in her life and she prided herself on her resiliency and control of her emotions. But she still regarded her last child as her baby and found herself saying aloud, in a choking voice, 'My poor baby boy!'

She pulled herself together almost at once, opened the door into the hall and made her way to the telephone which was housed in an inconvenient and draughty alcove below the stairs. The local operator, recognizing both the number and the voice, put her through at once. The delay at the Admiralty was scarcely longer, even though she had asked to be put through to Admiral Sir Henry Jackson who had recently succeeded Jackie Fisher as First Sea Lord. 'Harry? Yes, yes, good morning,' she began briskly. 'But tell me where my son is. I wish to see him and to learn the nature of his injuries . . .'

Richard's father was at sea on that June morning, 1915, on the bridge of his rusty, dirty, tramp steamer, south-south-west of the Blaskets, off the coast of County Kerry, 51° 28'N, 11° 18'W. Thanks to Clemmie's insistance, the message about his son was fuller than it would otherwise have been: 'The Lords Commissioners of the Admiralty beg to inform . . . Seriously wounded but out of danger. Your wife is at his bedside. You will be informed if there is any change in his condition.' For almost two minutes the shorts and longs rang out in the diminutive wireless room of the *Duchess of Marlborough*.

There could, of course, be no reply, not even an acknowledgement that the signal had been received. For the ship was under the severest wireless silence as she steamed slowly towards no destination at all, except – it was earnestly hoped by all on board – a prowling U-boat.

So Richard had stopped a packet, poor fellow. His mother would see that he got the best attention. Well, the boy was having a busy war and no mistake. Busier than my war at present, Buller told himself as he sucked out his empty pipe and surveyed the sea that spread out in an oily calm to every horizon, empty except for a single steamer with smoke trailing from its funnel, heading no doubt for Bristol. It felt as if they had been at sea for a year without sign of the thin stick of a periscope cutting through the water, feared by every merchantman in the eastern

173

Atlantic, longed for by the captain and crew of HMS *Duchess of Marlborough*.

7 August 1915. The Great War (as it had come to be called) had run for one year and three days and looked as if it might last for ten more years. Richard, convalescing in the garden at Wyston Court, let the newspaper fall from his hands, and he dozed off again to the sound of a reaper working through a field of wheat beyond the box hedge and the cries of children following it. The newspaper's headlines told of further landings on the Gallipoli peninsula – '20,000 men ashore', 'Few casualties', 'A great victory'; though the news from the Russian front, where German troops had captured Warsaw, was less encouraging. Very little about the Royal Navy, except a list of casualties, 'The Secretary of the Admiralty announces the following casualties . . .' – names of officers killed, wounded and missing. Six weeks earlier Richard had read his own name in one of these lists, among a dozen more, and had not quite believed it – 'It's like reading your own obituary!' he had said to Helena.

Richard continued to be surprised at his need for sleep while his body restored itself. His mother came out now, dressed in a long white cotton dress and a rather dashing broad-brimmed hat into which she had set some poppies. She automatically dead-headed the roses she passed as she crossed the lawn to the corner under the giant cedar where Richard lay in the shade. She was reassured to find him asleep, picked up the newspaper and returned to the house. His nurse friend had forty-eight hours' leave and was coming to stay for the week-end, and it was just possible that Lucy might be coming over from France for a few nights. Richard had made a wonderful recovery but he still tired quickly and Clemmie wanted him to be fresh for the evening.

★ ★ ★

Helena and Lucy arrived at Cirencester on the same train from London, both thankful to be away from the sounds and smells, and the constant giving-out, that work in hospital wards entailed. Helena was as curious to see where Lucy and her brother had been brought up as Lucy was to revive old memories and meet old friends. But the first thing that Lucy noted in Cirencester was the absence of familiar faces, especially among the young men. The two young porters were no longer waiting to carry bags, and only old Dagwood, who had been working at the station since the line had opened (or so it was said), could be seen. There were no taxicabs at the station entrance, only a single wagonette, already full, and – thank Heavens – the old family coach with Bessie and Belinda in the shafts and Mills to take their bags and welcome them.

There was a hushed air about the old market town, in peacetime bustling all day long with open stalls in the marketplace selling everything from fresh fish from Bristol to shoes and farmers' breeches. Now a number of the shops were shut, unable to find anyone to serve customers, and there were fewer people in the streets, and those there were appeared subdued as if in mourning for friends or relations lost in the fighting. A civic hall had been taken over as a recruiting-centre, with two elderly soldiers standing outside in khaki uniform handing out leaflets, the front of the building decorated with Union Jacks and posters – 'Your Country Needs YOU.'

Richard rose to his one usable leg when he heard the sound of hooves and steel-rimmed wheels on gravel, slowly by contrast with the dogs who were up and running like a flash. His shoulder had only recently healed enough to allow him to use crutches and he still moved cautiously on them and with some pain. But he was there to greet the two girls in the hall, smiling as they exclaimed at his progress and told him how well he looked. 'I'm running a race with the dockyard maties at Harwich working on the

175

Arrow and I'll bet I'm fit for sea before she is,' Richard claimed. He kissed his sister and, in this public place, shook Helena's hand. They were both in summer travelling clothes and had left their uniforms behind, at Amiens and Guy's Hospital respectively.

Clemmie gave them a few minutes to themselves in the hall, and then came downstairs and welcomed her daughter and Helena, who indicated Richard and exclaimed, 'But he's walking about! Look at him. You must be a wonderful nurse, Lady Buller.'

Clemmie demurred, giving Helena credit for what she had done for her son in the early days after his arrival at Guy's, then led her upstairs to her room. 'Dinner is at eight, but come down as soon as you like. I know Richard will be fretting to talk to you.' And Clemmie went to her own room, happy and reassured at what she had seen of this new friend of both her son and daughter.

Richard heard the voices murmuring, sometimes distantly, then less distantly, like people talking in a gusty wind. Helena's voice was the clearest. She was talking about her childhood, spent in so many countries. But a happy childhood with loving parents and nursemaids, an ayah called Mahada in India, Sarah in Hong Kong – 'such a lovely roly-poly Chinese lady!' Then Clemmie's deeper voice, crisp but affectionate: 'Dear Rich – fast asleep like a baby. He sleeps out here every afternoon. Nature's way of healing . . .'

There had been roast wild duck for luncheon, served with an orange cream sauce and hock, with great fresh peaches from the hothouse afterwards. They had eaten in the summerhouse open to the garden. Helena seemed already to be part of the household so compatibly did she slip into her role at Wyston Court. Debutante girls in London, daughters of neighbouring landowners in Gloucestershire – none of these girls and young women had

176

Richard taken seriously. They were no more than puppets in his memory by contrast with Helena Cochrane, whose voice he could half hear before it faded away entirely.

But Richard failed to take with him into unconsciousness the serenity and sunny contentment of a summer day on the lawn at Wyston Court. Increasingly of late, in inverse ratio to the repair of his body, his mind was becoming afflicted with the memory of the cruel and savage sights he had witnessed before the fight that had put him out of action. It was as if his subconscious was rebelling at the prospect of a return to the slaughter he had witnessed in so many places – the South Pacific, the South Atlantic, the North Sea and France. His dreams seemed to express despair and disgust which cast a black shadow across his life, yet failed to conceal the specific sights of gaping wounds and severed limbs. In hectic succession, like the rapidly turned pages of a photograph album, he saw the white, bloated body of a German sailor from the *Nürnberg* being cast back into the rising seas alongside the hove-to *Glasgow*, three dead troopers spreadeagled across barbed wire side by side like divers in a race to perdition who never even reached the water, or the helmsman of his own destroyer folded in two with terrible symmetry.

The contrast between these scenes of ruthless warfare and the sunlit garden of Wyston Court when he awoke – ancient cedar trees, dahlias and rose-beds, dogs lying stretched out in the shade, the horses with their heads over the fence – was so startling that for a moment reality was the dream and the warm, safe, comfortable garden the fruit of a striving imagination.

His mother and sister were no longer there. Helena had drawn up her chair closer to him, just as her nursemaids must once have done to their charge years before in the role of protector. She had a book in her hands but this was lying on her lap when Richard first identified her, opening his eyes briefly, then for longer, to confirm the truth of what he saw.

'You've been as restless as your destroyer must be in the North Sea,' Helena said. She smiled at him.

'It's nice to be on dry land, especially here. And especially with you, although I'm afraid you are not having a very exciting week-end.'

'I haven't come here for excitement.' She looked at him more seriously. 'You were having horrible dreams, weren't you?'

'How do you know?'

'Because I spend some of my working life beside the beds of wounded soldiers. Remember?'

'Yes, of course.' He turned away his head, trying to draw an opaque curtain across his memory.

Helena reached down for his crutches. 'Exercise time,' she said briskly, 'Nurse Cochrane does not wish her patient to stiffen up. Lying down all afternoon indeed. Bad therapy!'

They walked across the lawn to the horses, who were nodding their heads against the flies and whickering at Richard. He reached for some carrots in his pocket and gave one to Helena who scratched between the ears of one of them and waved away the flies. But her mind was elsewhere. 'Don't imagine you're unique with your nightmares,' she remarked.

It sounded so nearly a rebuke that Richard bridled. 'I don't imagine anything of the kind. And how do you know that I have nightmares? As a matter of fact I sleep extremely well.'

'Don't protest too much, my dear,' she said softly. 'I want to help, don't you see. I have watched you asleep here, and in hospital. I know how troubled you are and frightened that it will show when you're back in your ship.'

'I'm not frightened,' Richard said unaggressively.

'Of course you're not. I know that. But you might be disgusted by it all – all this killing and maiming. I am, too, when the wounded start pouring in after a push. It isn't

178

nice for anyone, especially the wounded themselves, as you know.'

They left the horses and walked down a stone path towards the stream, the infant River Thames, that flowed through the lower part of the garden. Neither spoke for a while, as if absorbing the words of the other. Richard sat down on a bench, thankful for the relief from the ache of his right shoulder.

Helena stood, watching trout steadying themselves in the current. 'It's always better to say things, Rich,' she said. 'And let's be thankful we can, unlike these poor fish.'

'Perhaps they've got their own way of saying things,' he said, watching her and feeling ripples of tenderness like the stream's wash running through him. Then he said, a touch helplessly, 'I think it's the waste of it all that really troubles me. I'm sure that doesn't bother my father, nor any of those old Bullers over the years, fighting the Americans and the French and the Spaniards and Dutch. They weren't so fussy.' And then he added quickly, 'Not that I think they should have minded. It's just that I can't *help* minding and being horrified, and . . .'

Richard ran out of words and Helena moved the crutches aside and sat beside him. 'It does seem like waste, doesn't it?' she said, her hand on the hard plaster of his leg. 'But I don't think it is. It's payment, I think, for keeping what we have. A sort of rent. I don't mean just this,' she said, indicating the house and garden. 'I mean the way of life of all the people, the freedom of all the people in Cirencester, and London, and the whole country. All those Buller ancestors were fighting for the same thing, and I bet some of them paid the price of keeping England's freedom – from Napoleon's tyranny a hundred years ago, and the Kaiser's tyranny today.'

Helena paused, and laughed apologetically. 'Goodness, I sound like a recruiting officer calling for volunteers.

179

"Rally to the colours, all you men worthy of the name!"'
she mocked herself.

'Not at all,' said Richard. 'I love to hear you talking like
that. I *should* understand it all as a professional sailor but
you make it sound just right.' He smiled at her. 'And your
nice voice helps.'

He kissed her, and when they broke apart he said, 'Will
you take the dogs for a proper walk – across the fields?'

They had been showing impatience for activity, and now
they went bounding off eagerly, leaping the stone wall,
followed by Helena.

At lunch on Sunday Helena looked round the table and
said, 'Well, this is lovely. Now I've met nearly all the
family. Lucy and Richard in Amiens, Harry for a few
minutes when he was passing through the town. Your
mother here in this house. That just leaves your father.'

Clemmie answered, 'You're the nicest guest, Helena.
And I know Archy would love to meet you. But I'm afraid
that will have to wait. I think he's at sea somewhere. But I
don't even know the name of his ship. I just write to him at
Devonport, and sometimes get letters from him there. It's
so different from peacetime when I always knew where he
was and of course the name of his ship.'

Then, half an hour later, as Clemmie was about to pour
some coffee while they were all sitting round a table in the
garden, a strange pony and trap came clip-clopping up the
drive, and out of it stepped Buller carrying a small
Gladstone bag – sure sign, Clemmie recorded at once, that
his stay would be a brief one.

Buller was in uniform, looking bronzed and fit and
exceedingly cheerful. He embraced Clemmie and Lucy
and shook Helena's hand, then turned his attention to
Richard, who had struggled onto his crutches. 'Well, three
actions in a year! There're not many officers who can claim
that record. And the Hun thought he could do for you!
What a hope!'

'And what have you been up to, Father?'

Buller patted the dogs' heads and glanced round the garden, which was at its summer best, a glorious blaze of colour. He said to Clemmie, 'I think I'll change and have a hack, my dear, if you don't mind? I've been sitting in that train for too long.' He turned back to Richard and smiled mysteriously. 'Up to? Oh, I've been away at sea – like you.' And that was all he would say.

XII

Double-Deception

A heavy Atlantic beam swell causes the *Duchess of Marlborough* to pitch and roll heavily in a stomach-turning and almost continuous corkscrew. Even Rod Maclewin, who in more than thirty-five years at sea has never been sick, turns away from the billycan of hot onion soup offered to him on the bridge. They have been at sea for a month now, without a sign of the enemy. Under pressure from the United States, which had lost many innocent civilian lives in attacks by U-boats, German submarine warfare has relaxed in intensity. But there are still many raiders at sea, and it is known that others are leaving German ports to make their way circuitously to the Mediterranean, and the Dardanelles, down the west coast of Ireland.

It is here that the *Duchess of Marlborough* has been operating in the hope of picking up one of these boats. Rod and Buller have already learned some valuable lessons. First they have discovered that the U-boat commanders, like all successful hunting animals, have learned caution and canniness. At night the ether is thick with their wireless signals, warning each other in code of the position of enemy warships they may have seen and of any suspicious patrolling vessels. Any U-boat which suspects that it has been observed informs all other U-boats in its vicinity, and itself makes off in an unlikely direction and refrains from attacking any vessel for a time.

For hunter and hunted alike, this is a war of words, transmitted and received in a number of codes, a war that occasionally and suddenly flares up into violence. At posts on shore, secret direction-finding devices, undreamed of a few years earlier, are sometimes able to locate accurately the position of a transmitting U-boat. At sea, wireless telegraphists, German and British, can judge approximately the range of the enemy by the volume of the message. Then this new electronic war of words bursts into a war of sudden action, and a sinking ship is heard to cry out in anguish – 'SOS steamship *Zanzibar* torpedoed and sinking in position . . .' and sometimes the message is cut short, perhaps by rising water, or by a German shell striking the wireless room.

It is not only a war of words and a war of sudden action. It is also a war of nerves. And for no other men is the strain greater than for the crew of the *Duchess of Marlborough* which, day and night, seeks out the most dangerous areas and contrives by every means to invite attack.

The ship takes a heavy green, once again soaking all those on the bridge. A red light shines out briefly beside the wheelhouse door, for although outwardly a run-down tramp in need of a lick of paint, the *Duchess of Marlborough* bristles with electrical and other devices to make the running of the ship as efficient as any RN man-o'-war. Rod places his mouth close to the mouthpiece beside the light and reports: 'All's well, sir, and no change. We're taking a lot of water for'ard but no damage.'

Rod resumes his watch. He has lashed himself to the bridge-rails as a precaution against being thrown against them and in order that he can hold his glasses with both hands. His careful sweep of the horizon reveals nothing more than white-flecked rollers and driving spume. They are seventy miles from Ireland and the nearest land to the west is the American continent.

Rod will not allow himself to admit to it, but a four-hour watch under these conditions stretches his endurance to the limit. At fifty-three it is scarcely surprising. He was asked before the war whether he wanted to take retirement, but war is what he has been preparing for all his life and he is determined that his contribution will be a useful one. However, the strain is taking its toll and he feels a sort of general malaise contrary to his usual general fitness and the dizziness and loss of appetite continuous heavy seas cause.

Rod feels a tap on his shoulder. The helmsman is pointing at something off the port beam. It is only intermittently visible when it rises out of a trough and very faintly at that. But he should have spotted it. No doubt of that. It is the shape of a triangle. Gone now. No danger in that – a fishing-boat, surely, having a rough time of it, too. And there it is again, for a second only as it is lifted up and plunges out of sight with not a sign of its hull.

U623 had been at sea for almost as long as the *Duchess of Marlborough*, travelling up the west coast of Denmark inside the German minefields, and then up the Norwegian coast, well inside territorial waters where the danger from British patrols was known to be greatest. On 27 June, off Bergen in dirty weather, U623's commander, Käpitan-Leutnant Hans von Grüber from Hildesheim, sighted a four-funnel enemy cruiser turning at the end of its patrol line. It was no more than two miles away and von Gruber ordered a crash-dive, their first of the voyage. In practice they had never bettered thirty seconds. The U-boat's commander was satisfied, and relieved, to observe that this time it took no more than twenty-four seconds.

Cruising on the surface at their economical speed of eleven knots, U623 headed west and then south-west between the Faroes and the Shetlands and south through that part of the Atlantic known as Rockall Deep. They were some 150 miles off Malin Head on the north coast of Ireland when they met the storm that the *Duchess of Marlborough* endured two days later and which affected all shipping heading in and out of the North Channel for or from Liverpool and Glasgow. At one point, in order to give his men a rest from the frantic tossing of the little 600-ton submarine, the commander gave the order to dive. At ten fathoms they entered a new world of peace and silence, relishing a meal taken sitting down at the hanging mess tables.

U623's orders were to proceed without diversions to the eastern Mediterranean, refuelling and collecting instructions at neutral ports *en route*. Only worthwhile targets were to be attacked, the torpedoes to be reserved for warships in the Aegean.

U623 spotted little shipping, even in the busy shipping-lanes west of the North Channel but von Grüber was constantly aware of the danger of attack from British men-o'-war which in poor visibility and heavy weather could appear as suddenly as that British cruiser had done. To deceive look-outs he therefore rigged a mast and single sail similar to that of British trawlers aft of the submarine's conning-tower. It was an object of much hilarity amongst the submarine's company, and Leutnant z. See Braun, U623's young comic, cast out a simulated herring-trawl when the sail was set for the first time, to the cries of '*Du Witzbold*!' – 'You wag!'

At 3.15 p.m. on 15 August, still in heavy seas, the officer-of-the-watch sighted a single-funnel vessel steaming north on an opposite course to their own. When the commander was informed and climbed to the conning-tower he was struck by the ship's curious deck cargo forward and remarked on it to the officer-of-the-watch. The ship was flying the red ensign and was remarkable in no other way. But it was the sight of the lashed truck, suggesting an unusual cargo in the ship's hold, that decided von Grüber to attack. He therefore ordered an alteration of course to intercept the *Duchess of Marlborough*, and action stations. The single 7.5-cm deckgun was manned with some difficulty, its crew lashed to a running-line.

The crew of U623 approached their first target in a state of tension and excitement, a rating on the conning-tower giving a running description of the scene down the voice-pipe to the crew members below. At 3.25 the U-boat began to flash by signal-lamp the international signal to halt. Von Grüber was thankful not to have to fire a shot across the steamer's bows, ammunition being precious at the start of a long operation. The *Duchess of Marlborough*, her name clearly legible at the bows, hove to at a range of 500 metres and began to blow off steam. Von Grüber ordered her company to abandon ship, informing them that he would open fire in ten minutes.

The crew in U623's conning-tower were better able to watch what followed than the gun-crew, who were at a lower elevation and even this close saw the ship only intermittently. But they, too, watched, half in wonder and half in amusement, as the British skipper, inverted pipe clenched between his teeth and carrying a parrot-cage, clambered into the boat, followed by his motley crew, scrambling for a place, raising their arms in disarray and lowering the boat from its davits in violent jerks fore and aft, almost tipping them into the sea. Von Grüber's second-in-command asked him if he really intended to take them on board, arguing that they would soon be picked up by another vessel.

'It will not be for long. We'll put them ashore at Lisbon,' von Grüber replied. He ordered the helmsman to bring the submarine close alongside the British steamer, apparently abandoned now by its crew and wallowing in the swell. The lifeboat was equidistant between the steamer and the submarine, the crew pulling manfully but with little co-ordination, and von Grüber heard the skipper's voice, carried on the wind, cursing his men.

The U-boat's gunnery mate had been allowed six shells to sink the *Duchess of Marlborough*. If she did not go down she would be abandoned and the petty officer would be disrated. The long barrel swung round and steadied on the target, its elevation matching the U-boat's roll. He was about to open fire when the appearance of the target was suddenly transformed. The swift raising of the white ensign and lowering of the 'red duster' signalled the change, but, at almost the same second, the chicken-house amidships and the steering engine-house aft which had been blowing off steam through a small funnel, collapsed, revealing deck-guns which were already firing. The most alarming change occurred forward where the big truck magically divided as if on hinges and a gun as big as their own opened fire.

Kapitan-Leutnant Hans von Grüber's sight of the enemy lasted scarcely half a minute. In that time he saw the muzzle flash of the two 12-pounders, saw the first shells fall short, sending up waterspouts twice as tall as his own wireless masts, heard the clatter of a Maxim gun and the crackle of small arms-fire as well as the percussive impact of the two 12-pounders.

In that thirty seconds he struck the emergency alarm which sounded the klaxon above and below decks and shouted '*Unter Deck!*' to those in the conning-tower beside him. The gun-crew just forward of the conning-tower were racing for the hatch after firing one futile

187

shot. The long, shark-like bows of the submarine were just beginning to dip deeper into the sea when the first of the shells struck the hull of U623 aft. The second struck low down in the conning-tower. This 12-pounder shell alone would have doomed the submarine, but more followed – three more and then two right aft, destroying the twin screws and the horizontal and vertical rudders.

Von Grüber was killed by two Maxim gun-bullets before a shell killed all those still alive in the conning-tower. Only three men succeeded in getting below before the hatches shut, but like all the submarine's complement who were not on deck, their death took longer. The pressure cracked the hull of the U-boat at forty-two fathoms, taking it apart piecemeal as if it were being subjected to hammer-blows; and this detritus, like autumn leaves, floated down to the Atlantic sea bed 1,450 fathoms deep.

Only one success was granted to U623 in her first and only attack. But it was an important one. With remarkable presence of mind the wireless telegraphist had succeeded in transmitting a brief message *en clair* before succumbing: 'Being attacked by English warship in disguise of merchantman . . .'

At the end of the week when Buller packed his Gladstone bag and kissed Clemmie good-bye, his wife knew no more about what he was doing than when he arrived to find two of his children and a pretty dark girl staying at Wyston Court. Clemmie knew that if he could tell her anything he would, but all he volunteered was that he was operating from Devonport in a small boat. 'Makes a change from a battle-cruiser,' he had said. At first Clemmie presumed that he had been demoted as a result of displeasing Winston Churchill and their Lordships, the Commissioners of the Admiralty. But the hierarchy had long since resigned, been discredited or moved elsewhere, and (as Clemmie could read in the newspapers) all Buller's gloomy foreboding about the Dardanelles operations were being realized.

Secrecy about the *Duchess of Marlborough* and her success remained iron-tight at the Admiralty and at Devonport. But with the decision to step up the numbers of decoy ships, or Q-ships as they were officially referred to, whispers began to be heard about the vessels and their volunteer crews whose clothing and slack public appearance and behaviour aroused curiosity and sometimes outrage at naval bases. What were these 'mystery ships' that could sometimes be seen, like slovenly beggars on parade with a Guards regiment, skulking in corners of a dockyard, dirty and neglected in appearance, and often with their decks obscured by tarpaulins? In wartime you were not supposed to ask questions, but you could not prevent people from speculating.

Like thieves in the night, the German U-boat commanders were becoming increasingly cautious and canny as new measures were devised to locate and sink them. Minefields and nets across the Straits of Dover had closed the short Channel route from bases in Germany and Belgium to the Atlantic shipping-lanes, which was the reason why U623 had been obliged to take the long route round the north of Scotland. Vessels of the Auxiliary Patrol, manned by reserve officers, multiplied in numbers. Bombs, exploded underwater at pre-set depths, and later known as depth-charges, were increasingly used against U-boats when they were seen to submerge. And unconcealed guns fitted to merchantmen deterred U-boats from surfacing and using their own guns, forcing them to fall back on their limited supply of torpedoes.

But most feared by the U-boat commanders were the decoy ships. The last despairing signal from the doomed U623 had been picked up by a sister ship some forty miles farther north following on the same route to the Mediterranean. Word spread rapidly among the U-boat commanders about these patrolling wolves in sheep's clothing, and Q-ships became victims of their own eagerness to be attacked. Lone decoy-colliers and decoy-tramps like the *Duchess of Marlborough* were stalked cautiously by submerged U-boats, torpedoed and left to sink, leaving the 'panic party' to return for the gun-crews, and then drift and be picked up by another passing ship, or left to starve or drown.

The *Duchess of Marlborough*'s next patrol was abortive, and other Q-ships patrolling the Western Approaches and the western entrance to the Channel either failed to make a killing or were themselves sunk.

On a Sunday late in November 1915, Captain Herbert Richmond took the train from London to Plymouth, and in the afternoon met Buller and Rod Maclewin in an office provided by the superintendent of the Devonport dockyard. He had announced his intention of arriving in a telephone call to Buller, who had recently returned from an arduous and stormy patrol when he had caught neither sight nor sound of a U-boat, but had picked up the victim of one torpedo attack and had taken off the crew of another merchantman that was slowly sinking.

Buller greeted his fellow captain warmly. 'Well, Bert, was U623 just a flash in the pan? Has your idea gone sour, do you think?'

Richmond thought not. 'Even if we don't ever get another, the Q-ship campaign will pay off.'

'What makes you think that?'

'Because of what our undercover people in Germany have learned, and from prisoners from two U-boats we sank recently in the North Sea.' It seemed that the arming of merchantmen and the existence of Q-ships was adding to the strain of U-boat crews and leading them to be much more cautious about approaching innocent-looking lone merchantmen. Hove-to on the surface at night, the ether was thick with German signals from U-boats exchanging information about the position and characteristics of suspicious vessels.

'What we need is a few more sinkings like your first. That'll really smash their spirit.'

'Not so easy, Bert. We're having no luck at all.'

'Then we've got to be cleverer. Let's have your ideas.'

Buller looked across the desk behind which his old friend was sitting, and then at Rod, who had remained silent so far. He laughed and said to Rod, indicating Richmond, 'He's supposed to be the brainy one – Naval War Staff and all that. Or is he just an armchair critic?'

Richmond's sense of humour was not famous in the Royal Navy, and he glared at Buller and told him sharply, 'We're fighting a war for our lives, not running a music-hall.' Then he seized a sheet of paper and, serious and business-like, began to write swiftly on it, talking as he did so. 'Let's list the reasons why a U-boat commander won't come near you. 1. He's had a description of you from another U-boat who was suspicious. 2. You've been seen in the same area twice before and the question is asked, "What is his destination and why doesn't he go there?" 3. There are too many people on the bridge – I know you've got to keep a keen look-out but most merchantmen have only the helmsman and the officer-of-the-watch on the bridge. 4. You've got one or more suspicious-looking structures on your deck, and they could conceal guns. 5. . . .'

For the next hour the three officers worked out measures to counter these give-aways, and even Captain Richmond, who did not readily show satisfaction in anything, said with something close to a laugh, 'Devilishly cunning, gentlemen! We'll nab a Hun yet.'

Then they retired to dine with the admiral superinten-dent of the dockyard and his charming wife and daughter.

191

The strain of the past months eased. Rod, who had been suffering from it badly, began to feel cheerful and optimistic, and refilled his glass three times as the port went round after the ladies had retired. They talked, inevitably, about the war which was increasingly, month by month, consuming the attention of almost every family in the land, and consuming their lives too in tens of thousands of tragic cases.

As the junior officer present, Rod Maclewin would never have suggested a toast under normal circumstances. But now, with the heavy fumes of cigar-smoke and port in the air, he stood up and, addressing the admiral, asked, 'May I suggest a toast, sir? To our sons and to their safety.'

The admiral had three sons serving in France, Rod had a son, Tom, serving in the Harwich flotilla as an ordinary seaman, and of the Buller boys, Richard was now back with his destroyer and Harry was heavily engaged in a new push in France, the Battle of Loos. 'To our sons, and their safety.'

When the *Duchess of Marlborough* sailed from Devonport on 8 October 1915 she was full of new tricks, which had all been practised sedulously by her crew. A number of the crew – all volunteers – were new, too. With her extra armament, she needed more men, and others, less resistant to the strain of storm and of playing the part of live bait, had been given duties elsewhere. Outwardly the ship looked very much the same, but on the forecastle, in place of the truck disguise which Buller believed had outlived its purpose, there was a hatch. The whole forecastle had been built up to a height of three feet, which partially concealed the new big 4-inch gun Buller had winkled out of the Ordnance Department.

With this gun, one direct hit should be enough to sink any U-boat. The barrel of the gun and the upper part of its mounting had two means of concealment. Sandy Marchant had thought up the simplest idea, which was to put an upside-down fifteen-foot whaler on it, firmly secured, or so it appeared, but capable of being thrown off in a few seconds. This disguise appeared perfectly natural; but as an alternative to confuse the enemy, lengths of heavy tarpaulin could be hung over the derrick above as if drying on a line.

The steering engine-house aft had been redesigned to accommodate a long-barrel 12-pounder, and at the extreme stern was a fully exposed 2½-pounder, a fitting so common now on merchantmen that its absence could appear suspicious. Judging the chicken-hatch trick to be overworked now, the Maxim gun was concealed in a contrived extension of the ship's upper deck cabins, made of light wood and completed with a dummy door, a brass handrail and 'port-holes', all of which could be flattened with a single pull on a wire trigger.

Finally, a dummy funnel was carried for changing the ship's silhouette during the night, being rigged rapidly with funnel stays, and, like the real funnel, capable of carrying various markings to alter the ship's identity. By a simple trap and feed-pipe, some of the real smoke from the engine-room could be diverted into this light metal dummy.

The *Duchess of Marlborough* was given a patrol area off Ushant, and a high-powered new wireless-receiver to take in signals from Naval stations with the latest news of sinkings and likely whereabouts of U-boats. The free-ranging days of their first patrol were now over, and the whole Q-ship exercise was tightly controlled by the Admiralty, with as many as thirty Q-ships at sea at any time.

For ten days Buller kept the *Duchess of Marlborough* on her east-west patrol line west of Ushant. For forty-eight hours they would steam on a westerly heading, then at nightfall the crew changed the appearance of the ship to make her unrecognizable to any U-boat which had previously spotted her or had received by wireless her description from another U-boat. A funnel was added or dismantled, two scarlet rings added where previously there had been, say, a white diamond on the funnel. Another name-board for the ship was slipped into the cleverly concealed grooves at the stern. The manner of concealment of the 4-inch forward gun was also altered and the silhouette of the wheelhouse was adjusted by means of stout canvas screens. Buller even changed his hat and encouraged anyone on the bridge to do the same thing.

Rod admired Buller's capacity for keeping the spirits of his men as high as he did by making these changes as much like a pantomime between scenes as he could. But the savage late autumn weather and the strain after only a week at sea inevitably began to show. It was not easy to remain a sitting duck, day and night, when you knew that all about you ships were being sunk, often without warning, and men were dying in hundreds as a result of exposure or drowning or, violently, from shell or torpedo explosion. Every day the wireless picked up the plaintive SOS signals, often followed by urgent appeals for rescue as the ship was sinking.

On this October patrol Rod again felt the tension tightening like an enclosing wire net. He ate very little and several times found himself nodding off when on watch, an unforgivable offence which he had never committed before. He was sick several times in the privacy of his cabin, and wondered anxiously about the pains in his stomach. A voice kept telling him, usually when he was waking up in his bunk, 'You've had enough. Your nerves are cracking and you're becoming a liability in the ship.' Then his own disciplined voice of an officer of long standing would as stoutly deny the charge and order him to pull himself together. He would open his eyes to the familiar sight of his austere, diminutive cabin, the steel deck three feet above his head, the grey light of another Atlantic dawn percolating through the thick glass of the porthole, which, inevitably and all day and night long, poured with seawater.

Once Buller spoke to Rod about his condition. 'You look pretty washed-up, old man,' he told him one evening. 'You'd better take some leave after this patrol. That nice wife of yours'll feed you up and put you to rights.'

'I'm all right, thanks. You know what we always say – better at sea.'

A Saturday morning. Steaming east into a north-east wind. Bitterly cold on the bridge. A heavy sea running, as always, the forecastle taking a heavy green every few minutes as the bows plunge down like a shovel into the water. In every direction a spume-dashed grey and white sea, the horizon scarcely discernible against the grey sky of endless scurrying clouds. The *Duchess of Marlborough* (temporary alias *City of Newcastle*) drives on at eight knots, her wake astern at once swallowed up into the restless pattern of the ocean.

Sandy Marchant is officer-of-the-watch, with an hour to go on this bitterly cold and uncomfortable bridge. But his spirits have never slumped on this patrol, not once, and he has been thanked by his captain for his example of stoicism and optimism. He is feeling optimistic at this moment. Twice he has been handed reports of U-boat sightings not far distant, and in the night, he has been told, two conversations between U-boats were picked up, and they were not far distant either, judging by their volume and clarity. This has often happened before on patrols with no outcome. But this young lieutenant has a well-developed talent for forgetting old disappointments. And this time his optimism is justified.

The torpedo was sighted first at a range of some four hundred yards. It was travelling at thirty knots on a bearing of 275 degrees, trailing the distinctive white wash which had signalled the end of so many merchantmen in this war. Sandy Marchant did a quick calculation and ordered a rapid change of course to starboard so that the torpedo would strike them abaft the engine-room rather than in the engine-room, which would certainly lead to the death of the duty stokers and engineers. Then he pressed the alarm and called out over the intercom, 'Torpedo coming! Action stations! Torpedo coming!'

A sharp turn to port instead of to starboard would have led to the torpedo missing altogether, and even after all their training it still seemed unnatural to court disaster in this way. But that was what they were here for, and this was the opportunity they had been awaiting.

The torpedo struck with an enormous explosion sending a column of water and smoke and wreckage high into the air. The ship gave a convulsive shudder that sent everyone on the bridge crashing to the deck. Sandy pulled himself to his feet, already bleeding from a cut to his head, and almost at once Buller was at his side with the bo'sun, Petty Officer Len Drage, who was acting the part of captain. He had a megaphone to his lips, and the real-life drama had already begun when he called out, 'Away boats! Abandon ship!'

The entire ship's company of forty-five officers and men, with the exception of one rating killed instantly by the explosion, now began to play their part. The boat was rapidly losing way, blowing off steam and making great volumes of smoke, too, to simulate a hit in the engine-room and to conceal partly what was going on. The 'captain' made a rapid descent from the bridge and joined in the general chaos surrounding the two boats as the derricks were swung out, manned and lowered clumsily and with much shouting towards the turbulent sea. Some of the men were carrying bundles of clothes and other possessions, and some of these were allowed to fall into the sea amid further cries of anguish.

Rod joined Buller and Sandy Marchant on the bridge, all crouched down now out of sight. 'What are things like below?' Buller asked.

'What you would expect. We're taking in a lot of water in the stern and it looks as if the engine-room bulkhead is going to give way.'

'Good.' Buller knew that if they had not been fatally damaged and in imminent danger of sinking they might be shelled, and that was the last thing they wanted. He had already made out the U-boat's periscope, like the fin of a killer-shark relishing its victim. It was travelling west to east at a range of half a mile, evidently examining them carefully.

Buller handed his glasses to Rod and told him to keep a sharp watch on the U-boat through the observation hole cut into the bridge panelling. He made his way by the concealed route to his cabin, seized from the safe the ship's papers, code books etc., secured them to their weight and returned to the bridge.

All guns and torpedo tubes were manned but not one of the crew moved, silently sweating out the time before the submarine surfaced or their ship went down. This was the moment for which they had been trained over and over again. But now reality had its own sharp flavour, its own piercing pressure. Lying with his cheek resting on a deck-rivet beside the 4-inch gun mounting, Able Seaman Charlie Richards, married, two children, muttered between his teeth, 'Come on, you bloody Boche! Time to come up for air,' and was kicked by Gunner Duff.

Half an hour later, with the two panic parties resting on their oars as their boats rose to dizzy heights and fell into the trough of the waves, the U-boat moved slowly away as if she had had enough. Buller watched in exasperation. They were taking in a lot of water astern where the seas were frequently breaking over the stern rails threatening the 12-pounder crew. He thought they might last another thirty minutes. The drill *in extremis* was to despatch an SOS *en clair* giving their position, which was known approximately anyway. Then, disposing of the papers in the sea, they would abandon ship and take to the single raft, the carley float, available for all the gun-crews.

'She's surfacing, sir,' said Rod, 'and it looks as if they're manning the gun.'

Evidently impatient and anxious to get away, the U-boat commander had decided to finish them off with shellfire. The long, low dark shape of the U-boat was clearly visible on the surface now. It was barely two miles distant and well within range of their own 4-inch gun. But the enemy made a poor target, especially in these high seas, and there would be time for only three or four shells before she crash-dived out of sight. No, Buller decided, they would have to stick it out and hope she came closer.

The first German shells fell short, sending up white geysers of water close to the two boats and confirming how difficult firing conditions were. The firing began spasmodically, but soon settled down to a rate of about six rounds a minute. Buller could see clearly the muzzle flash and the shell coming straight at them on a low trajectory. It was a curious sensation and he concentrated on observing the fall of shot clinically as a veteran gunnery specialist. One screamed just overhead and the next struck the ship no more than a dozen feet forward of the bridge with a terrific crack. Buller was certain that it must have hit the concealed Maxim gun, utterly destroying it. The familiar faces of the gun-crew manning it raced through his mind agonizingly. At the same time he worried that the explosion had revealed the true nature of their target.

'Go down and see if you can do anything for those poor fellows,' Buller ordered Sandy. 'But don't for God's sake show yourself or we'll all be killed.'

The ship shook from another hit, somewhere aft, and there was a third explosion close to the waterline right below them. The U-boat appeared nearer, as if closing for the *coup de grâce*, and Rod said, 'Do you think we should have a crack at her now, sir? Otherwise she's going to take us to pieces.'

'No, we must hold it a little longer.'

The U-boat was bows on, range little more than a mile, seas breaking over her heavily. For a moment, Buller's admiration went out to her crew, a thousand miles from home, suffering the appalling risks of their calling, the gun-crew soaked to the skin and freezing cold. Then he thought of the hundreds of merchant sailors they had already killed, and of his own men dead or dying about the ruins of their Maxim.

When the U-boat turned to bring herself beam on at a range of 750 yards, Buller made up his mind. The 12-pounder crew would soon have to retreat from their gun or drown at it and it looked as if the cautious U-boat commander was not coming any nearer. He reached over and punched the button which activated the 'open fire' klaxon.

The silence which had been sustained by the crew of the *Duchess of Marlborough* for nearly an hour was instantly broken by the sound of collapsing timber and metal sheeting and the shouts of men relieving their lungs after the long ordeal. The white ensign was run up, and exactly as it fluttered out in the strong wind, the two big guns opened up simultaneously. Buller saw that the gun-crew aft were already standing in water and having difficulty in working the gun at all. But they were still getting off a round every ten seconds, and the deeper-throated 4-inch was thudding out shells with the same regularity.

Buller turned his glasses swiftly onto the target, already half-screened by the water of near misses, and already half-submerged. He could just make out the last of the gun-crew racing for the hatch and disappearing as the water closed over their vessel. 'Surely that was a hit!' Buller exclaimed aloud. 'Oh God, don't let her get away now.' The stern was up high, but not unnaturally high as if from a hit; just the natural angle for a crash-dive. One hit now, from the 4-inch, and she would be finished. A tall column of water arose from the sea at her stern, barely a dozen yards distant. Another shell struck the sea just short. And when the water cleared like a turned-off fountain the dark shape of their tormentor had disappeared, and Buller felt sick with disappointment and exasperation.

For another hour Buller and his men stuck it out in the faint hope that the U-boat would reappear to finish them off. But why should it? Buller asked himself. Its target was clearly doomed and it was many months since a U-boat commander had taken the trouble to rescue his victims, the law of the sea flouted so often that no German bothered with it any more.

But Buller had underestimated the venom and urge for revenge of this U-boat commander. Within minutes of the abandonment of the *Duchess of Marlborough*'s after 12-pounder gun because of the rising sea, the U-boat manoeuvred to a position astern of the ship. Buller saw the periscope at a distance of no more than three hundred yards. Then the vessel heaved herself out of the sea, water pouring off her deck in a white torrent, figures appeared on the conning-tower and the big gun and the machine-gun were manned.

Buller recognized now what they were in for and ordered a wireless SOS to be transmitted, giving their position and announcing the presence of a U-boat. The shelling began at once and there was nothing they could do to defend themselves. The ship was out of control, wallowing in the ocean, her only surviving gun unable to bear. Now the U-boat opened fire at point-blank range, steadily, in no haste at all, but with deadly effect. They could see the crew working the gun, talking and laughing, then choosing which part of the ship to hit. From time to time the machine-gun fired a burst and in exasperation but with no visible effect, some of the *Duchess of Marlborough*'s ratings fired rifles in reply.

'We won't be able to stand this much longer,' Rod remarked. On the bridge Buller had been thrown down twice as a result of hits. The funnel had been shot through and through, the mainmast toppled over the side, the wireless aerial destroyed. The ship was being torn apart, progressively dismembered, while her crew were helpless to reply. An able seaman lay dead at Buller's feet and everyone else had been sent below except Sandy Marchant and Rod.

A burst of machine-gun fire rattled on the armoured sides of the bridge and the ship shivered as if in unbearable pain from another hit on the port side. 'Will you go below and tell everyone we're abandoning ship,' Buller ordered Rod. 'You go with him, Sandy.'

'We don't want any heroic stuff from you, sir.' The lieutenant held his arm. He had been wounded in his left shoulder by a splinter and there was a damp patch on his

201

torn coat. Even he could not any longer find anything to laugh at, and his face was drawn and tense. 'No sinking with the ship for the honour of the service,' he told Buller firmly. A shell burst amidships, knocking them sideways. 'That'd be a silly waste. You're too valuable to the service, sir.'

Buller shouted at him, 'Go and get that carley launched and don't worry about me. I'll join you when I can.'

The scene on the maindeck was terrible. All the surviving uninjured crew had collected in a corner of the mess quarters, doing what they could for the wounded they had managed to move. The air was heavy with the stench of coal dust, cordite, oil and blood. Sandy glanced at the men, who were looking at him, awaiting orders as if only he might have the power to stop this merciless shelling and ease their burden of pain, suffering and fear.

Petty Officer Stephen Wallace's face was smeared with blood and oil but Sandy recognized him and said, 'We're abandoning ship, Mr Wallace. Will you see to the carley float and get any men you can into it?'

'Ay, ay, sir.' There was instant movement among the survivors and awkwardly, for the deck was now at a steep angle, the wounded were helped or carried towards the bent and twisted stairway to the upper deck.

The firing was only intermittent now as if the U-boat, like a suddenly weary beast of prey, had tired of its cruel game. But every few minutes a shell was fired and one rating was shattered with splinters and killed instantly before he could get to the rail. The carley float was in the water, rising and falling against the side of the ship. Two men had succeeded in getting into it and were attempting to control it while others climbed down the lines thrown over the side. Sandy helped a leading seaman with a broken leg to get down; for this man his life depended on the strength of his arms and his will to survive the cold and the danger . . .

There was Buller, thank God, stout and hatless, his thin surviving hair blowing in the wind, a dour figure showing an air of defiance and confidence in spite of defeat and the destruction of his hopes and his ship. Three men were still manning the 4-inch in case the wind turned their ship enough for them to get in a round or two, but now Buller himself ordered them over the side with the rest. 'We'll have to leave that bastard for another day,' he said, encouraging them as they grabbed a line and in turn slipped down to the raft.

A burst of machine-gun fire from the U-boat, a voice near at hand crying out, 'Why can't they leave us be, sir? They've done for us.'

'Not yet they haven't, Smith. Get down there with the others.'

Another voice, 'Come on, sir.'

'I'll be with you. I'm just checking below.' Buller had glanced down at the raft and seen no sign of Rod among the sitting and sprawled figures. There were others missing, many shipmates he would never see again, but Rod had been safe a few minutes ago. 'Rod – Rod Maclewin!' Buller shouted down an alleyway. 'Where are you?' There was light pouring in from shell-holes and Buller's voice echoed hauntingly like a voice in an abandoned tomb. He ran, avoiding the litter of the shelling – scattered lumps of steel, some clothing, lumps of coal, more steel litter. A body lying across the alleyway. Ordinary Seaman Macpherson from Dundee, a good man, face unmarked, torso best not looked at. 'Rod! Where are you?' Buller glanced in to the torpedo flat, the tube loaded with a 14-inch torpedo, useless now. He felt the ship take a lurch, sharpening even further the unnatural angle. A hand on his arm. He turned. Sandy Marchant, as white in the face as poor Ordinary Seaman

203

Macpherson. 'Come on, sir. There're a number of men missing, but we must put off.'

The *Duchess of Marlborough* shook herself again, whether from another hit or another lurch towards the bottom, who could tell. 'Rod, Rod—' But Buller was coming, running back along the alleyway, up the stairway. The bo'sun was by the rails, waiting for them, calm as if seeing off an admiral's gig, holding out the rope for Buller like a ceremonial gift. 'I think she's going, sir.'

There were twenty men in the carley float, half of them uninjured. 'How could there be so many after what they had been through?' Buller wondered through his anguish and the agony of loss and the burden of responsibility for these survivors – *his* men. They were not overcrowded. The carley could take thirty, they had hard rations and water, and they would rig a mast and sail later. Some wag shouted, 'They probably think we're just another panic party.' The real panic party had left the parrot behind, and he was in a bad temper after all the noise, his defiance like a many times repeated parody of their own desperate defiance: 'Damn the Huns, and good-day to you, sir. Damn the Huns and . . .' 'Shut up, Pol!' an OD shouted.

The U-boat, black and low as a crouching puma, was still cautiously hove-to astern of the sinking ship, the men on deck leaning from side to side with the roll of their ship, victors gazing at the vanquished. The *Duchess of Marlborough* was slipping inexorably down, only the bridge and forecastle clear of the water, the abandoned big gun a hollow mockery, and top hamper from the after part of the ship rising and falling on the waves above the invisible stern.

'Shall we give 'er a cheer, sir?' The question came from a rating lying at Buller's feet, wounded in the side, propped up to witness the end.

'When she goes' Buller gazed at what was left of his ship, recalling the time, so many years ago, when the *Victoria* went down. Then he had lost consciousness and Rod had caught him and brought him safely to a boat. Oh Rod – the fire and storm they had been through together!

The waves broke over the raft, soaking them. The bo'sun had organized a bailing party. 'Keep at it – we're going to be all right.' The two boats were heading their way, already within earshot. And the U-boat was moving at last, anxious now to get clear of the area in case they had got off an SOS with the position.

Buller could see that the gun-crew had been stood down but many more of the crew had come up on deck, lining the rails like holidaymakers on a pier awaiting the fun. The U-boat, a small vessel, half the size of a destroyer but sleek and deadly, with a sting that could sink a battleship, was heading north, picking up speed. Too late, it was coming abeam of their doomed ship and Buller saw that the U-boat would come close to them. He suddenly feared for the lives of his men again, for the machine-gun was still manned and he did not put it past these Germans to shoot at them before leaving the scene.

Buller could see the faces of the German crew. Most had grown beards and all were in stout waterproof long coats and sou'westers. Some were grinning and pointing at them. One simulated operating a movie-camera, winding the handle, his mates watching him and breaking into laughter when he was knocked sideways by a wave. Others were waving an ironic greeting and shouting, but Buller, mercifully, could not distinguish the words. Then, as he had feared, he heard a riffle of machine-gun fire, saw the spark of its muzzle. The men in the raft ducked low, but Buller saw that there was no need. The gunners were teasing them, firing around the raft with short bursts, egged on by their shipmates. The submarine slipped by, gathering speed, off to seek new prey, uncaring for their fate, its machine-gun firing one last burst in farewell.

The *Duchess of Marlborough* was taking her time to go down, brave Duchess. But she was nearly gone now, only the forecastle remaining above water, and the seas washing over the deck as if preparing her for what must soon come.

Across the water there came the sound of an explosion. A single explosion. And then another, as if the 4-inch magazine was going up, to hasten her end. 'God, sir!' 'Well, I'll be buggered . . .' and 'Oh Christ . . .' The exclamations about Buller were like an unmelodious chorus rising from the lurching raft. Buller had his eyes on what was left of his ship and only turned when one of his men seized his arm. Then he saw the tall waterspouts, one just over, the other short of the U-boat.

The firing was not swift. There was only one man at the big gun and a 4-inch shell weighs 25 pounds. But if any man knew how to load, lay and fire a 4-inch naval gun it was Rod Maclewin, even if he was working it at forty-five degrees with the waves lapping about his feet. 'Just the best damn gunnery officer in the Fleet,' as Buller had boasted to the captain of the sunk *Blücher* earlier in the year. 'And an old friend of mine.'

Through his glasses, Buller could recognize without any trouble at all the stocky figure going about his business as Buller had seen him time and again at gunnery drill as well as in action. 'The best damn . . .' The third shell, like the third German salvo at the Battle of Coronel, found its target. The U-boat was almost a mile distant, the crew pouring down the hatches like bolting rabbits. They had no time to man the gun, scarcely time to say a prayer. Rod got the third shell off before the U-boat had time to dig in its nose for a crash-dive, and it struck just forward of the conning-tower, sending up a massive cloud of dark brown smoke and debris.

It was enough, more than enough, to seal the U-boat's fate. She heeled hard to starboard, sweeping off a dozen men, appearing to lose none of her speed until an explosion, bright yellow, tinged red, black smoke now, a holocaust out of proportion to the size of the vessel. A brief glimpse of severed ends of the U-boat rising like twin tombstones, a second smaller explosion, a ball of steam and spray and more smoke rising and carried away at once on the wind as swiftly as a last evidence of the submarine itself. It was over in fifteen seconds, and the sea where she had been was as clean and clear as if nothing had happened.

The *Duchess of Marlborough*'s final descent was quieter and more dignified but also swift and without further hesitancy. Buller thought he saw Rod wave an arm in farewell but he could not be sure for there was much spray as she turned over to reveal her red bottom and keel.

Buller stood up and hailed the nearer of the boats, ordering it to head for the position where she had gone down. But he knew that there was no chance of finding anything. No one could survive for more than a few minutes in this bitterly cold, rough sea. Several Germans floated past them in the next half-hour, like discarded bundles, white and limp, but that was all.

One of Buller's men died, too, to add to the toll of this long-drawn-out deadly game of tit-for-tat in the wastes of the Atlantic. Buller gave his attention to the survivors, the wounded and the uninjured, getting the raft organized and the men's spirits lifted after their ordeal. That was what he had to do now, and the men responded, silently aware of his grief and his pride.

'You couldn't ask for a better end, sir, could you?' an

able seaman said. His teeth were chattering, his lips blue, his cheeks white and drawn.

Buller looked at him and smiled, and nodded. When he spoke it was to himself. 'Rod was always quick onto the target, and he needed to be today – God have mercy on his soul.'

The destroyer *Thistle* found them, the two boats and the carley float, before it was too dark to get them safely on board that evening. Then they headed for home.

XIII

The Fellowship of the Sea

Conversation on the bridge of HMS *Arrow*, 3.10 a.m., 31 May 1916:

> *Lieutenant-Commander Charles Anderson* DSC: A little birdie tells me that we may be onto something this time. (He is a Scotsman from Elgin, 'little' sounding 'leetle', and 'birdie' as if spelt with three rs.)
>
> *Lieutenant Richard Buller*: Well, I hope you're right, sir. But I don't need to remind my commanding officer that we've heard about these little birdies before. What makes you think the Hun's on the rampage this time?
>
> *Anderson*: My private wireless. It picked up Admiral Hipper talking to Admiral Scheer. 'Och ay,' he said. 'It's time we made another raid. Got strafe England. *Auf wiedersehen.*'
>
> *Sub-Lieutenant the Hon George Hoste*: I think the skipper's right. You can almost smell the blighters.

The Battle-Cruiser Fleet had left the Firth of Forth soon after ten p.m. on the evening of 30 May with orders to proceed east across the North Sea in order to rendezvous with Admiral Jellicoe's battle squadrons at two p.m. the following afternoon in a position south of Norway, 56° 40′N, 5°E. To the crew of these vast British fleets, numbering twenty-eight battleships, nine battle-cruisers, and seventy-nine destroyers, it looked like being just another sweep, and they believed that they would be back at their bases the following day. There was little apprehension or excitement. Almost every man had given up hope of drawing the German Fleet out for a straight fight. And Charlie Anderson, the eager young new commander of the destroyer *Arrow* of the Battle-Cruiser Fleet's flotillas, was one of the few officers experiencing any sense of expectation that, after nearly two years of war, they might be in for a fleet action – the longed-for new Battle of Trafalgar.

By contrast with the weather on the *Arrow*'s last operation before she was damaged, it was a calm, warm, still night. The light wind from the north-east was starting to back to the north-west but there was no threat of poor weather, only a risk of mist. But then, when was there not a threat of mist in the North Sea?

Sunrise was due in an hour and a half and already there was a faint orange glow on the eastern horizon. Richard could make out the silhouettes of the six battle-cruisers on the port beam, Beatty's flagship *Lion*, *Princess Royal*, *Queen Mary* and *Tiger* – 'the cat squad', as they were nicknamed – and then the slightly smaller *New Zealand* and *Indefatigable* forming the 2nd Squadron; thirty-two 13.5-inch guns and sixteen 12-inch guns in all. They were keeping perfect station as they had all through the night, speed nineteen knots, black smoke streaming from their funnels and drifting south towards the *Arrow*'s flotilla.

Astern of these two battle-cruiser squadrons but not yet visible in the darkness of the west were the four new fast battleships of the 5th Battle Squadron, the *Queen Elizabeth*'s sister ships armed with mighty 15-inch guns but not quite so fast as the battle-cruisers. Far to the north, Admiral Jellicoe's battle squadrons, after leaving their bases before midnight, were also steaming east to the rendezvous, twenty-four more dreadnoughts headed

210

by three battle-cruisers, the most powerful single naval force ever to put to sea.

Eight bells rang out in the *Arrow* and the destroyer went through the ritual of watch-changing. Nineteen knots was a comfortable speed for the destroyer, decks vibrating gently with the steady revolutions of her turbines and she was rolling no more than a Thames barge coming down-river on the tide. The helmsman's bearded face reflected the increasing glow of light ahead, his eyes dropping with the regularity of a pendulum to the compass. No one had spoken for half an hour. Now the commander said, 'I'm going to put my head down for a bit.'

'Shall I call you if we sight the enemy, sir?' asked Sub-Lieutenant Hoste with mock innocence.

'Enough of your cheek, young fellow.' And he disappeared below.

'You'd better shut your dear little eyes too, Georgie, or you won't be able to stay awake for the party,' said Richard.

The young sub, suddenly serious, asked, 'Do you really think there's going to be a show?'

'Who knows! But they do say that the new German C-in-C is more offensive-minded. Anyway, you get some sleep.'

Now Richard was the only officer on the bridge. He relished the feeling of responsibility and the knowledge that if a crisis arose he would have to deal with it alone until the commander could be summoned. A signal-lamp was flashing from the bridge of the destroyer ahead, too fast for Richard to read, but the *Arrow*'s signalman repeated it aloud as if speaking slowly from the page of a book. The battle-cruisers were signalling to one another, too, a constant succession of routine messages punctuating the half-light.

At half an hour before sunrise, the protective flotilla on

the port beam of the battle cruisers could be seen, and the ships of the 5th Battle Squadron, five miles astern, exposed the stately and reassuring silhouettes of the world's most powerful battleships. Richard had a friend in the flagship *Barham*, a gunnery officer commanding one of the 15-inch turrets and he wondered if he, too, was experiencing any sort of premonition about this day, the last in May. Tomorrow was the anniversary of that famous victory in 1794 of Admiral Richard Howe, the Glorious First of June. There had been a Buller there too, of course.

At precisely ten minutes to five, the edge of the sun lifted up over the horizon to the north-east. The sea at once took on a sharper, dappled definition of light and dark grey. Long shadows formed behind masts and funnels and the ships themselves, and Richard had to shade his eyes when he scanned the water ahead in the eternal and vigilant search for a periscope or a more distant smudge of smoke. The steward appeared with cocoa, the handles of the mugs hooked neatly between thumb and forefinger.

'Thank you, Taffy, that'll go down well.' Richard took the wheel from the helmsman so that he could drink in comfort. In this mellow orange sunrise light he appeared to have a ginger beard. 'Thank you, sir. I reckon it's going to be a warm day, sir.'

All through that long May morning the Battle-Cruiser Fleet continued on its easterly course until by noon it was more than half way between the Scottish coast and the northern tip of Denmark and the Skagerrak, the gateway to the Baltic between Norway and Denmark. The weather remained fine and visibility good for the North Sea. For the 14,000 men who manned these ships it was an enclosed world of their own, swift-moving but with no destination beyond the eternal seas. No other world might have existed. No smoke, no sign of a sail smudged

212

the horizon. Even the wireless was silent, the ether carrying no more than the crackle of static. Early in the war the Germans chattered away all the time amongst themselves. Now they had learned their lesson, and it was a daunting thought that the whole German High Seas Fleet might be at sea and only just out of sight.

The morning routine of the ship was carried out as if they were on exercises, and Richard made an inspection of the guns with the gunner. On his way up from eating an early lunch, he met his commanding officer and asked if there was any news. 'Not the noo,' was the answer. 'But just remember, laddie, there's nine hours of daylight yet for a scrap.' Richard paced the quarterdeck for half an hour, talked to a couple of ratings who were making some adjustments to the number 2 torpedo-tube, and returned to the bridge.

Soon after two p.m. every ship in the fleet, battle-cruisers, light cruisers and destroyers, broke into a sudden activity of signalling, the hoist originating in the flagship and at once spreading in acknowledgement with the competitive speed of long practice. 'Fleet turn six points to port in succession onto course three six zero.' As the fluttering flags were hauled down, executing the order, the *New Zealand* and *Indefatigable* which were at some distance to the north-east, and the *Lion* and her consorts and all the protecting flotillas in turn put their helms over so that by 2.15 p.m. the Battle-Cruiser Fleet was steaming north towards its rendezvous with Admiral Jellicoe's Grand Fleet.

They had reached the limit of their sweep and would soon be returning to base. Officers and men throughout Beatty's Fleet accepted phlegmatically, even fatalistically, that the operation was another abortive one to add to the many in which they had all participated since two summers ago. On the bridge of the *Arrow* where all the officers except the engineer-lieutenant were again

213

gathered, young George Hoste glanced at his commanding officer but judged it discreet to remain silent. Richard understood what George was thinking and, nodding his head in the direction of Anderson, who was leaning on the bridge-rail staring ahead, said quietly, 'Lost in his thoughts!'

At that moment they all heard through the open door the sound of morse dots and dashes from the W/T office abaft the bridge platform. The silence on the air had lasted for so long that now the staccato shorts and longs startled them and made them turn towards the source of the sound. Richard, swifter at reading W/T Morse than the lamp, spoke the words to himself as they came over the air, repeated once. It carried the call sign of the *Galatea*, a light cruiser scouting twelve miles to the east – and the message was what they had all given up hope of ever hearing: 'Enemy in sight. Two cruisers probably hostile in sight bearing ESE course unknown.'

As recently as fifteen years ago, this scouting vessel would have had to retrace its course back towards the fleet to despatch a visual signal, no doubt losing contact with the enemy while doing so. Now, with the miracle of wireless, the whole Battle-Cruiser Fleet was made aware that the enemy was near at hand. Commodore Edwyn Alexander-Sinclair in the *Galatea* was able to report on every development, the range, bearing and course of the enemy, the increase in the number of ships, the fact that he was opening fire, that his fire was being returned.

A few minutes later the W/T messenger handed the commander a copy of the latest signal, and Richard read it with him, '. . . a large amount of smoke as from a fleet bearing ENE . . .' Not just two cruisers, perhaps a Fleet! At once the *Lion* signalled by flags for the Fleet to turn ESE in order to cut off the enemy from his base to the south, and speed was increased. The helmsman put over the wheel to Anderson's order. The tilt of the deck as the

Arrow heeled over, the new urgency in the increasing sound of the turbines, the roar of the fans from the engine-room exhausts, the noise of the klaxons bringing the gun and torpedo crews to their stations, the renewed rattle of Morse messages from the W/T office – all this sudden activity honed a new edge to everyone's eagerness and alertness.

'There's a singular sight for ye, young fellow,' Anderson said to George Hoste. 'Take a good look – maybe it's a joke or maybe it's history.'

The *Arrow*'s Division was racing past HMS *Engadine*, a once graceful passenger-liner converted into Admiral Beatty's seaplane carrier with a massive hangar built aft. Not only was she a singular sight but amongst all these men-o'-war heading towards the enemy, she was hove to. And the *Arrow* was close enough to her to observe the reason for this. From the big ship's stern a crane was lowering a seaplane onto the water. Briefly Richard put his glasses onto the machine which was already gathering speed, a frail little biplane which looked as if its floats must crumple as they leaped from wave-top to wave-top. But she left the water safely, climbed rapidly, banked and turned north 500 feet above the *Arrow*, already outpacing the fastest destroyers. Richard gave a wave but the pilot and observer were too busy and the machine was soon lost in the scattered low cloud and mist which, in the past minutes, had descended upon them.

A keen-eyed look-out on the *Arrow*'s after searchlight platform was the first to sight the enemy, and the bearing was rapidly transmitted to the commander. It was a minute before Richard could make out for sure the dark shapes – five of them – on the eastern horizon. Beside him Anderson said in confirmation, 'Ay, that's Hipper, that's the "baby-killer" all right. And he won't get away this time, the bastard.'

'Are you sure they're German battle-cruisers, sir?' George Hoste asked.

'As sure as Edinburgh's the capital o' Scotland.'

'Then it's six to five in our favour – not counting the 5th Battle Squadron. And we've bigger guns.'

The commander lowered his glasses, held Hoste's shoulder and turned him towards the west. 'And just consider Hipper's advantage,' he said grimly. There was no need to say more. The *Engadine*, now five miles distant, and some of the 5th Battle Squadron's leading destroyers, were sharply distinguishable against the light of the afternoon sun by contrast with the indistinct shape of the enemy to the east. Simply by their favourable position, the Germans had won the first round in the tactical battle. Richard recalled his youthful advice to those elderly gunnery officers of the *Canopus* after the Coronel disaster – 'Don't get into a position we found ourselves in – clear for the enemy to sight, fire and spot, while he remains invisible to you.' It was not as bad as that now. Just nearly as bad.

Richard turned his glasses back onto the big enemy ships. The last time the battle-cruisers had met in combat, it was his father who had taken part; now it was his turn. The Battle of Dogger Bank had been a pursuit action, a chase as the Germans raced to get home in face of a superior enemy. This time Admiral Beatty could cut them off and destroy them at leisure – and surely he must do so with his great superiority. But as Richard saw the big German ships, still some sixteen miles distant, turn through 180 degrees onto a southerly heading, he said to Anderson, 'They're making a run for it again, sir.'

'Very wise, too. Though they'll no' get away.'

'Do you think we'll be sent in, sir?' Richard asked.

'Not for a while yet, laddie. Our smoke would make it even more difficult for the gunlayers, and the admiral'll be wanting to get at him with his big guns awhile.'

216

It was a quarter to four. The opposing battle-cruisers had been in sight of one another for fifteen minutes, with the range gradually closing. The *Arrow*'s flotilla, at close to maximum speed now, with decks vibrating so that it was difficult to get a steady view of the enemy through glasses, had drawn ahead of Beatty's flagship, which was leading the two squadrons of battle-cruisers onto a southerly course. The *Arrow*'s 4-inch guns were trained on the enemy but at this range it was no more than a gesture of defiance. The *Arrow*'s sting was in those two torpedo-tubes, which were also trained towards Admiral Hipper's ships, but, as Anderson had indicated, they were unlikely to be ordered in to attack at this stage.

This was to be a gunnery duel, the culmination of years of training and more years of scientific development by gunsmiths and scientists in the skills of optics, metallurgy and ballistics. And at 3.47 precisely, at a range of some 15,000 yards, this duel was opened without further ceremony or preliminaries. The line of five distant enemy ships was suddenly lit from end to end with the bright yellow sparks of muzzle flashes, and the brown cordite smoke rose in the air to blend with the black funnel smoke.

Anderson was counting off the seconds – 'twelve, thirteen, fourteen . . .'. As he said 'eighteen', tall columns of water arose from the sea, every one an overshoot on the west side of Admiral Beatty's line. But before the shells arrived, the *Lion*, *Princess Royal*, *Tiger* and the rest with guns close to maximum elevation, returned the fire with two-gun salvoes, the barrels seeming to punch out the half-ton shells before they kicked back on their recoil. By watching closely, you could just make out the projectiles rising in their trajectory on their long passage through mist and low cloud towards the enemy, followed in a few seconds by the deep concussive roar of their detonation.

Richard had his glasses on the British flagship, and he knew that he would never see a braver sight than this of HMS *Lion* slicing through the shell-torn water at maximum speed, bow waves rising high, foaming wake astern, turrets trained on the German line, a multitude of white ensigns and the flags of the latest signal hoist streaming out. The Germans were firing ripple salvoes with clinical accuracy, and it could be only a matter of seconds before they made a hit. Anderson had been right; the light conditions were strongly favouring the Germans, whereas the British fire appeared ragged with most of the shells long overshoots.

Yes, there was the first hit, amidships, dead on Q turret of the *Lion*. Richard saw the flames and smoke and debris rising from the tremendous explosion. But she did not falter, firing steady salvoes with her remaining guns. Seconds later, from far down the line of battle-cruisers, there appeared a yellow flash many times more brilliant and deadly. It was difficult to identify the victim. Anderson, from the starboard wing of the bridge, shouted out, 'They've got the *Indefatigable*!' Another enormous flash lit up the sky, followed by a dense, billowing cloud of black smoke that dwarfed every ship in the Fleet. Now they were only five in number.

All the time the range was closing, the noise becoming ever more deafening, the shellfire more devastating. Far astern, the great dark shapes of the ships of the 5th Battle Squadron could just be made out through the drifting smoke and low mist, replacing the lost *Indefatigable* with four ships of double her gunpower. And this gunpower was making itself felt in the German line, the 15-inch shells sending up waterspouts significantly taller than any others. And it was good shooting, too; the last German ship was taking a terrible hammering. But still Hipper's battle-cruisers kept up a steady and accurate fire.

'Oh God! Oh, God, have mercy on their souls!'

Richard called out, unheard, in anguish. The Germans had struck again, a concentration of shells from two of their ships hitting the *Queen Mary*, third in line. The catastrophe was much nearer this time, a horrifying display of the power of high-explosive shell. She took three or four hits dead amidships, a blast of red flame shot up twice as high as her masts, revealing with indecent clarity the 26,000-ton battle-cruiser's agony of death. Then a merciful, all-concealing gout of black smoke rose twice as high as the flames and swallowed the ship, so that, when the smoke drifted away on the breeze, the surviving battle-cruisers had all passed by her grave and there was nothing left to see. It was swift, total extinction.

Anderson turned away, an older man; then at once resumed his role as commander, back straight, glasses on the enemy. Now they were coming! He called out, 'They're sending in their destroyers. Close up the guns.'

Richard passed on the order. 'We'll be going in now!' It was inevitable, and a hoist from the *Lion*, still smoking amidships from her terrible wound, confirmed: 'Destroyers, attack!' Admiral Hipper, seizing the advantage from sinking two British ships, now hoped to multiply the damage with a mass torpedo attack. And it was up to the protecting British destroyers to halt it.

The *Arrow* was already at maximum speed and as she turned to conform with the other Division ships, she heeled over so that her gunwale brushed the water. 'Stand by the torpedoes.' 'Ay, ay, sir.' 'Hold your fire until you can't miss.' 'Ay, ay, sir.' 'Number One, stand by to select target. We're going for the big ships.'

Richard was on the forecastle, cracking jokes with the 4-inch gun crew who were out in the open without even the protection of a shield. He had never seen such a keen and tough bunch. 'Whites of their bloody eyes – right, sir?' The petty officer winked and Richard laughed.

'That's it – not long to go.'

Like deadly predators hell-bent on their prey, the little black German destroyers were racing at a slightly oblique angle towards them, smoke like raven hair in the wind. Richard watched them coming, reminding himself that these vessels were full of men as strung-up for battle as they were, guns following their advance. And what a speed it was! Closing speed of around sixty knots – faster than the family Rolls-Royce flat out. Like a scene flashed for his encouragement and support at this critical moment, he saw the lawn at Wyston Court last summer, and heard the sound of Helena's voice before she took the dogs for a walk – 'It's always better to say things, Rich.' Then it was all gone, the scene and the sound, in the tearing rush of wind and spume.

A four-funnel German light cruiser, dwarfing her charges, streaked out of the mist no more than three miles away, gun-flashes running from forecastle to quarterdeck. Shells punched the water around them like giant-thrown rocks. There was no evading them. Chance ruled here, out in the North Sea in this massive clash of arms. Shells struck, or failed to strike. Soaked, deafened, half-blinded, the gun-crews worked like swift automata, pumping shells at a black German destroyer that raced past not three hundred yards distant, firing back at them, then at another that replaced it, like moving targets in a shooting-booth.

The *Arrow* heeled over in an eight-point turn to bring herself on a parallel opposite course with the cruiser. There came an animal-like shout, *'Fire!'*, and both torpedoes hissed from their tubes and splashed into the water. Richard never saw the result. All that he saw was the loader at the 4-inch gun beside him fall, his body skating across the steel deck into the scuppers, and Richard raced to take his place, thankful for the activity. The cold greased shell was cradled in his arms as he had been trained at Whale Island, and he plunged it into the smoking breech, followed instantly by the cartridge, as the empty shell case from the previous round was ejected to clatter onto the deck and roll with the others, adding their own metallic sound to the chorus. Slam shut the breech. Layer presses the trigger. Then again, and again.

There had been no order in this battle within a battle from the moment of contact. In half a minute it had become a shambles, the little boats swarming hectically like fish at feeding time, the firing of guns and torpedoes depending on fleeting identification. Richard, in a brief pause while awaiting more shells from the magazine, saw a German boat hit by a torpedo and break into two as if severed with an axe, and a second later they passed a large twin-funnel British boat that was sinking by the stern. Then the shells for the 4-inch arrived, six at a time in a sling carried by two ratings. He had loaded only the first when an order arrived to report back to the bridge, and his place was taken by an able seaman.

Richard never reached the *Arrow*'s bridge. As he ran across the forecastle, with the deck tilting at thirty degrees on a full rudder full speed turn, he glimpsed through the smoke and spume the bows of a destroyer. It was coming straight at them like an arrow, the identification V27 just visible, torpedo-tubes projecting port and starboard forward of the bridge, forecastle gun depressed to fire at them at point-blank range.

Avoidance was impossible, a collision inevitable. Richard's impression of its shape and detail was no longer in time than the click of a camera's shutter. He threw himself to the deck. The *Arrow* was hurled sideways like a toy kicked by an angry child. The metal tearing was like a scream of agony before death. Tight-embraced in their death pact, the two destroyers came to a standstill in a cauldron of hissing steam and gouting smoke. Torn metal settled against torn metal, smashed bulkheads arranged

221

themselves in lunatic juxtaposition against deck plating or shattered turbine-blades. The hissing of steam died to a murmur and the sound of water, ebbing and flowing, filling and spilling in and out of the shattered wreckage, was in tranquil contrast with the shouts of men giving orders and of other men crying out in pain.

Richard, crawling unharmed to his feet, saw a riddled funnel with the *Arrow*'s markings collapsed over what had once been the German boat's bridge, now identifiable only by the wheel, amazingly intact and vertical. A torpedo-tube, British or German, lay like a giant discarded cigar across the *Arrow*'s crushed twenty-five foot whaler. In this maelstrom of catastrophe German and British sailors, like members of dazed boarding-parties, passed from one wrecked ship to the other. First-aid parties were recovering the injured, German and British, where they could be found, and, above the shouting of petty officers' orders, the two commanders' voices echoed in a deeper note through megaphones – 'Launch the gig if the whaler's finished', and an order in German which Richard could not understand.

Both ships were going down fast, still in tight embrace, while the crews struggled, sometimes German and British in concert, to get anything into the sea that would keep them afloat. Richard took command of the carley float party. It had become jammed between dented deck-plates and with three ratings he attempted to pull back the metal. Others came to help but the water was rising swiftly, washing up to their waists, and the task had to be abandoned. George Hoste was among those clustered about the locked carley float. 'What about the dinghy – has that been hoisted out?' Richard asked.

'Smashed – so's the gig.'

There was the sound of tearing metal again, as if the two boats were struggling to wrench themselves apart before going down. Richard was puzzled why the sea had turned black, then remembered that all German destroyers were coal-burning and the bunkers had split open like the *Arrow*'s oil-tanks, spreading the stinking fuel with the coal dust into an odious compound. Men who had committed themselves to the water were already black as they struggled to keep afloat. A pair of German ratings, uniforms clinging to their bodies like old-fashioned swimming costumes, stood hesitantly on the smashed roof of a deck-house above Richard and George. They each had an oar from a boat and were about to jump. One of them grinned at Richard and spoke in English. 'Not very good for the swimming, eh officer? Do you come too?'

Richard smiled back, 'Good luck!' In the last moments before their boats went down, the camaraderie was complete, British and German attending to the wounded of both nationalities, being helped into the water and given fragments of wreckage which, in most cases, would only prolong the agony of their end.

'The Huns have got a boat launched,' said George, the nickname already sounding anachronistic.

'We'd better get clear – come on,' Richard plunged into the sea, came to the surface and kicked out. The oil was like a cloying net, every movement demanding twice the normal strength. Richard was a good swimmer but he knew he would never last for long in this choking, stinging and stinking sea.

He never saw the two boats going down; he could hardly see anything, and when he attempted to wipe the oil from his eyes he only smeared it into a thicker glutinous and impenetrable paste across his vision.

Panic threatened to seize him. A hand on his shoulder seeking his support, pressing him down further, caused the panic to recede and his sense of responsibility as an officer to assert itself, even at this critical moment. 'Easy now – I can't see you, but stay beside me and we'll swim together.'

His voice, muffled and choking though it sounded, appeared to calm his companion. Reaching out with his right hand in a clumsy breast-stroke, Richard felt a resisting shape. A floating body? No, more like a rope. It must be one of the many bundles of hammocks used as splinter protection against the searchlight platform and emergency wheel aft on the *Arrow*. But it had buoyancy strength and Richard reached out and dragged his companion towards it. As the long bundle fell into the trough of a wave, he half threw him onto it and himself put his arms and shoulders across it.

The support the hammocks gave the two men was marginal. Oil-soaked water washed over them chokingly and frequently, and each wave that broke across them threatened to tear them off. They should not have lasted five minutes, that they lasted for ten was a small miracle of survival. At the eleventh minute the German ten-metre whaler, the only boat launched by both ships, succeeded in manoeuvring alongside them, and they became the fourteenth and fifteenth men (German and British, it made no difference) to be saved by this boat. They were also the last. Such was the margin for Richard and his fellow survivor.

Strong arms of men speaking German, the guttural tone accentuated by the efforts they were making, dragged Richard bodily over the gunwale and he collapsed into the bottom of the boat. After a moment he felt a cloth wiping his face. At first he could still see nothing and with a wave of shock followed immediately by acceptance of the disability, he thought he was permanently blinded. But the thick curtain became lighter, became no more than a net, and this too was drawn aside to let in the daylight so that he could make out first shapes, and then detail.

Richard's face was close against another, like two lovers in bed. This other face was a grotesque mask of black oil

224

mixed with coal dust, the eyes looking into his. He realized then that this was his companion in the water who had almost drowned beside him, then had lain across the merciful hammock beside him, and been dragged into this boat beside him. His left arm was half across his face, and on the sleeve of his uniform was a single wide gold stripe with the insignia of the German crown above it.

At a cost of two ships sunk and more damaged, Beatty's destroyers had thwarted the German torpedo attack and had themselves hit one of the German battle-cruisers. Four destroyers in all were sunk in that bloody and confused *mêlée*. As Richard, the German lieutenant he had saved, and the mixed complement of Richard's shipmates and ex-enemies sat or lay in that overcrowded whaler, the embattled fleets thundered south, at one moment firing as furiously as ever at one another, at the next evidently losing contact in the smoke and mist. The quality of German shooting fell off after the brilliant opening and several of the German big ships took a severe battering though none was sunk and all were able to maintain their speed.

But at 4.30 the whole complexion of the contest was transformed by a signal from a British scouting cruiser racing ahead of Beatty's battle-cruisers. Out of the haze to the south there suddenly appeared the masts and superstructures of more German heavy ships. Rapidly, they formed the shape of a battle fleet cruising north in line-ahead formation – no fewer than twenty-four battleships, the whole of Scheer's High Seas Fleet. It was the first time it had been seen since the outbreak of war, and at 4.38 p.m. the British cruiser signalled by searchlight, 'Have sighted enemy battlefleet bearing approximately SE, course of enemy N . . .'

Far away in the Admiralty in London this message was picked up and passed to the First Sea Lord and his staff. Even the restrained and unemotional Captain Richmond and the more reserved First Lord, Arthur Balfour, could not conceal their excitement at the prospect of a great clash of arms in the North Sea. 'Blinker' Hall and his minions in Room 40 heard it and checked to see if any further German wireless messages had been intercepted. At every east coast port facilities were prepared for the reception of damaged men-o'-war, hospitals warned of possible casualties and tugs ordered to prepare for sea.

Still far to the north of the High Seas Fleet, Admiral Jellicoe heard it and made final preparations for action in the cool, laconic style for which he was so well known. Soon the news had reached every ship in the Grand Fleet. 'Action imminent!' 'The Huns are at sea!' 'The High Seas Fleet's been sighted!' Jellicoe's formal general signal to his Fleet at 4.47 p.m. ran, 'Enemy's battle fleet is coming north', followed by 'Fleet action is imminent.'

As for Beatty, who was closest to the enemy fleet – so close that he sighted the leading battleships even as he turned towards his scouting cruiser – he recognized the trap into which he was about to fall and ordered a reversal of course in order to evade it. Now his function was to draw his old antagonist, Hipper, and his new and far more powerful foe, Scheer, north and into the open and expectant jaws of his C-in-C, Jellicoe.

And so, through that late misty afternoon of the last day of May, the surviving British battle-cruisers and the 5th Battle Squadron steamed north close to the scene of the destroyer action, luring the whole German fleet towards its threatened destruction.

Sitting up now in the bottom of the tight-packed whaler, Richard heard the dull boom of gunfire, sometimes close, sometimes more distant, and saw the horizon intermittently lit up as if a series of thunderstorms were rolling about the North Sea. There was little

226

talk among the men. Those who were not preoccupied with the pain of their wounds or the discomfort of the cold and their filthy condition, were suffering from the inevitable aftermath of the crisis they had so recently endured.

But if little was said as the battle raged about them, Richard remained aware of the camaraderie which had rapidly developed among his fellow survivors as soon as they ceased to be adversaries. Later, as they began to recover from the shock of battle and the loss of so many of their shipmates (assisted by two bottles of schnapps that were passed round), several of the men began to talk, some in halting German or equally halting English. Sitting close to Richard, a German gunnery rating who spoke English well and stumbled only over technical terms, began a discussion with a British opposite number from the *Arrow* who had manned one of the 12-pounders. Yes, they agreed, no amount of gunnery practice can prepare you for the reality when everything happens so swiftly.

No vessel was in sight except a distant badly damaged and listing British destroyer. Once a four-funnel German light cruiser passed them at a distance of two or three miles, travelling at a great rate, her 4.1-inch guns at full elevation and with smoking damage from a shell hit on her forecastle. The German lieutenant beside Richard was sick over the gunwale several times, and between these bouts closed his eyes as if in desperate need of sleep. But once he opened his eyes fully, smiled at Richard, and said, '*Danke, Kamerad!*'

The main firing was now from the north, and it rose rapidly in intensity until the horizon was illuminated by a continuous pulsating glow.

By skilfully continuing to lure the German Fleet to the north, Beatty succeeded in bringing it to within some twenty miles of the British main Fleet, whose proximity remained unsuspected by the German C-in-C. Then the British battle-cruisers turned east to screen from the Germans with smoke this imminent threat. The ruse worked brilliantly. Shortly before 6.30 p.m. the German Fleet, still believing that it had trapped Beatty's battle-cruisers, now found itself confronted by the entire strength of the British battle squadrons forming line of battle ahead of them, and greatly outnumbering them.

The first and last dreadnought fleet action opened with a devastating cannonade the like of which had never before been heard. And it was the glow of this battle that the mixed complement of the German whaler observed.

Like the effect of a dry log thrown onto an already blazing fire, the light of distant battle was intensified by an even brighter yellow and red splash of colour in the evening sky. It was repeated twice more in the next minutes followed by deep booms which could only signify the death knells of three ships – and no doubt all who were in them. 'Gawd 'elp 'em, the poor buggers!' exclaimed one of the *Arrow*'s stokers sitting in the stern of the boat.

In their private world the whaler's company became aware that the apparently drifting British destroyer was actually heading towards them. Richard could make out men at the rails preparing to hoist out nets. A German petty officer who had assumed command of the whaler ordered half a dozen men to fit the rowlocks and take up oars in order to close the distance between the destroyer and themselves.

They were alongside by eight p.m., the whaler rising and falling on the destroyer's starboard beam and having to be fended off by the oarsmen. Then nets were cast down and hands seized them amid sharp orders in German.

Richard looked up at the destroyer which was listing so steeply that the thought crossed his mind that the additional weight might capsize it. A dozen ratings were at the rails, and one of them shouted indignantly, 'They're all 'uns, sir.' Another called, 'Put 'em back where they belong – we don't want no 'uns.'

Cupping his hands Richard shouted back angrily, 'I'm a British officer – and we're all *survivors*.' He knew that the sailor's threat would never have been carried out, but after what he and the rest of them had been through he found the half-serious ribaldry hard to bear. 'Come and give the wounded a hand and look smart about it.'

In the half-light of the end of that terrible day a British light cruiser took the damaged destroyer in tow after taking off all the survivors, injured and uninjured. Richard, washed and in borrowed uniform, made his way to the cruiser's wardroom. There was only one officer there, the ship's paymaster, an RNR lieutenant who looked as pale and haggard as the rest of the ship's officers after little or no sleep the night before and a gruelling day of pursuit and action.

He commiserated with Richard at the loss of his ship and so many of his men. He shook his head over his pink gin. 'There'll be a lot of naval widows on both sides of the North Sea after today,' he said. 'How did those Huns you had with you behave?'

The question was a genuine rather than a hostile enquiry but Richard again found himself bridling. 'The Germans?' he said in correction. 'Oh, they did what we would have done. They made room for us in the boat and looked after us – just as you're looking after them now.'

'It's funny really,' said the lieutenant. 'When you meet them they seem the same as our fellows.' He arose from his seat and said, 'I'm sorry to leave you. It's been a long day and I'm going to turn in.'

Richard's own weariness had disappeared as if he had gone through some barrier and would never again need rest, so he went up on deck. It was a warm summer night, so dark that there was no horizon and the towed destroyer astern could be identified only by the single masthead light. They were making no more than seven knots. There was little sound above the hum of the cruiser's turbines and the faint wash against the hull.

Richard stood at the stern near some sailors on duty by the towing capstan and looked south into the black night. The faint thunder of gunfire still came across the sea and there were just discernible distant flashes. Then a sudden, more intense glow lit up the sky. He knew it could only mean that another ship had blown up and he echoed the prayer of the sailor in the whaler – 'Gawd 'elp 'em, the poor buggers.' Be they British or German.

He felt desperately sad for the loss of his captain and the cheerful young George Hoste and the many more of the *Arrow*'s brave company who had gone down in their ship. And he felt, too, that he had, through his own ordeal and through what he had witnessed during this day and night, now laid, once and for all time, the ghost of his own fears and uncertainties. Above all, he wanted to tell Helena of the cure she had set in train – 'It's always better to say things, Rich.' But in this case he knew he never would, and that he would never need to because she would know.

XIV

The New Order

'Gunnery, gunnery, gunnery! Big guns, high speed – they're all that matter. Hit first, hit hard, and keep on hitting!' Admiral Fisher beat his desk with his fist three times so that the portrait of Nelson in its silver frame and the silver ink-well vibrated as if a gun had been discharged three times.

Fisher glanced first at Buller and then at his son. Addressing Richard he said, 'Your father is here because he knows more about gunnery than anyone in the Navy. You are here, like David, to "sit thou at my right hand", Psalm 110, and tell me all that you saw, because you were *there*. All that I know of the great battle is what I have read in the newspapers. No one tells me, no one consults me. So *you* shall tell me all that you know and all that happened at the great battle. From the admirals I shall hear only lies and excuses. But "out of the mouth of babes" (Psalm 8, of course) and out of the mouths of junior lieutenants shall the truth be found, Oh Lord.'

Richard glanced at his father who smiled and nodded encouragingly; and Richard began to deliver his account of what he saw, 'I was serving as first lieutenant of the *Arrow*, sir, in one of Admiral Beatty's three flotillas . . .'

Richard described the preliminaries to the battle-cruiser action, the sighting of the German light cruisers, and then Hipper's big ships.

'And where, pray, was the 5th Battle Squadron at this time?' Fisher asked.

'About ten miles distant to the north, sir. Or so I understand. I believe that there was some difficulty in getting a signal to those big battleships so that they were absent when the gunnery duel began.'

'And at what range was fire opened by Admiral Beatty, young man?'

'15,000 yards or thereabouts.'

Jackie Fisher raised his eyes and his arms to heaven, then glared at the two officers as if they were an audience of hundreds and declaimed as if he were in a giant auditorium: '15,000 yards! So I arm the Navy's battle-cruisers with 13.5-inch guns that can range to 23,000 yards, 6,000 yards greater than any gun the German battle-cruisers can boast. Admiral Beatty also has as support thirty-two 15-inch guns with a range of 28,000 yards. And he waits until the enemy has *his* range of 15,000 yards before he begins the action!' He turned to Buller as if he were a student at an examination. 'And what is the chief advantage of out-ranging the enemy, Archy Buller?'

Buller grinned like a first-term student at HMS *Excellent* gunnery school. 'So that you may destroy your enemy at leisure while he is helpless to harm you.'

'Exactly!' Fisher's keen brown eyes swung to Richard. 'And is that not what you observed first at the Battle of Coronel where von Spee outgunned poor Kit Cradock? *And* at the Falkland Islands where my beloved greyhounds annihilated von Spee with their 12-inch guns and were scarcely scratched themselves? My greyhounds were never built to stand in the line like the battleships of my beloved Nelson [and he pointed to the portrait] in a slogging match. They were designed and built by me to scout and with their superior speed and gunpower to destroy the enemy at *their* choice of time.'

The old admiral rose from his seat and paced up and down, brows furrowed, his fine head thrown back. Both Buller and Richard were surprised by the sudden silence yet certain that, when the flood-gates were reopened, the waters would pour forth in a torrent. And so they did, in a torrent of sarcasm and accusation.

'Admiral Beatty with his lightly-armoured ships kindly waits until Admiral Hipper can hit him with every advantage of light in the Germans' favour and keeps his 15-inch-gunned heavy battleships which are heavily armoured over the horizon. I suppose he thought it was not fair to give the enemy no chance *at all* to keep out of his range and then blow up all Hipper's battle-cruisers like overfed pheasants sitting on a wall. Like Saul's son, "his hands were feeble".'

Richard, unable to restrain himself, rose from his seat and said, 'No, sir, that is not true. He may have been mistaken – I was not beside him and do not know – but he was as brave as a lion. It is reported that when he saw his second battle-cruiser blown up he said "There seems to be something wrong with our bloody ships today" and then ordered a turn of two points *towards* the enemy.'

'Young man, sit down,' Fisher ordered, and did so himself, at the same time offering his cigar-box to Buller. 'You are right to correct me. Admiral Beatty *is* a brave man. But there was nothing wrong with his ships. He just did not handle them correctly. Continue your account. I understand Hipper attacked with his destroyers and you counter-attacked with your destroyers.'

Richard gave an account of the skirmish between the battle lines, concluding, 'Unless you were there, sir, it is impossible to imagine the difficulty of identifying the enemy, let alone recording his bearing and speed and bringing your guns to bear. It was like trying to arrest a gang of thugs in a London street in a pea-souper. With respect, sir, from all I have heard since, Admiral Beatty

233

performed brilliantly to hand the German High Seas Fleet to Admiral Jellicoe, on a plate, so to speak, sir, ready for carving.'

Buller was listening to his son with pride in his heart, admiring the way in which he refused to be bullied and was resolved to speak the truth as he believed it. Drawing on the fine Havana he had taken from the box and blowing out the smoke, he said in support, 'I think that is well put, sir, don't you?'

'Very well, very well. "Surely I *am* more brutish than *any* man . . ." You will recall Agur's confession – Proverbs 30. But such folly on that evening when Jellicoe should have gobbled up Admiral Scheer, leaving not a bone on the plate! Instead he lets him get away, loses him in the night, and the next day Scheer is back safely in harbour claiming a great victory. "And why didn't Lord Fisher put on more armour?" the ignorant will cry out. "*Hang Lord Fisher!*"'

Encouraged by the support of his father and his own tactical victory over the formidable Admiral, Richard declared, 'Safely in harbour, sir, that is true. But not undamaged. His newest battle cruiser, Admiral Hipper's flagship, is at the bottom of the North Sea, and I hear that the others will be unable to put to sea again for many months. And the only battleship to be sunk was German, besides a number of light cruisers. It was not a Nelsonian victory, sir. It is as if the Spanish and French fleets at Trafalgar escaped back into Cadiz instead of surrendering *en masse*. But will they ever dare to come out again? Judging by the way they fled at the sight of our battle fleet, I judge not, sir. It has been a great victory at Jutland at relatively little cost. I suffered the loss of many loved shipmates, sir, and six thousand more British sailors and almost as many Germans were lost. But think of the number of dead if there had been a full-scale fleet action! Twenty, thirty, forty thousand – and I have seen too much of death and suffering.'

Fisher smiled broadly at Buller. His puckish, mischievous grin was well known amongst his friends and admirers though it could appear and disappear as swiftly as the sun in squally weather. 'This boy of yours, Archy. This young fellow, this junior lieutenant. He may turn into quite a remarkable man if he does not get a swollen head.' He turned his attention directly towards Richard. 'How many actions have you seen, Richard Buller?'

'Four, sir. I have been very lucky, sir. Not only did the good Lord spare me, but the Germans *saved* me!'

'I like that. Like Hezekiah, Archy Buller, the Lord was with your son, "*and* he prospered whithersoever he went". As for you, you have your bar to your DSO for your last Q-ship action. But, like me, your career is over. Too old, Archy. Look at me. Dragged out of retirement twice and where do I find myself? In an office in Berkeley Square running something called the Board of Invention. What I must invent is some way of dealing with superannuated admirals. But this fellow, this *young* Buller, he has everything before him. Hooray for youth, I say.'

Like the moment of sighting the enemy battle-cruisers a month earlier, Richard knew that this was another moment in his life he would never forget, as Admiral Fisher, who had done more for the Royal Navy than anyone since his own hero, Horatio Nelson, stood up and offered his hand in congratulation. Then he took from a drawer in his desk a large photograph of himself in full dress-uniform, wrote on it and handed it to Richard.

Richard read, in bold, clear, rounded handwriting, 'For Richard Buller, scion of a great naval family. May he reach the top. For King and Empire and the Royal Navy. Fisher of Kilverstone A/F.'

Richard and Helena were married on a sunny, faintly

misty, October day in 1916, with the leaves of the plane trees in the London squares and parks turning golden and beginning to fall. It was as considerable a naval and social occasion as the conditions of war allowed. Serving Bullers from far and wide who were able to get leave attended the ceremony and the reception in Clarges Street. There was a naval guard of honour at the church porch, and among the officers who extended swords beneath which Richard and Helena walked from the porch was one rating included at the insistence of Buller himself – young Tom Maclewin, Rod's only son. And at the reception there was one woman, without title or wealth or social standing of any kind, and who was the special concern of Clemmie Buller, Rod's widow and Tom's mother, Rosie.

Clemmie Buller felt a special responsibility and fondness for Rosie Maclewin, who had experienced more of life's worries than she had known and whose husband had shared so many of her own husband's dangers. Brave Rod Maclewin who had given his life for the Navy and the nation he loved! All he lacked, poor Rod, was that seam of luck, like gold, and a seam so narrow in the rock as scarcely to be visible, which Bullers possessed and which had saved the life of her younger son and her husband.

'He knew he was going to die,' Rosie Maclewin had told Clemmie, who had then asked if Rod had had a premonition. 'Oh no, Lady Buller, he left a letter for me to be opened if he did not come back. He had been feeling so ill that he had visited a specialist under an assumed name and had been told he had no more than six months to live. So I would have lost my Rod soon anyway.'

'And do you find that a consolation?'

'Yes, it is a support. But, oh dear, I should have liked to have seen him once more. A medal is all very well, but . . .'

236

After the award of the Victoria Cross posthumously to
Rod had been gazetted, and Rosie had come to London to
receive the award from the King, Clemmie had
accompanied her to the Palace and helped her through
the ordeal. It was typical of Rosie's good grace, good
sense and stalwart character that she was now behaving
with complete naturalness in this company on this
occasion, and Clemmie's heart went out to her in her
bereavement.

Archy was now at Clemmie's side, already pink with
champagne as she knew he would be, enjoying every
moment of the occasion, charming the women, joking
with his fellow officers, kissing the bride more than once.

'How's your glass, dear?' he asked, nodding towards a
waiter.

'Not as full as yours, Archy, but quite full enough.'

'Do you know, Clemmie,' he said, ignoring the hint,
'what Jackie Fisher said to me the other day?'

'Knowing our Jackie, a great deal.'

'Yes, yes. But he said my career was over. That I was
too old for anything – that we were both superannuated!
Superannuated! Me, Archy Buller?' He patted his
considerable stomach with the large hand not engaged in
holding a glass of champagne. 'As fit as ever I was.
Fisher's seventy-five, I'm only just over fifty. I think they
ought to give me back my ship – I mean my battle-
cruiser, don't you, Clemmie?'

Clemmie Buller said, her thoughts elsewhere, 'Yes,
dear. Now who is that woman talking to Admiral Wilson?
I'm sure I know her . . .'

For two more years after Richard Buller's wedding, the
war at sea maintained its relentless course towards its
inevitable conclusion. It was a war of blockade and
counter-blockade with even fewer major battles than

237

during the period up to the Battle of Jutland. The British blockade of Germany and her allies became so tight and impenetrable that it was as if the Royal Navy had built a dam across the North Sea between Scotland and Norway, and another across the Channel between France and England. This had a throttling effect on Germany's food-supplies and raw materials for making war, while on land Germany's great armies wearied of breaking through into the heartland of France, which they had so nearly accomplished in 1914.

But if British sea power was grinding down the will and the means of Germany to continue the war, Germany's new undersea power came close to throttling Britain to death before her own blockade could prove effective against Germany. The U-boat offensive against Allied shipping which Buller had helped to fight in 1915 was no more than a preview of what was to come as German shipyards launched bigger and better U-boats, and set about the destruction of Allied trade more and more relentlessly so that by April 1917 the monthly loss of shipping was over 880,000 tons. Britain was already on short rations and at this rate would be starved into surrender by the end of the year.

The slide to disaster for Britain and her Allies was halted only by the introduction of a strict convoy system, and other desperate measures. Archy Buller, appointed now to the Naval War Staff and raised to flag rank, was deeply involved in the administrative side of this battle against the U-boats, while fretting restlessly for a sea command again. It never came his way. 'You must learn to be satisfied with what you have already done, dear, and be thankful that you have survived,' Clemmie once remarked by way of consolation. 'You have had more luck than most naval officers and I'm not sure that you have always deserved it. But I'm glad you had it all the same so that we can grow old gracefully together.'

They both laughed at this, and Buller made his customary wordless reply: the pop of a cork of Veuve Clicquot.

And so it was left to Richard Buller to maintain the family reputation at sea in the second half of this long and terrible war. Early in 1917 he was given his own destroyer, the hardest worked of all RN ships. With the introduction of convoys, his ship was withdrawn from the Battle-Cruiser Fleet, and, until the end of the war, through fair weather and foul – mostly foul – worked the Western Approaches, escorting home and escorting out the great armadas of shipping that were the lifeblood of the Allied cause.

On a stormy August day in 1917, Richard's attention was drawn to a man-o'-war which had recently joined the convoy as an additional escort. Its configuration was unfamiliar, and so was the flag it was flying as the little vessel dipped into a deep roller, leaving only its mastheads in sight. The flag was the Stars and Stripes. The American destroyer was being signalled by the convoy's commodore whose broad pennant was flying in a light cruiser at the head of the convoy: 'Welcome! We need you, and more like you!'

The United States had at last entered the war in April, and as that great nation began to train the armies that would soon be arriving in France, it was at sea that the first effect of American power was felt. It was sorely needed and gladly given.

On 9 April, Admiral William Sowden Sims USN had arrived in London to act as liaison officer between the US Navy Department and the British Admiralty, and to examine how best the American Navy could help the Allied cause. The need for escort vessels for convoy work was the first priority, and the American 'four-stacker' of the *Alwyn* class which Richard Buller was to witness joining the convoy escort three months later was among the first of the vessels to fill this great need.

It was also agreed that the US Navy would contribute a Battle Squadron to the Grand Fleet at Scapa Flow. Buller was closely involved in arrangements for this reinforcement. He had known Sims before the war when Sims had come to London to make a study of RN gunnery practice, and the two officers had got on well. Now, in the hard circumstances of war, they were to meet again at the Admiralty. This time Buller suffered no constraints on what he could tell the American. Their professional relationship developed into personal friendship, and when Admiral Sims travelled north to Scotland in early December 1917 to greet the arrival of the American Battle Squadron at Scapa Flow, Buller travelled with him and was introduced to the American admiral commanding the squadron, Hugh Rodman.

Seen against the massed British dreadnoughts at Scapa Flow, the four American battleships appeared to be a very puny contribution. But there were warm expressions of welcome hospitality by the Grand Fleet, and the Americans proved to be equally friendly and as anxious to learn from these war-experienced battle squadrons as the British were to teach them. The US Navy, forged out of the Revolutionary War for independence, and a fierce foe of the British again in 1812, now worked closely and eagerly with the Royal Navy against the common enemy.

Less than one year later, the German High Seas Fleet, its ships filthy from neglect, manned by crews who had recently mutinied, steamed to surrender to the Grand Fleet, now commanded by Admiral Beatty. In this momentous and solemn meeting off the Scottish naval base of Rosyth, the American battleships made their own special contribution.

Buller was a guest of Admiral Rodman on his flagship, the battleship *New York*. As the German battleships and battle-cruisers steamed slowly between the lines of the victorious Allied fleets, Hugh Rodman remarked, 'This is a proud day for you, Admiral Buller. The greatest victory for your Navy in all time, I guess.'

Buller did not answer at once. The great German battleship *Kaiser* slipped past, the German national flag lowered, the white ensign flying above it, her slovenly crew leaning on the rails and staring expressionlessly at the smart line of British battle squadrons. After the *Kaiser* the *Prinzregent Luitpold* and then the *Kaiserin*, all the fine ships which had for almost four and a half years acted as a hidden threat to Britain and her Empire. And here they were, scarcely two cables-lengths away, the breech-blocks of their guns removed while the conquering ships had their guns loaded and manned in case of trouble.

'What would your Admiral Nelson have said at this sight?' Admiral Rodman enquired. 'He was a man of peace I've always heard, and if Trafalgar could have been fought and won without a gun being fired and a man hurt, perhaps he would have welcomed it. And the saving of his own life!'

Buller, recalling the bloody and noisy battles in which he had been engaged during so much of his long naval career, could not help feeling that this was a tame end to the greatest war in history, whatever Nelson might have thought.

The American admiral was speaking again, speaking lightly, 'Or would you have preferred to see all those German dreadnoughts sunk, going down in smoke and flames under the broadsides of the British Navy?' Rodman laughed, and Buller turned and smiled at the American. On the decks of the British flagship, *Queen Elizabeth*, three cheers were sounding out from the crew, and other ships were taking up the chorus of triumph and praise for the C-in-C who had brought them safely through the war.

241

'Oh no,' he said, with a slightly mischievous smile, 'we Bullers have always been men of peace, too.'

Sometimes it seemed to Buller that he had spent more than half his life on ships' bridges, legs set apart to balance himself with the roll, hands clasped behind his back, watching the rise and fall of the prow and sweeping the horizon with his glasses. Mighty battleships digging their bows into an Atlantic storm, elegant white-painted cruisers in tropical waters, wicked little black-painted torpedo boats of the 1890s, with no more than a sketchy canvas screen, 'butting through the Channel in the mad March days' like John Masefield's coaster – for Buller the ocean viewed from any ship was no enemy, even though it could consume him in seconds and sometimes had nearly done so. As a ploughman lives with the earth he tills, so, neither loving nor hating it but accepting the relationship like a long marriage, the ocean was a landscape with which Buller had long come to terms.

From the bridge of a man-o'-war the sea was also like a canvas upon which was painted Buller's life as a sailor, sometimes in violent colours, at other times in mellower hues – as now, steaming west through calm seas towards the setting sun. Buller was conscious of this and was also experiencing a curious and welcome absence of any feelings of responsibility for this ship, this big Cunarder bound for New York. He was, in fact, a guest of the captain on the bridge where he was welcome at any time as the most experienced sailor in the ship.

For the first time in his life, however, Buller was making an ocean crossing in the role of a diplomat rather than as a sailor. Promoted to full admiral and raised to the peerage with a KCMG, Sir Archibald Buller was *en route* to Washington with the British politician and diplomat, Arthur Balfour. Balfour, who had been First Lord of the Admiralty at the time of the Battle of

Jutland, was now acting as head of the British mission to a Washington conference concerned with naval disarmament.

'This time tomorrow we'll be raising Nantucket, Admiral. Are you looking forward to seeing New York?'

Buller turned to the liner's captain, a short, jaunty man with a full white beard, ten years younger than Buller. 'Yes, I am. In forty-five years of naval service I was never on the North American Station, and a very cushy station it was, too, from all accounts: up north to the St Lawrence in summer, New York in the autumn and the West Indies when winter really set in. But we'll only have three days in the city before we go down to Washington to start work.'

'You won't be standing any nonsense from those Yankees, will you, my Lord? We don't want to be giving away our Navy after winning the greatest war in history.'

Buller looked down at the captain and smiled ruefully. 'No, I don't think we'll be doing that,' he said. 'But beggars can't be choosers. We may have won the war but it's made our country almost as poor as Germany. We've been too busy fighting to realize that now when it's all over the United States has become the richest country in the world. And we owe that country millions of pounds. What's more she feels she needs a Navy as powerful as ours.'

The coxswain turned the wheel a few spokes to the right, and then eased it back again to conform with the compass-reading in the illuminated binnacle before him. Lights were going on all over the giant ship and it was warm and calm enough for a few passengers, in long dresses and dinner-jackets, to be strolling on the upper deck.

'But what does she want it *for*?' persisted the captain.

'To defend herself, just as we've always needed a navy to defend ourselves and our sea routes.' They walked

243

together to the port side of the bridge and out into the warm evening air. Some five miles distant an east-bound steamer was heading out into the Atlantic, *en route* for Europe, smoke streaming from her two funnels, safe now from U-boats.

'But America has no enemies. We're at peace now,' said the captain.

For an answer, Buller pointed to the sun, at that moment cut in half by the horizon ahead of them. 'What nation does that remind you of, Captain? That sun may be setting but the rising sun of Japan is what America fears. I'm only a simple sailor, but I have seen the Japanese Navy in action at Tsu-Shima. That victory gave them confidence and they believe that they can rule the Pacific Ocean if they build a big enough navy. That's what's worrying the Americans – and why President Harding has proposed this conference.'

The captain nodded his head. 'I've no doubt you're right, Admiral. But it will be hard to bear if our Navy has to be cut down to the size of the American and Japanese navies after all our sacrifices.'

Buller said, with a new jocular note in his voice, 'I've always held, Captain, that both to offset depression as well as to celebrate some cheerful occasion, there is nothing to equal a bottle of Dom Perignon. Shall we split one to start off the evening? You have a very good '08. I gather from the chief wine-steward that there is not very much of it left, and it would be a pity if it got into the undeserving hands of the passengers you will be picking up in New York.'

Archy Buller surveyed the scene about him and felt thankful that he had chosen the Royal Navy as a career and not politics or the diplomatic service. For weeks the delegates of the world's great naval powers, closeted in the Pan-American Union Building in Washington, had been wrangling and 'speechifying', as the Americans called it, struggling to maintain as big a navy for their country as they could, even if they could not afford it, while denying as far as they were able the claims of other nations.

There they sat, the five delegations, led by Senator Henry Cabot Lodge and Oscar Underwood for the United States, Baron Shidehara for Japan, Senator Albertini for Italy, M. Briand the French premier for France, and Arthur Balfour for Britain – and all, on this December morning of 1921, looking more cheerful than they had since they had first sat down to argue and wage a war of words. The reason for this was that an agreement had at last been reached on the most important part of the agenda.

The Washington Agreement fulfilled all the fears for the future of the Royal Navy and marked in sharp statistical terms the rise of two great naval powers. Buller's great-grandfather had taken part in the defeat of the combined Franco–Spanish Fleets off Cadiz; when his grandfather had joined the Royal Navy the American Navy was no more than a handful of frigates; during his own father's period of service the Royal Navy really did rule the waves; and in Buller's own time as a junior officer when there were 'war scares' over Russia and France in the 1870s and 1880s, the power of the Royal Navy remained almost as great as that of the rest of the world together.

Now, as the price of four and a half years of warfare at sea with ultimate and complete victory, the Royal Navy was being cut down to the same strength as that of the United States. Although Buller had been involved in every fought-over stage of the negotiations, on this December morning when the preliminary agreement was made known outside the conference he found it hard to believe that the Royal Navy was no longer the greatest navy in the world. In round figures the ratio of strength between the chief naval powers' battle fleets was in future to be 5:5 for Britain and America, 3 for Japan and 2 each for France and Italy – 'The 5:5:3:2:2 Treaty' as it came to be called.

Arthur Balfour was on his feet now, a tall, handsome figure with a fine, ringing, patrician voice, extolling the virtues of the treaty regarding the Pacific: 'Japan's friendship with Britain has stood the test of two wars,' he was saying. 'Something closer unites us than the mere words of this Treaty . . .' And then of America: 'All my life I have been a consistent advocate of the most intimate and friendly relations between the two greatest branches of the English-speaking race. You can therefore see how deep is my satisfaction when I see great powers put their names to a treaty which for all time will lead to peace in the territory where the treaty breathes . . .'

After the meeting broke up there was a reception with the American delegation as hosts. Buller had enjoyed as warm hospitality in Washington as he had during those few days in New York, and no warmer hospitality than from Admiral Fergus O'Donnell USN, a third-generation American naval officer whose ancestors came from Scotland. Buller had spent the last three week-ends at his home outside Washington and they had become warm friends. Now, as the mass of delegates drank their mint juleps and highballs, the American came alongside and asked Buller how he felt now that the treaty was signed, the Pacific Ocean was safe and war had been made remote by the drastic cuts in naval power and expenditure.

'I hope Mr Balfour is right,' Buller replied, 'and that it *will* be peace for all time in the Pacific, and everywhere. But as a simple naval officer I'm not so sure. When politicians want something they have been known to tear up treaties – it's easier than sinking a battleship.'

The American laughed. 'There aren't so many to sink now. We're scrapping four good ships and sixteen more we've already started to build.'

'What are you complaining about, my friend?' Buller asked without bitterness. 'We're sending twenty-two to the scrapyard, bringing us about level with you in a few years' time.'

They were both feeling the heat in the crowded room, and they agreed, too, that they had heard enough of the clamour of many voices. 'Why don't we get away from here,' the American suggested. 'We can be at my home in half an hour and we can solve the world's problems on the way.'

It was crisp and cold outside with a clear moonless sky. In two weeks it would be Christmas and the stores were brightly lit – and open for late shoppers. Admiral O'Donnell drove the big Oldsmobile himself, down Pennsylvania Avenue and past the White House where President Harding would shortly be giving a dinner to the delegate heads of the conference.

'We've both been battleship men,' the American said, continuing the subject of their earlier conversation. 'Battleship men for most of our lives. And we've both got sons in the Navy. But I wonder if battleships are going to count very much when our boys become admirals – or captains even.'

'You're thinking about the submarine, I expect,' said Buller. 'My old friend Jackie Fisher, who died last year, was saying nearly twenty years ago, "Look at the submarine. When it is perfected, we do not know what a revolution will come about. Once they were the weapon of the weak. Now they loom large as the weapon of the strong." Then he'd quote from the Bible to drive home his point. Well, we know now about the revolution – they nearly did for us in the Great War. And before he died Fisher was prophesying underwater dreadnoughts with

247

great guns – the battleships of the future.'

They were already leaving behind the lights of the city and heading out into the countryside. The American clearly enjoyed driving and, keeping his eyes on the ribbon of road ahead, said, 'And while we're onto prophecies, Buller, don't forget that we sank a surrendered German battleship, and a real tough one too, with a few aerial bombs last year in an experiment just off the coast here.'

Buller laughed. 'You mean we should have been talking about submarines and aeroplanes all these last weeks instead of battleships.'

'All the gas, gas, gas! All for nothing!'

'Jaw's better than war, so they say. And so long as the US Navy and the Royal Navy don't pick a quarrel we'll be all right.' It was not a question of 'standing any nonsense from those Yankees', as the liner's captain had declared. It was more a question of remaining friends.

Author's Note

Like the earlier *Buller's Guns* and *Buller's Dreadnought*,
this is a work of fiction. But, as readers will have at once
recognized, the story is set against real events and
features sailors and prominent figures of the time. The
tragic event off Chile and the victory off the Falklands
took place as described, including such details as Admiral
Cradock's oranges and the deception practised by the
unfortunate engineer commander of the *Canopus*. The
account of the Dardanelles bombardments is based,
rather more freely, on historical records and eyewitness
accounts, as is the Battle of Jutland. Archy Buller's
Q-ship adventures are also based on several real actions, in
particular those of the remarkably gallant Gordon
Campbell VC DSO. Except for the *Glasgow*, the ships in
which Buller, father and son, served are fictional.

There are always hazards in presenting real-life
characters in an historical novel. Objection may be taken
at the less-than-sympathetic picture of Winston Churchill.
But this is the high-handed and less experienced
Churchill of 1914–15, who was widely distrusted in the
Royal Navy and lacked the general approbation and
admiration he rightly attracted twenty-five years later.

The Washington Conference of 1921–2 was a more
complex and longer-drawn-out event than the account
here indicates. It nevertheless marked the drastic
reduction in the relative strength and standing of the

Royal Navy and the end of Britannic omnipotence at sea. Archy Buller and his sons and future grandsons will now have to adjust themselves to a new role and status for the service they love, and the mastery of new weapons. For the fighting ship as a gun platform is receding in importance, and in 1922 the signs are already clear that the future arbiters of sea power will be the aircraft-carrier and the submarine.

THE END

BLITZFREEZE
by Sven Hassel

THE FUHRER'S COMMANDS WERE SIMPLE – FORWARD TO MOSCOW!

And so the mighty Panzer regiment thundered into action – killing, raping, burning their way across the great wastes of Russia . . .

But this was to be the bloodiest of all Hitler's wars – a war where Russian infantrymen threw themselves before the oncoming tanks, where women fought as savagely as men, where German guns killed Germans and Russians alike, mangling them indiscriminately into tattered hunks of meat . . .

And finally Porta, Tiny, Barcelona, all of them – caring nothing for who should win the war – thinking only of their own survival – began the long retreat – back through the corpse-littered plains where blood and bodies were already frozen beneath the winter ice . . .

0 552 09761 6 £1.95

BULLER'S GUNS
by Richard Hough

Archy Buller and Rod Maclewin joined the Navy for reasons as different as their own backgrounds.

Rod came from the slums of Tyneside and for him, the Navy was the only alternative to hunger and despair. For Buller, too, there was no alternative. For generations, every Buller boy had left the great Cotswold estate to become an officer, many of them to win honour and celebrity.

As both lads grew up and rose in rank, fate and war brought them together time and again, until a bond was sealed in the burning heat of the South African veldt . . .

Set in the majestic floodtide of Victorian imperialism, when arrogance and self-indulgence, suffering and poverty were taken for granted, and when foreign uprisings were settled by gunboat or bayonet, this is the first novel in a series featuring Buller, intrepid adventurer in the navy of his day . . .

0 552 12003 0   £1.50

THE LAST BATTLE
by Robert Jackson

For the Luftwaffe, April 1945 was a bloody twilight. Their battered remains were being ruthlessly swept from the skies by swarms of Allied fighters as the last battles were fought over the ruins of Berlin. George Yeoman, commanding a squadron of brand-new Meteor jet fighters, had a desperate mission to carry out in the last days of the Reich. A group of enemy scientists, working on Germany's atomic bomb project, were in hiding in Berlin, now encircled by the Russians, and it was vital that they should not fall into Russian hands. When the scientists attempted to escape from a Berlin lake in an old German flying-boat, Yeoman's squadron was briefed to intercept them and force them to land in Allied territory . . .

0 552 12226 2   £1.50

SS STUKA SQUADRON 2: HAWKS OF DEATH
by Leo Kessler

The sons of German–Austrian aristocracy, the men of the *Black Knights* had joined the SS not simply because they believed fervently in the Fuhrer's 'New Order' but also because it represented for them a means of getting back to the top.

Fanatically dedicated, arrogant and ruthless, they believed themselves to be the world's greatest gift to the German Air Force, and fought to gain the prestige and importance they thought was their due. Vengeance and victory was their goal; nothing – and no-one – was going to stand in their way . . .

Second in this savage war series.

0 552 12285 8   £1.50

SEVEN MINUTES PAST MIDNIGHT
by Walter Winward

The compelling novel of a perilous plan to snatch one of the highest-ranking Nazis from Hitler's infamous Bunker. The Horsetraders – a small team of British and American crack-commandos. The Operation – a simple trade-in: life and liberty for double-agent 'Valkyrie' in exchange for vital information about Stalin's post-war ambitions and the location of Germany's hidden gold reserves.

But only when they were actually in Berlin would one of their team – a woman – be able to recognize 'Valkyrie'. And as Berlin crumbled and blazed all around them as the Russians moved in, the Horsetraders discovered that one of their own team was a fanatical Stalinist agent . . .

'SPLENDIDLY DETAILED POST-WAR THRILLER . . . CREATES A MOST INGENIOUS CLIMAX'
British Book News

0 552 11551 7   £1.25

A SELECTED LIST OF TITLES AVAILABLE FROM CORGI BOOKS

WHILE EVERY EFFORT IS MADE TO KEEP PRICES LOW, IT IS SOMETIMES NECESSARY TO INCREASE PRICES AT SHORT NOTICE. CORGI BOOKS RESERVE THE RIGHT TO SHOW AND CHARGE NEW RETAIL PRICES ON COVERS WHICH MAY DIFFER FROM THOSE ADVERTISED IN THE TEXT OR ELSEWHERE.

THE PRICES SHOWN BELOW WERE CORRECT AT THE TIME OF GOING TO PRESS.

☐	12686 1	The Commissar	**Sven Hassel**	£1.95
☐	11976 8	O.G.P.U. Prison	**Sven Hassel**	£1.95
☐	09761 6	Blitzfreeze	**Sven Hassel**	£1.95
☐	08603 7	Liquidate Paris	**Sven Hassel**	£1.95
☐	12003 0	Buller's Guns	**Richard Hough**	£1.50
☐	12226 2	The Last Battle	**Robert Jackson**	£1.50
☐	12148 7	Tempest Squadron	**Robert Jackson**	£1.25
☐	12105 3	Operation Diver	**Robert Jackson**	£1.50
☐	11987 3	Mosquito Squadron	**Robert Jackson**	£1.25
☐	12216 5	SS Stuka Squadron 1: The Black Knights	**Leo Kessler**	£1.50
☐	12285 8	SS Stuka Squadron 2: Hawks of Death	**Leo Kessler**	£1.50
☐	12407 9	SS Stuka Squadron 3: Tank Busters!	**Leo Kessler**	£1.75
☐	12408 7	SS Stuka Squadron 4: Blood Mission	**Leo Kessler**	£1.95
☐	12510 5	Wolf Trap	**Frederick Nolan**	£2.50
☐	12119 3	The Canaris Fragments	**Walter Winward**	£1.75
☐	11940 7	The Ball Bearing Run	**Walter Winward**	£1.50
☐	11551 7	Seven Minutes Past Midnight	**Walter Winward**	£1.25
☐	11186 4	Hammerstrike	**Walter Winward**	£1.00
☐	12514 8	Cougar	**Walter Winward**	£1.95

All these books are available at your bookshop or newsagent, or can be ordered direct from the publisher. Just tick the titles you want and fill in the form below.

CORGI BOOKS, Cash Sales Department, P.O. Box 11, Falmouth, Cornwall.

Please send cheque or postal order, no currency.

Please allow cost of book(s) plus the following for postage and packing:

U.K. CUSTOMERS—Allow 55p for the first book, 22p for the second book and 14p for each additional book ordered, to a maximum charge of £1.75.

B.F.P.O. and Eire—Allow 55p for the first book, 22p for the second book plus 14p per copy for the next seven books, thereafter 8p per book.

Overseas Customers—Allow £1.00 for the first book and 25p per copy for each additional book.

NAME (Block Letters) ....

ADDRESS ....

....